Praise for T

NATIONAL B

"A beautifully written and satisfying tale."   —*Winnipeg Free Press*

"Ghosts weave in and out of the smoke, decades-old passions are re-examined, life-changing options present themselves, life and loss continue, unabated. *Turtle Valley* is both haunting and haunted (as it's both a romance-mystery and a ghost story) and it carries powerful magic all its own."   —*The Hamilton Spectator*

"*Turtle Valley* has all the hallmarks of the author's previous best-sellers. . . . It zooms into the heart of rural life, with its family ties and rivalries, while ripping open the doors of family closets and letting the insecurities, eccentricities and dark secrets pour out. . . . Another suspenseful page-turner."   —*The Vancouver Sun*

"As with most celebrated fiction in this country, a sense of place is as important as the characters. . . . There is a homespun, 19th-century quality to Anderson-Dargatz's work."   —*Calgary Herald*

"*Turtle Valley* lives up to Anderson-Dargatz's gothic reputation, with ghosts dashing out from behind the farmhouses, mysterious flocks of ladybugs clinging to the ceilings, stoves leaping to life at strange hours and horrible secrets hiding in the family well. . . . It's a tense, passionate story of family and memory, haunting and history."   —*Vancouver Courier*

"Anderson-Dargatz is skilled at peeling back the layers of love, commitment and confusion that most families experience."   —*The Globe and Mail*

"Part mystery, part memory story, part eco-conscious tale, but a rare take on illness in the context of a marriage is what makes *Turtle Valley* a winner. . . . Gripping."   —*NOW* (Toronto)

Also by

GAIL ANDERSON-DARGATZ

The Miss Hereford Stories
The Cure for Death by Lightning
A Recipe for Bees
A Rhinestone Button

Turtle Valley

Gail Anderson-Dargatz

VINTAGE CANADA

VINTAGE CANADA EDITION, 2008

Copyright © 2007 Gail Anderson-Dargatz

Published in Canada by Vintage Canada, a division of Random House of Canada Limited, Toronto, in 2008. Originally published in hardcover in Canada by Alfred A. Knopf Canada, a division of Random House of Canada Limited, Toronto, in 2007. Distributed by Random House of Canada Limited, Toronto.

Vintage Canada and colophon are registered trademarks of Random House of Canada Limited.

www.randomhouse.ca

Library and Archives Canada Cataloguing in Publication

Anderson-Dargatz, Gail
Turtle Valley / Gail Anderson-Dargatz.

ISBN 978-0-676-97886-5

I. Title.
PS8551.N3574T87 2008   C813'.54   C2007-906938-X

Book design: Kelly Hill

Printed and bound in Canada

2 4 6 8 9 7 5 3 1

For Mitch and for all my family and friends in the Shuswap,
a place I will always call home.

Go, go, go, said the bird: human kind
Cannot bear very much reality.
Time past and time future
What might have been and what has been
Point to one end, which is always present.

T.S. ELIOT,
from *Burnt Norton*

1.

THE FIRE ON THE HILLSIDE shimmered in the night like a bed of dying embers in a fireplace. Pretty. Not frightening at all. The smell of woodsmoke in the air conjured ghosts of past campfires. Wieners and blackened marshmallows. Watery hot chocolate. But the fire was crawling across the top of our mountain, and was now beginning to head down the slope as well, threatening this valley of farms and acreages. Several huge columns of smoke loomed over the Ptarmigan Hills, blackening out the stars.

Across the field, Jude passed under the yard light, carrying a box from his kiln shed to the Toyota pickup. If I could see him, he could see me standing here in my mother's kitchen in the T-shirt and panties I had worn to bed. I reached for the switch intending to turn off the light so he wouldn't notice me as I watched him, but I changed my mind and pressed my hand to the glass of the window instead. The smell of cumin on him as we danced in the Turtle Valley hall all those years ago. The heat of his hand at my waist. His thigh against mine.

A bird bashed into the pane and I gasped and jumped back. It was a junco, scared off the mountain by the fire, I imagined. When it flew away I saw a figure reflected in the window, an old woman standing beside the door to my parents' room behind me. I swung around to see who it was, but I was alone in the kitchen. My mother's whistles and Dad's snores still rang from behind the closed door to their room. When I looked back at the window I saw only my own face mirrored hazily there, but I had seen the old woman, there had been someone in the room with me, I was sure of it.

I grabbed my father's robe from the bathroom and put it on as I started my search through the house for the woman, opening my sister Val's old room first, where my son, Jeremy, slept on one of the two single beds, his face flushed and his hair wet with the heat. Then I eased open the door to my parents' room, careful not to bump the fire extinguisher that hung by the door, as it often fell from its housing when someone brushed by it. My mother was curled into herself and nearly falling off her side of the bed, her eyes moving beneath their lids in dream. My father spooned her; his arms and legs were outlined under the covers. Then to my childhood room, where my husband, Ezra, snored, his arm hanging off the side of the double bed. I opened the door to the parlour, which my mother used only for storage now.

The boxes and bags stacked on the piano. But there was no one else in the house.

I checked to make sure Jeremy was all right one more time, stopping a moment to smooth his sweaty forehead, then went back to the kitchen, where I turned on a burner and placed a small pot of milk on the stove in an effort to calm myself. The *Vancouver Sun* I had picked up that afternoon at a gas station in Golden now sat on the table; on the front page a headline about this fire read, *If you have 10 minutes to flee a forest fire, what do you take?* The whole of Turtle Valley had just been placed on evacuation alert, and if the fire did take a run down that slope toward the valley, we would be given only a ten-minute warning to get out. Not nearly enough time to salvage my parents' precious possessions. So we had begun to gather them now, for storage at my sister Val's place in Canoe, just outside of Salmon Arm, until the threat of evacuation was over.

All around me cardboard boxes and garbage bags were stacked hip-high. But even before this fire, the house was not simply cluttered but tumultuous, each room full of my mother's accumulated thrift-shop finds of wicker baskets, dishes, bags of yarn, and stacks of books, as well as her contest winnings. My mother entered competitions of all kinds, and her mailbox was jammed with junk mail as a result. But she did sometimes win. There was a ceramic geisha from a contest advertised on a box of mandarin oranges; a barbecue from a local grocery store; an exercise bike from a sporting goods store. These items sat about the house unused, gathering dust and cat hair. She never gave them away as gifts, as both Val and I wished she would.

Ezra, Jeremy, and I had arrived in Turtle Valley earlier that evening, after driving all day from our farm outside Cochrane,

Alberta, to help load my parents' things and deal with their farm animals. As we passed through Salmon Arm, we had seen a crowd of tourists on the pier, watching the Martin Mars water bomber as it picked up water from Shuswap Lake to dump on this fire. Twenty or more firefighters in full gear, grimy in soot, were gathered at the Tim Hortons that we stopped at for washrooms and donuts. When we entered Turtle Valley, making the skip from pavement to the reddish gravel of Blood Road, we saw neighbours sitting out on lawn chairs, drinking beer and watching the fire creep over the hills above. The sun, shining weakly through the plumes of smoke, cast a thin yellow light over the trees of the hillsides, the pastures on the benchlands, and the farms in the narrow valley bottom. On one lawn, children jumped on a trampoline as a light dusting of ash fell around them.

I turned off the burner, poured the milk into a cup, and carried it to the window, where I stood for a time looking out at Jude's yard. He carried another box to his truck, loading up his possessions for storage elsewhere, out of the path of the fire, just as we were. I hadn't spoken to him for nearly six years. He had once come over to my parents' place for coffee any time he saw our truck in the yard. But that last visit with him had been our first since Ezra's stroke, and Ezra had still been very often confused, and prone to blurting out whatever thought came to mind. During a lull in the conversation he had asked Jude, "You come here to glance at Kat, don't you?"

Jude's cheeks reddened. "Well, yes, I came to see Kat. And you, and Gus and Beth."

I put my hand on Ezra's. "He comes over to visit Mom and Dad often. He's not just here to see me."

"You still want her, don't you?"

Jude pushed back his chair. "Maybe I should go."

"No, please, Jude," I said. "He doesn't know what he's saying. It's the stroke talking."

"It's okay. Lillian is expecting me back home for lunch. It was good to see you Kat." He nodded. "Ezra." I watched him walk over to his place, following the path that wound past the old well. After that I waved to Jude when I saw him in town, or as I drove by his place on my way to my parents' farm, but he didn't come over during my visits home anymore, and I never summoned the courage to face him or Lillian, to stop in on them and say hello.

The fire extinguisher slipped from its mount on the wall and crashed into the open box below. I startled and turned, expecting to find my mother, as she often knocked that extinguisher down when she left her room, but there was no one there. I listened a moment to see if the noise had woken Jeremy, but the house remained still.

When I picked up the extinguisher to replace it, I saw the corner of my grandmother's carpetbag lying beneath a stack of my mother's writings in the box. This carpetbag was the one my grandmother carried in that last photograph of her, a picture taken by a street photographer who made a living snapping shots of people as they strode along the sidewalk in Kamloops. She was not expecting to be photographed—her brow was furrowed and her face was tense because, my mother told me, her hips and knees were so badly worn that each step she took was painful. Her outfit was very much of her time: the sensible black shoes, the big round buttons of her coat, the carpetbag slung over one arm. She had sewn the bag herself from flowered upholstery fabric, and fashioned it with curved wooden handles varnished the colour of butterscotch. Even though it wasn't quite the sort of valise Mary Poppins carried, as a child I had begged my mother to let me play with it. But she always said no. "My mother was a very private woman," she told me later, when I was in my twenties. "No one looked in her handbag, not even my father."

"Surely she wouldn't have minded us looking at her things once she was gone," I said.

"I mind." And she had kept it hidden from me, in her room.

As I pulled the carpetbag out of the box, my grandmother's billfold and dozens of dead ladybugs fell from inside it to the floor. The insects often overwintered in this house, creeping inside in the fall through the many cracks in the door and window frames, and gathering into swarms within unused dresser drawers, just as they did outside under piles of leaves and other litter. But I had never before seen them in such great numbers.

I picked up my grandmother's wallet. It was fat with bits of paper: shopping lists and receipts, the obituaries of lady friends, a few of the community notes my mother had written for the Promise paper. A tiny worn photograph—not much bigger than a good-sized postage stamp—was wrapped inside a carefully folded news story. It showed a slim, sharp-featured man, dressed in a white shirt with braces and armbands, leaning on a shovel. On the back, in my grandmother's hand, was written: *Valentine, June 1945, in his garden.* Valentine Svensson, my father's uncle. I unfolded the news story. My grandmother had written the date on the clipping: *April 1, 1965.*

PRESS-TIME NEWS FLASHES
TURTLE VALLEY MAN MISSING

A private search in the Ptarmigan Hills revealed no
sign of Turtle Valley resident John Weeks. Well-
known area woodsman Valentine Svensson under-
took the search along with his nephew Gustave
Svensson last night on horseback. They were doing
so at the request of Mr. Weeks's wife after Mr.
Weeks failed to return from a late evening hike into
the hills. Mr. Svensson says he plans to continue
the search today and overnight if necessary, saying
that his efforts last night and early this morning
were hampered by heavy rainfall.

This newspaper story was about my family. John Weeks was
my grandfather and his wife was Maud Weeks, the grandmother
who had owned this carpetbag; their daughter, Beth, was my
mother. Gustave Svensson—Gus—was my dad. I looked out the
window at the Ptarmigan Hills where my father and great uncle
had searched for my grandfather. Against the night sky the fire
on the ridge was the corona of the sun seen in an eclipse: flames
like solar flares licked up into the black. Why hadn't my parents
ever told me the story of how my grandfather was lost? They
were both such great storytellers; it seemed so unlikely that they
would forget to tell me this.

I searched through the rest of the contents of the purse,
looking for other newspaper clippings that would tell me when
my grandfather was found, but there weren't any. Instead I was
surprised to find a tiny jar of sweetly scented rouge, something

I never would have guessed my grandmother owned. The blush still carried its vibrant red colour; its perfume was spicy, flamboyant, not words my mother used to describe my grandmother. I hadn't known her; I was only a few months old when she passed away of a heart attack inside the greenhouse not far from the house.

I put everything back in the bag and went to the window to finish my hot milk. My grandmother would have looked out this window to see Valentine walking across his yard, just as I now saw Jude carrying another box to his truck. My parents had inherited that land on Valentine's death and even now, more than twenty years after they had sold the place to Jude Garibaldi, they continued to graze their small herd of cattle there, as they had when they farmed the land with Valentine. I could just make out the rooflines of the crumbling log home that had once belonged to Valentine, and a second two-storey farmhouse that had been left incomplete and never lived in, and was badly weathered by the time I played in it as my parents drank coffee with my great-uncle. There were many loose floorboards in that house, and I would pry them up with a hammer, searching for treasure. I found one of my Uncle Valentine's old MacDonald's tobacco cans under there once, but it was rusted shut, and I was on the hunt for dimes and marbles, so I left the can where it was, and never thought any more of it.

Movement pulled my attention to my grandmother's ancient greenhouse, a shadow dancing against the dirty glass walls. The old woman? I hunted through the kitchen junk drawer until I found a flashlight and then slipped on my runners to step out onto the porch stairs. The lilac bush beside me was strung, as always, with clear Christmas lights; I plugged the cord into the outside socket and the bush lit up, casting a circle of light around me. Jude was crossing his yard, carrying another box to the truck. When he saw the lights on the lilac bush go on, he stopped and shifted the box in order to wave. I waved back. He stopped a moment looking my way before continuing on to the truck.

The potting shed was the entrance to the greenhouse, and as I passed through it, I lifted cobwebs out of my way. "Hello?" I said and shone a light into the corners. The shelves of pots, the crunch of dry soil and pot shards beneath my feet, the smell of dust and smoke. A spider sped over the back of my hand and, after taking a moment to enjoy the panic and tickle, I shook it off. Then I stepped over the threshold into the greenhouse itself. But the place was empty. My mother had not grown anything here since my grandmother's death; Maud had had her heart attack here, and my father had found her body lying on the dirt floor.

I heard the jingle of keys shaking within a pocket, and the crunch of footsteps on the gravel driveway, and I stepped outside. "Jude, is that you?" The footsteps stopped. I scanned the dark driveway—the haze of smoke in the flashlight's stream—but couldn't see anyone. Nevertheless, I heard footsteps, running toward me. I ran onto the porch and into the kitchen, closing the door behind me and locking it, and then listened, breathing hard, for footsteps on the porch. When I finally turned away from the door, I found that my grandmother's chair was rocking by itself, and every burner on the stove was on, glowing red.

2.

WHEN I BROUGHT MY SON into the kitchen for breakfast the next morning, I found my mother, Beth, sitting in her mother's rocker, scribbling with a purple pen that smelled of green apples, a child's pen, on a pad of sentimental stationery adorned with butterflies. Judge Judy presided from a television set that flickered on a wire trolley in front of her. At her feet the ancient black cat I'd named Harrison wore a harness and was tied, like a dog, to the table leg, so it wouldn't run out an open door. This cat was my fault. Jude had given it to me when it was a kitten, and a year later, when I moved to Vancouver to go back to school, wishing to keep nothing of Jude or that past, I left

Harrison on the farm with my mother. The cat was now nearly sixteen years old and its hair was dull, sticking up at all angles and falling out, and yet my mother had reported only a month before, in one of her daily faxes, that Harrison had caught eight mice under the porch over a single weekend while tethered to the railing. I wondered about the need for that harness; surely the elderly beast wouldn't have wandered far. Still, my mother feared it would run out the door and leave her.

Jeremy rubbed his eye with a fist and yawned as I led him by the hand to the kitchen table. "Grandpa!" he cried when he saw my dad, Gus. He settled into my father's lap, wrapping his arms around him. My father had once been portly and hairy, his eyebrows so long they curled over his glasses, but now he was nearly hairless, and thin. Within his bony face his eyes were especially startling, an unearthly aqua that didn't look quite real, as if he were wearing coloured contact lenses. A lovely colour that Val inherited. I have deep brown eyes; my grandmother's eyes, Mom told me.

For twenty years my father had been battling prostate cancer and it appeared that he was now losing that fight. Between our previous visit, in May, and this one in early August, he had lost his ability to walk unaided. Now he required our help to get from his bed to the bathroom, or to the kitchen table. His skin had taken on a yellowed transparency that allowed us to see the deep blue veins that ran like rivers and their tributaries over the backs of his hands.

"Does Grandma get a big hug too?" my mother said, holding out her arms.

I ran my fingers through my son's blond curls. "How about you give Grandma a hug?"

But Jeremy shook his head and retreated into my father's embrace, and my mother shrank back into her rocking chair to hide in her writing pad.

"Beth, will you look at that," my father said, to draw my mother out of herself, I think, and she glanced up to see a huge Martin Mars water bomber appear from the smoke over the Ptarmigan Hills, as if manifested by some elaborate trick. I lifted Jeremy onto a chair to see, and opened the window slightly so he could better hear the deep drone of the plane flying overhead.

"I don't understand how the fire got so big so fast," Mom said. "But then it's been so hot and dry." She pointed her pen at me. "Kat, you saw the lightning strike that started it, didn't you?"

"We only just got here last night, Mom. We were in Alberta when the fire began."

"Oh, of course; what am I thinking?" Her hand fluttered to her mouth as she turned to my father. "Now who was it that saw the lightning strike? Was it Val? Or one of the neighbours? Or was someone talking about it in the paper?" When my father didn't answer, she went back to scribbling on her pad of paper. I made out the words *lightning* and *forgotten*.

I poured Jeremy a bowl of Cheerios and he sat at the table. "I think there might have been someone inside the house last night."

My mother looked up. "Oh?"

"I saw someone reflected in the window, an old woman in the room behind me."

"It's the warped glass," said my father. "I've seen all kinds of things in it. Likely it was your own face."

"No. It was an old woman, standing beside your door. I thought maybe she was confused, disoriented in the panic of the fire, and had entered our home thinking it was hers."

Val had told me how many of the elderly in her care, their brains riddled like wormy wood, had roamed away from home. They never went far, because their minds flitted, like a toddler's, from one fascination to another, from the sparkle of mica flecks in a boulder to the bob of a Steller's jay feeding on the head of a sunflower. Val said she always found these lost souls within a mile or two of their homes, most often lying on the ground, curled in sleep.

"Like Mrs. Simms," said my mother.

"Yes." Mrs. Simms had once babysat me, and now required supervision herself. She had wandered up to my parents' house one afternoon that past spring. Mom found her standing on the porch looking through the screen door, wavering back and forth unsteadily. *The look on that woman's face,* my mother had written in her fax as she described this visit, *as if she were a rabbit caught in a car's headlights.*

"When I ran back to the house, all the burners were turned on."

My mother touched her cheek. "Had you been using the stove?"

"I made myself a hot milk. But I wouldn't have turned all the burners on."

"I've done that and forgotten," Mom said. "I must have forgotten."

"It couldn't have been you, could it? Turning the burners on?"

"Val says I'm forever doing that. Other times I'll come into the kitchen and the stove will be on. I don't remember doing it.

It's a strange thing to be this forgetful. It's like there's another person living in the house, a person I never see, doing things, and then I find them done."

"A ghost."

"Boo!" said Jeremy.

"Could it have been Jeremy?" said Dad. "Turning on the burners?"

"The first thing I did was check to see he was okay. He was fast asleep. You were all asleep." I put a piece of bread in the toaster for myself. "I guess Ezra could have been sleepwalking. He's done it before." During the weeks following Ezra's stroke six years before, he once rose from bed to urinate in our clothes closet, thinking, I suppose, that it was the bathroom. I saw him in the half-light, the erotic stance of a man peeing. In the morning I scrubbed the stain from the carpet with Nature's Miracle, a cleaner I had picked up at the pet store to remove the stains the previous owner's dog had left behind. I never told Ezra about that incident. He had already suffered too many indignities.

"We better lock things up tonight," Dad said. "There's always the chance of looters at a time like this."

"Was anything missing?" Mom asked.

I waved at the bags and boxes on the floor around us. "How would we know?"

Mom staggered up from the rocker, setting it rocking, and grabbed the broom from the corner. As she began to sweep the space not occupied by boxes, cat hairs lifted into the spill of light from the window. From the television Judge Judy ranted on. "I meant to tidy up before you came."

"It's fine, Mom."

"The cleaning ladies haven't come for a couple of weeks."

"It's actually been a couple of months. I'm sorry I had to cancel them."

"Oh, well, it's better they aren't coming. Val can always come over and help. You know it costs her nearly two hundred dollars a month to keep Penny and Carol coming?"

I glanced at my father, who gave a little nod as if to say, *I know.* I had no idea Mom had become so forgetful. "I paid for the housecleaners, Mom," I said. "I just couldn't afford to anymore after Ezra lost his last job."

"The house is looking better, though," she said. "Don't you think?"

I looked around the room with her but didn't say anything. With almost each trip home I found Mom had made changes. She'd thrown out a couch and put two chairs in its place, or painted the bathroom walls green, only to repaint them blue before my next visit. This time she had put up wallpaper trim along the top of the kitchen wall: sunflowers and roosters. Layer after layer of my mother's renovations hid the home my grandmother knew. Yet there were vestiges of that past here: the white damask linen on the table under the clear plastic tablecloth; the elderly green kitchen scales that sat on top of the cupboard; the round, beautifully carved breadboard that hung on the partition wall that separated the kitchen from Val's old room. My grandfather built the wall, but he didn't have it meet the ceiling. It was meant to be a temporary wall, my mother had told me, and at the time John Weeks built it, he intended to put on an addition that would have been my mother's room. He would then have taken down the partition, to enlarge the kitchen to its original size. But he never got around to starting the project.

I took the breadboard down from this wall. "We can't forget to take this." Specks of dried dough from my grandmother's last day of bread-making were trapped within the elaborately and deeply carved foliage that rimmed its edge. Except for times when Mom took it down to accommodate her renovations, the breadboard had hung on that partition, unused, since the day of my grandmother's death nearly forty years before. The surface was sliced and nicked, as one would expect, but the marks were in the direction of the grain more often than not. My grandmother's habits were recorded there in wood.

"I've never been able to keep house," my mother said. "My mother always kept this place spotless. It seemed like every time I came in the house I'd find her on the stepladder, wiping off the top of that partition, as if anyone was ever going to see the dust up there. She was so very organized, like you, Kat." Mom leaned on her broom for a moment and nodded at me. "You came into this world to replace your grandmother." Because I was born just a few months before she died, and I looked so much like her, my mother had given me Maud's wedding band. But Val had known our grandmother, as she was fifteen the year Maud died and I was born, and I'm sure she resented me getting that ring. I wore it next to my own wedding band.

"I came across Grandma's carpetbag in that box last night." I pointed to where the bag sat now, on top of the box. "It was full of dead ladybugs. I guess a swarm of them overwintered in it."

"My mother always called me her ladybird," said Mom. "Even when she was in her seventies, I was still her little ladybird."

"Lady *bird*," Jeremy said and laughed. "It's not ladybird, it's lady*bug*. Ladybug, ladybug, fly 'way home!" he sang. "Your house is on fire. Your children all gone."

"That's what they call them in the old country," my mother told him.

I glanced at my mother. "I took a look through the carpet-bag."

She pushed the small pile of dirt into the corner before propping the broom up there as well. "I wish you hadn't. Those were her private things."

"I know, I'm sorry. I was just curious." I watched her as she brushed crumbs off the counter to the floor with a dishcloth. "There was a photo of Uncle Valentine in her wallet. It was wrapped up in a newspaper story that says Grandpa was lost in those mountains and Dad and Uncle Valentine went to find him. Why didn't you ever tell me about that?"

My father coughed, and I patted his back. "The smoke," he said, and coughed again, holding his chest. I closed the window.

"How long was he lost?" When my mother didn't answer I said, "Your father was found, wasn't he? He died of a heart attack, right?"

"Yes, his heart."

I could form no mental image of my grandfather's face. There were no pictures of him in the house and so I had no idea what the man had looked like, though my mother claimed to have inherited his lantern jaw, a fact she was unhappy about.

"So why didn't you ever tell me that he'd gone missing?"

Dad reached over and took my mother's hand so she'd stop fidgeting with the dishcloth. "Wasn't anything to tell," he said.

"Why would Grandma carry Valentine's picture?"

"Valentine and Maud were old friends long before your mother and I married," Dad said. "He built that greenhouse for her."

"Yes, but why would she carry *his* picture and not others, not of her own husband or children, or grandchildren for that matter?"

My mother picked up her pad of paper and pen and sat back in the rocker. "Every spring Valentine would hunt out the wild yellow and purple violets and bring her a little bouquet. I remember my mother once glancing at me as she told my father that I'd picked those violets while I was bringing in the cows. It's the only real lie I can remember her telling."

"Were she and Valentine more than friends?"

My mother looked up at me. Her cataracts made her blue eyes milky, ghostly; she appeared to be looking not at me but through me. "My mother was a very handsome woman. Even when she was in her sixties she attracted the attention of men as she walked down the streets in Kamloops. I remember one day just before you were born, when she and I were shopping and she happened to smile at a gentleman who opened a door for her—just a courteous smile, there was nothing flirtatious about my mother—and he turned and followed her, and attempted to strike up a conversation. She rebuffed him, politely, of course."

I tucked my hands in my jeans pockets, and looked out at Valentine's cabin and the unfinished house. Then I found myself staring at my own face mirrored faintly in the window, where the lilac boughs blocked the light. The imperfect glass created an image that was rippled and hazy, but I could still make out my long nose and full mouth, dark hair and brows. My reflection was the likeness of Maud as a young woman, and yet over the course of these six years since Ezra's stroke, I had lost all confidence that I could inspire passion in the way she evidently had.

"But you've got to remember the times they were living in," Mom said. "I can't remember Valentine ever calling her anything other than Mrs."

I turned. "Mrs.?"

"Just Mrs."

My mother began scribbling again. She wrote of the conversation we had just had, I know. It was her habit to chronicle even the smallest details of her life immediately after they transpired, but she wasn't present for these moments any more than tourists who view their vacations through the lens of a camcorder. Nevertheless, if I understood little else about my mother, I thought I understood this, because writing was one thing we had in common. I assumed she wrote to preserve the moment, to stop its fleeting, to stop its loss. Of course these were only projections. I had never asked her why she wrote so obsessively. I assumed she was driven to write down the details of her life for the same reasons I wrote: to make sense of things, to give the random events of life meaning, and to remember—as memory was such a mercurial companion, and one not to be counted on.

3·

I POURED JEREMY ANOTHER BOWL of Cheerios, and then stood near the window eating my toast as my parents watched Judge Judy. In the yard, Ezra rearranged the boxes and bags of my mother's things in the back of our truck, trying to make more room. A T-shirt and jeans had become his new uniform, now that he was farming again. They replaced the dress shirts and pressed pants he had worn to teach English at the college before he'd suffered the stroke. But even when he taught for a living, he had moved with the sureness of one accustomed to physical labour; his big farmer hands never lost their calluses as he continued to garden and keep a few chickens and sheep on our acreage in Chilliwack.

A few months after his stroke, he had carved in wood a life-size likeness of one of his callused hands, and had given it to me as a gift, a hand nearly twice the size of my own. The muscled back of that hand; the bulging scar on the thumb where he had cut himself chopping wood. The carving of the hand felt very much like Ezra's real one: rough, warm, and protective. On his good days. This carving stood on its wrist on the wooden table that served as my writing desk, a table Ezra had also made for me. He had fashioned both from pine and left them unvarnished, so the hand appeared to be one with the table, as if someone had been caught within, drowning in wood.

Yet another helicopter flew toward us, dragging an orange bucket by a tether. As it flew overhead it shook the windowpane, and I pressed my hand against the glass to feel the vibrations. All morning, helicopters and air tankers had made one run after the other, from Shuswap Lake at Salmon Arm, where they filled up with water, to this valley where they dumped their loads on the fire. Two more helicopters dropped their buckets on the hills above now. Below, at the foot of the mountain, a flatbed truck carrying a bulldozer rumbled along the road heading up the valley to the fire. Regular traffic had been diverted away from Turtle Valley and only local traffic and firefighters were permitted on Blood Road. Driving in the opposite direction to the flatbed truck, a string of pickups, loaded with personal possessions, were heading out of the valley.

My mother left her television program to stand by the window with me. "My father would have hated this," she said. "All this noise. It's like a war zone." She stared for a time at Jude's yard, at Valentine's cabin and the unfinished house, then she turned to me. "Jude stopped in just before you arrived yesterday, asking for you. He heard from Val that you'd be coming down. I didn't want to tell you in front of Ezra."

"What did he want?"

"There was something—I should have written it down. I imagine he wants you to phone him back."

"He has a box of yours," said Dad. "Something he found in his basement as he was packing up his stuff."

Mom sat back in her rocker. "Yes, a box, that's right."

"I can't remember leaving anything with him. Why didn't he just drop it off when he came?"

"I imagine he wants to see you again," said Mom. "Val must have told you Lillian left."

"When?"

"Last winter. She moved to Calgary. Her mother lives there, evidently."

"And Andy?"

"He went with his mother," Dad said. He pointed at his room. "Grab my wallet, will you? And bring my cards while you're at it." I retrieved his wallet and deck of cards from his bedside table, where he kept the few items that were his alone—his razor, his jackknife, his harmonica, his wallet, his deck of cards—as his bed was where he now spent the better part of his days. When I handed him his wallet he leafed through it until he found a business card. "Jude said to give you this. He wants you to pop over if you see the pickup in the driveway."

I looked down at the card. *The Jude Garibaldi Pottery. High-fired functional pottery and raku. Distinctive masks, lamps, vases and wall pieces.* He had written his cellphone number on the back. "He's not trying to sell his paintings anymore?" I asked.

"Hasn't for years," Dad said. "No money in it."

"But he's doing okay?"

"It shook Jude up pretty bad that Andy made the decision to live with Lillian. He makes the trek up to see the kid every couple of weeks. So he's been keeping to himself a lot lately. We see him over in his studio or kiln shed, working all the time. He never goes to the dances at the hall anymore." Dad sighed. "But then neither do I."

The ancient screen door squeaked open and I slipped the card into the front pocket of my jeans. As Ezra entered, my mother jumped up from her rocker like a child caught in a forbidden act. "I should be packing. You want coffee?"

But Ezra's attention was seized by the flickering images on the television set, Judge Judy lecturing.

"Ezra?" I said. "Mom asked if you want coffee."

"No, thanks. The day's flaming."

Since the stroke, Ezra spoke of his world with descriptions that were often more apt than common phrases. "It's too hot, you mean," I said, offering him the words as Ezra's speech therapist had told me to in the early months of his recovery, in an effort to help him regain his facility with language.

"Yes." But his eyes were focused on the television.

"Would you mind if we turned the television off for a while?" I asked my mother.

"Gus so likes his Judge Judy," she said.

"I don't," he said. "That's your show."

"Ezra can't concentrate on the conversation if that TV is on," I said. He had once described the feeling of being bombarded by the sound in nearly any environment as having his shirttail tugged by the hands of hundreds of persistent toddlers, all wanting his attention at once. "Everything is saying, *Look at me! This is important!*" he had told me.

My mother fidgeted with her teacup as her gaze slipped to Ezra. "There's lemonade in the fridge if you want some," she said to him.

"Ezra?" I said.

"What?"

"There's lemonade in the fridge if you want some. Glasses are over the sink." But he leaned against the kitchen counter instead, absorbed in Judge Judy.

I stood and poured glasses for Ezra, Jeremy, and myself and put them on the table. "Maybe you could sit over here, so you're not facing the television. So you can join the conversation." When he still didn't respond, I sipped my lemonade and watched a helicopter head out of the valley for another load. Sprinklers saturated the area around Jude's studio and home; the wind cast the water across the yard. But there was no sign of Jude, though both his pickup and his Impala were in the driveway. Likely he was still sleeping after working so late into the night, as he always had in the days leading up to a show.

"He's sleeping," said Jeremy.

"Who?"

"That guy." He pointed at Jude's house.

I put a hand on my son's shoulder and glanced at Ezra to see if he had been listening, but he was lost in the television. I didn't know what to make of these brief tears my son made in the fabric of my reality, where he seemed to reach into my own mind. I hadn't talked to other mothers about it, or even to Ezra, though I knew he saw it too, as he often raised his eyebrows to me at times like this.

In the pasture surrounding Valentine's old cabin, a lame calf stumbled far behind my father's small herd. The calf's mother bellowed from some distance away, trying to encourage it to catch up. "What's the matter with that calf?" I asked Dad.

"Something's haywire with the ligaments in its front legs. Born like that. I kept meaning to put it down. But now I can't get out of the damn house. I've got to do something about it before the cops come and tell us to get the hell out of here."

"I'll do it," Ezra said.

"What about Ernie?" I asked my father.

"Ernie?" Ezra asked.

"He runs that butcher outfit off Fredrickson Road."

"I doubt he could get to it any time soon," Dad said. "At the best of times you've got to give him a week's notice, and with this fire raging there'll be lots of folks trying to get their animals butchered so they don't have to find a place to pasture them."

Jeremy emptied his glass and banged it on the table. "More lemonade!" he sang.

"Just a minute, Jeremy." I reached across the table to the television set. "Can I at least turn this down?"

Ezra sat at the table. "I said I'd murder the calf. I'll do it this morning."

"We'll be packing, and you'll need to get some rest."

"You don't think I can fly with it."

"What about Uncle Dan?" I asked Dad. My mother's brother.

"I don't want Dan to see that gimpy calf," Dad said.

"He knows you haven't been well. No one's going to judge you for it."

"I said I'd do it."

"More!" Jeremy sang out. "More!"

"Jeremy, please stop," I said. But he banged the glass again, even as I tried to take it away.

Ezra slammed his fist on the table, upsetting my glass; a puddle of lemonade spilled to the floor. "For Christ's sake stop that!" he cried. "Why do you have to make so much frickin' noise all the time?"

Jeremy began to wail and I pulled him onto my lap, shushing him.

I saw my parents exchange a glance and then my mother turned off the television and lowered herself to her knees to wipe up the pool of lemonade. When Jeremy wouldn't stop crying, I turned him toward me, and held his face. "We need to be quiet for Daddy, Jeremy. He loves you. It's the noise making him mad, not you."

Jeremy wiped his face with his sleeve. "Yucky smells make Daddy mad too, like Grandma's perfume."

I laughed a little in embarrassment. The scent of her lavender powder. It was a thing I had just learned, that ever since the stroke, Ezra had to fight through even the distraction of smell in order to focus on a conversation or task. Until recently, I hadn't understood that the reason he sometimes withdrew from me, or became overwhelmed to the point of anger, was the scent I wore.

"My father was like that," Mom said as she pulled herself up from the floor using the table. "Noise overwhelmed him. When he was exhausted, he had to spend whole days lying in bed with those dark green blinds pulled down, otherwise he'd moan and cry out about the light. He expected to be waited on as a sick child does. If he wanted ice cream on a hot day, he got ice cream. My mother would crank our ice-cream maker until she was sweating and her arm gave out, and I would take over. We would do anything to avoid his anger. It was my job to scoop the ice cream out of the maker with that old ice-cream scoop and take him a bowl. I gave that scoop to you, didn't I?"

I nodded. A wonderful antique scoop with a wooden handle and the brand name *Gilchrist's* inscribed on the thumb lever. Though its bowl was dented as if it had been used as a hammer, the mechanism still worked smoothly.

Mom sat back in her rocking chair and took up her pad of paper again. "I still don't like ice cream. It makes me think of him on those bad days."

"I'm so sorry," Ezra said. The look on his face, now that the burst of rage had discharged, was like that of a man stumbling from sleep. He pulled Jeremy out of my arms and onto his lap, but in his effort to get away, Jeremy arched his back across his father's knees until his head nearly touched the floor. When Ezra sat him upright and tried to hug him again, Jeremy bit his hand. "Shit!" said Ezra.

Jeremy leapt around the table. "Shit! Shit! Shit!"

"Jeremy, come here!" I said. "We don't bite. Biting hurts. You say sorry!"

"Sorry, Daddy."

Ezra held out his hands, but Jeremy retreated into my arms. I looked up at Ezra. "Just give it a couple of minutes. He'll forget all about it." And within a moment he had.

Still sitting in my lap, Jeremy tapped the kitchen window behind me and pointed. "Who's that guy?"

I scanned the yard for what had caught his attention and found a man standing by the old well. When I was a child the site of the well was marked by four fenceposts, but it was now hidden within a small patch of poplars, wild rose, and snowberry bushes in the middle of the field. The man stood within this bush. By the stoop of his shoulders I guessed that he was elderly, and he was dressed in a jack shirt and black fedora, an outfit better suited to rainy spring days than this smoky August heat. The lenses of his glasses glinted as he looked in our direction.

"Mom, who is that?" I asked.

"Where?"

"There's an old guy standing by the well."

"Likely some looky-loo trying to get a better view of the fire," Dad said. "I expect there'll be a lot of people stopping along the road to watch."

My mother sat up to see. "He's by the well?"

"He was. I don't see him now. He must have gone."

"Are there any toys around here?" asked Jeremy.

"Why don't you go into my old room and see what you can find?" And he skipped off to play with the few old toys of mine that my mother kept there.

"We should be worrying over water places," said Ezra.

"You mean thinking of water sources."

"I understood him, dear," Mom said.

Ezra pointed his chin toward the old well. "Any water there?"

"The well is filled in," I told him. "Or partly filled in."

"I remember my father choosing the site for that well," my mother said. "I was maybe four at the time, five? He got it in his head that he wanted to build my mother a new house, so off we all marched into the field to find water."

It was a story my mother had told many times. He used a willow stick for his witching, because a willow is always seeking water, but he didn't have much luck finding any. The divining stick wouldn't point for him. When he got frustrated and threw it to the ground, my grandmother calmed him down, as she always did, and then used the divining rod herself to find a spot. He dug the well there, by hand. When my mother saw him inside that hole he'd dug himself into, he didn't look like the father she knew. He was all face, and his legs tapered down into boots that appeared too small for him. She was used to looking up at her father. But here she was looking down on him.

"Wouldn't it be painless to find water on this place?" Ezra asked. "There are all those marshes."

"All he had to do was find poplars," said Dad. "There's always water where there's poplars."

"He just didn't seem to have the knack for divining," said my mother. "It was hard enough for him to see what was *there*, in front of his nose, much less what was hidden underground." My mother glanced around the room. "In any case he never built that new place. My parents ended up living out their lives in the house we're sitting in now."

"So the well is dry," said Ezra.

"There was water in it once," she told him. "Though it never ran clear. But he filled the well in."

"Why would he do that?"

She hesitated a moment, then told him the story of how my grandfather had buried a mule there. A good puller named Nelly that my mother often rode. But as soon as my grandfather took the reigns Nelly would dig in her heels and wouldn't move. He'd beat her with whatever was handy: a willow switch, a single-tree, a two-by-four. When she kicked my grandfather in the leg that last time, he slashed her across the muzzle with a willow switch, then had my mother put a halter on her and lead her to the well while he got his gun, as the mule would do nearly any-thing that my mother asked of it. He threw off the boards over the well and had her back the mule to its mouth. When Nelly wouldn't take that last step back into the hole, he whipped the animal. Her body shuddered as she lost her footing, and she looked up at my mother as she fell, pleading.

My mother tried to pull the gun out of her father's hands, to shoot the mule, to put her out of its misery, but he yanked the gun from her hands. When she tried to walk away, he dragged her back by the arm and forced her to watch Nelly die. There was about twelve feet of water at the bottom of that well, and nothing on the sides for the animal to get a footing on. My mother couldn't see much of her, just the flash of her eye now and again, a bit of her muzzle in the water down there in the black. But she could hear her, thrashing and snorting.

"I listened to her drown," my mother said and she wiped tears from her eyes. "Then he told me to get the shovels and we spent the rest of the day shovelling dirt into that hole to cover her body. It was dark when we went in for supper. That well was deep even with the fill. When those boards that covered it began to rot, I worried you might fall into that hole. I told you, didn't I, never to go near it?"

"Yes. Many times." But like any forbidden thing, it was a fascination. I crouched in the grass to pick the shooting stars that grew only around the well's dark mouth. I threw stones into it, fluttered handfuls of white petals from the field daisies into it, and kneeled to sing into it, to hear my voice distorted by its depth. I thought of that well now in cross-section, the bony face of the mule pointing upwards like an arrow at odds with the layers of sediment around it. The animal's bones glowing white in the surrounding black. So much time had passed, and yet the well was still there, and the mule was there, the instant of its death locked in soil.

4.

WHEN I LONGED FOR HOME, it wasn't my parents' dark farm-house that I missed, but those trees and bushes: the poplar, spruce, and cottonwood, pin cherry, and saskatoon that lined the driveway and hemmed the homesite, protecting it from the devilish winds of the valley, winds that blew the trees now and would urge on the fire as well. The lilac, fragrant flowering Russian olive, and bright-berried mountain ash that dotted the yard. The cherry, apple, peach, and nectarines of the orchard. The erotic cleavages of the plums ripening on the tree that Ezra stood on a ladder to prune. The trunk of this tree was deeply scarred from disease, so like the photos I'd seen of the brains of

Alzheimer's patients; great parts of the curled tissue were dead and black. I had sat within this tree as a child, batting away yellow jackets as I tore the red skin of its fruit with my teeth to get to the warm yellow flesh within. But now plums hung from only two of its gnarled branches.

"What are you up to?" I asked Ezra.

"This plant needs a good prune."

"It needs to be uprooted and burned."

"It's still creating fruit."

"You have a prairie boy's sensibility. Not all fruit trees are worth keeping."

"Long as it's got fruit on it, I don't see the bother in trying to solve it."

"Can I have one?" Jeremy asked, pointing at the plums.

"Sure you can." I reached up to press one of the fruit to gauge its ripeness, and burnished the plum on my T-shirt before handing it to him. "It's not safe to be up on a ladder in these winds." Ezra didn't respond. "You promised Dad you would butcher the calf this morning."

He turned on the ladder to look down at me. "Why are you always trying to halt me from doing what I want?"

"I'm not. It's just, with the fire we've got other things—"

But he turned his back on me. I crossed my arms and looked away, across the field. Jude's Toyota was still in his yard along with his old Impala. "All right then," I said. "If you're taking a break from loading the truck you won't mind if I head over to Jude's for a few minutes." The muscles in his shoulders tensed, but he said nothing, and kept his back to me. "Evidently he's got a box of mine." I waited a moment longer, but when he still didn't respond I held out my hand to

Jeremy and we headed down the worn path that crossed the field to Jude's place.

"Where are we going, Mommy?"

"To see an old friend."

THERE WASN'T A NUMBERED SIGN or a name burned into wood at the entrance to Jude's driveway, as there was on the other acreages up and down Turtle Valley. Instead there was a metal sign from an old restaurant that Jude had found at some roadside secondhand shop on a trip through the Okanagan: on a red background, in bold white lettering, was the word *Home*.

Jude had built the house himself, erecting the post-and-beam structure the year he bought the property from my parents, and had continued to add on as his needs dictated. When his son, Andy, was born he put the bedroom onto the back, and he replaced the stairs with the ramp and veranda when Lillian started using a wheelchair. A brand-new addition now jutted from the roofline over the master bedroom upstairs. He had talked about building something like it years before, to replace the low, angled ceiling of the bedroom, on which he bumped his head.

I led Jeremy by the hand up the ramp to the veranda to knock on the front door. A boy mannequin stood guard at the living-room window. So he had kept the mannequins. I had teased Jude, back then, for being a pack rat, for never throwing anything away. "And you're too quick to throw things out," he told me. "When you're young you think everything is disposable, even friends. You can always get another. But it's not true, you know. With almost everything I've thrown away, I've come to regret it later."

The back seat from a car sat on the veranda as a couch, and an old television was perched on an upturned log in front of it:

the glass, insides, and back panel had been removed so that, looking into that television, I saw a view of my parents' farm and the burning hills above. Over the mountain the Martin Mars made another drop, casting a splash of lurid pink-red, the peculiar colour of tandoori chicken, across the trees.

I knocked again.

"Look at the lady," said Jeremy, and I turned first to Jude's truck, and then to the Impala, the car he had driven when we were together all those years ago. Another one of our mannequins, a woman, lounged in the front seat of the Impala, with her legs crossed and thrust lazily out the passenger window. She wore red stiletto heels.

"Isn't she funny?" I said.

I followed Jeremy down to the Impala and peered into the car. The pair of baby shoes Jude and I had bought together dangled from the rearview mirror. Aside from these booties and the mannequin, the car was pretty much as it had been when he had taken me out for drives. The sticker in the rear window that read *Don't believe everything you think.* The red upholstery. No seatbelts in the front seats. He had installed the ones in the back after I left for the coast, for Andy's car seat. I had felt I was floating, untethered, when I rode with him in that car. Unsafe. Thrilled.

I heard steps inside the house and led Jeremy back to the veranda. Jude opened the door with a sheet wrapped around his waist and legs, the white fabric trailing on the floor behind him. "Katrine!" he said. His chest and arms were still muscular, a gift of the physical nature of his work, though he had a slight paunch above the folds of the sheet. Noting my gaze, no doubt, he pulled in his stomach.

"I've woken you."

"No, it's okay."

He stood back to let me in and I stepped into the high, open living space. Jude had cut the beams for this house from the birch on this property. Potted plants hanging from those beams obscured the light from the windows, giving the room a cool, submerged feel, a relief from the oppressive, smoky heat outside. The kitchen floor had recently been stripped down to the subfloor; a pile of new tiles sat in one corner waiting to be installed. There was a new computer on the kitchen table. Otherwise the house was pretty much as I remembered it. There was the same ancient, tiny fridge, the size of a hotel room's mini-bar, the Fisher wood stove that heated the house in winter, the avocado electric stove for cooking. He'd baked pumpkin soup with aged cheddar in that oven for me, during a visit with him and Lillian, cooked and served within the pumpkin shell.

Above the living room a steep set of stairs led to the balcony of the bedroom. There was no wall between this bedroom and the living room below. I could see the raised ceiling of the new addition, and the bed, from where I stood. The high white ceiling, the wood trim around the new, large windows, the sheer white curtains. It was now a breezy, light-filled room, so different from the dark, cramped bedroom he had shared with Lillian.

"I should have phoned first," I said.

Jude tucked the sheets more firmly about himself. "No, I'm glad you came."

"Jeremy, this is Jude."

"Hello, Jeremy."

"Hi."

"I bet you'd like some apple juice," Jude said.

"Yes, please," said Jeremy.

"How about you? You want a cup of tea? Or are you drinking coffee now?"

"Just water," I said.

I watched him walk to the kitchen. The muscles in his back. As he handed the glasses to us, I glanced down at the sheet he wore. He laughed. "I guess I better put something on."

I took a sip of water and watched him climb the stairs, the sheet sliding upwards with him, then averted my eyes as he let the sheet fall.

"That guy's naked," said Jeremy.

"He's getting dressed. It's not polite to stare when someone is putting his clothes on. Look at this vase. Isn't that lovely? Jude made that. And here's a picture of that funny lady we saw in Jude's car. I took that photo."

The year I photographed that mannequin was a dry one, and lake levels had fallen so much that the newly constructed pier extended out into a mud flat rather than into water; the docks where houseboats usually moored were now sitting on mud. I worked as a reporter for the newspaper at the time, and was looking for a photo to gently lampoon this tourist town's vulnerability to the whims of the weather. So Jude and I talked the curator into giving us a few of the old mannequins stored in the basement of the town's museum, and we hauled them down to the pier and set them up in the mud as if they were tourists playing. A crowd gathered on the pier above us, cheering and clapping each time we set up a mannequin in a new position. With Jude I did any silly thing, without embarrassment. I could not have talked Ezra into it.

"That's you, Mommy!"

I looked up to where he pointed, at the wall above, and there she was, my young self, smiling. "Jude painted that," I said. "He paints, too."

"I used to," Jude said from his bedroom above.

"You've got a big tummy in that picture," said Jeremy. "You're having a baby, like Jeannie." Jeannie, our neighbour in Cochrane, took care of Jeremy on days when I worked at the paper; she was now eight months along. I'd have to find another sitter, and soon. "That's me in your tummy."

"No, honey." I was never as pregnant as that painting allowed. I never showed much. It was all projection on Jude's part.

"Where is that baby?"

Jude descended the stairs, tucking his white T-shirt into his jeans. "She flew away," he said. I shook my head at him, to warn him not to say anything more, but he didn't understand.

"Where did she go?"

"Someplace happy," he said.

"Is she at the zoo? Mommy, can we go to the zoo?"

"Sure. Let's go to the Calgary zoo when we get back home."

"Will your baby be there?"

"This is me too." I pointed at the series of paintings along the wall. "And that one. And that one." Then I turned to Jude. "You kept them."

"Yes."

"Didn't Lillian object?"

"I stored them in my studio, until she left. She took most of the paintings we had put up." He grinned and scratched behind his ear. "I needed something to cover the walls."

"You got any toys?" Jeremy said.

"Ask nicely."

"Please?"

Jude squatted down in front of him. "You like Lego? There's a box in Andy's room."

"Yeah!"

"Right through that door."

Jeremy looked up at me. "Go on." Together Jude and I watched as he ran down the hallway into Andy's room. Then we stood in silence for a time, as we both struggled to come up with something to say. In the other room, Jeremy dumped the Lego onto the floor.

"This fire's a hell of a thing," Jude said. "I just keep loading boxes and carting them off to Mike's place in town, but I don't know what to take, what to leave behind. Mike picked out a pipe wrench with the bottom jaw missing from one of the boxes, and said, 'What the hell is this?' The thing is, I remember taking the damn thing off my workbench in the basement and putting it in the box yesterday. As if it was some family heirloom I had to save."

I nodded. "I couldn't talk Mom out of packing her collection of baskets this morning. She bought the works at the thrift shop."

"Well, I guess we can be forgiven for not thinking straight, given the circumstances."

We both looked at our feet for a while. Listened to Jeremy's singsong murmurings in play.

"I should apologize," I said finally, "for how Ezra behaved, when you came over to visit that last time."

He shrugged. "I should have known it would cause problems for you. I hope this visit isn't an issue."

"No, not really." I put my glass on the table and sat, and Jude sat with me. I nodded at the Impala. "You kept the baby shoes."

"I just found them as I was packing stuff out of the basement. It seemed right, somehow, to hang them in the car. All those drives we took." On back roads, so we wouldn't be seen together. "She would have been sixteen this coming spring."

"We never knew for sure it was a girl."

"You thought so, at the time."

I pointed out the window at Valentine's unfinished house. "Every Halloween when I was a girl my great-uncle would fill that old house with jack-o'-lanterns, all lit up with candles, and invite me and my friends in there to tell us a story he'd heard from the Sami in Lapland, about the ghost of an unwanted baby murdered at the hands of his own mother in secret. He said the ghost baby was seen crawling across the snow, hoping for revenge or that the truth of his death would come out; hoping to be named so his soul could rest."

"The miscarriage wasn't your fault, Katrine. It wasn't anyone's fault."

"I still hide it, though. I never told Mom. She hasn't seen that painting you did of me pregnant, has she?"

He shook his head. "I always go over to their place to visit."

"Jeremy knows, now. He'll be asking questions."

"Does it really matter?"

"I never told Ezra either."

"Why not?"

"I didn't know how he'd react. I didn't tell anyone, not even Val, though she guessed about you and me at the time. I imagine the whole valley did. But you were still living with Lillian; I didn't know what was going to happen between us. And then

I lost the baby, and Lillian got pregnant, and I lost you, and I didn't want to talk about it. Not with anyone."

"I'm so sorry, Katrine. You don't know how many times I thought of phoning you after you left for Vancouver. I felt I had to stay with Lillian but it wasn't what I wanted."

"You don't have to explain it again." I looked down at my glass. "I only just heard from Mom and Dad that you and Lillian had separated. It must have been hard, to lose them both like that."

"I drive up to see Andy a couple of times a month. I'd go more often if I could afford it. I phone him nearly every day." He ran his thumbnail along a crack in the table. "Val told me a few things, about Ezra, what you had to deal with after he had the stroke."

"He's much better than he was."

He looked up. "So he's not fully recovered?"

"He'll live with some handicaps for the rest of his life. I doubt he'll ever be able to teach again."

"Your dad said he had trouble holding down a job."

"He's forgetful, and he has trouble catching on to new things. He often gets caught up in projects that don't really matter—like right now he's over there pruning trees—so things that do matter don't get done. Not many employers will put up with that."

The day Ezra lost that last dairy job, milking cows, he shuffled the distance between the truck and the garage, where I waited on the steps, and stood on the step beneath me to press his head between my breasts. His arms dangled at his sides and his shoulders heaved as he sobbed. The stink of the dairy around him. "They fired me," he said. "Ron said I was taking too long, making too many stumbles. I can't even do a shit job right anymore."

He had milked cows as a fourteen-year-old at his father's dairy. Worked the four a.m. shift half asleep, he knew the job so well. And hated it.

"I don't mean to complain," I said. "We were very lucky. Right after Ezra had the stroke, his doctor told me he likely wouldn't be able to talk, if he survived at all. One of the nurses suggested we both learn sign language. Can you imagine? The two of us, with perfect hearing, having to use sign language."

"Like my uncle after his stroke," said Jude. "All he could say was *Fuck* and *Apple Jacks.*"

"Apple Jacks?"

"His favourite cereal. He ran his business for years on those few words, with the help of his sons. They learned how to interpret. With just a change in intonation he could make *Fuck* and *Apple Jacks* mean just about anything." When I laughed he said, "There are all kinds of ways to get your message across. You remember I told you about that trip I took through the Canary Islands?"

I nodded. Some hazy recollection.

"There are people there who have a language of whistles, so they can communicate across the valleys. Their whistles overlap like the songs from a bank of mud swallows."

"That has got to be one of your tall tales," I said. "A tribe of whistlers on the Canary Islands?"

"It's true!" After our smiles faded he continued to hold my gaze.

"Kiss!" Jeremy called out from Andy's room.

Jude grinned. "I guess he heard us."

"Heard what?"

"Andy used to pick up on what I was thinking all the time when he was that age."

I blushed and shook my head. "Jeremy wasn't reading my mind."

"Then he was reading mine."

I sat back in my chair. "I hear you have a box for me."

"It's there, on the coffee table. Mostly cards and letters from our time together, I think. Don't worry. I didn't snoop. When I saw they were your things I closed the box."

"I'm not sure I want to look. I'll look at it later, when I'm alone."

He clapped his hands together. "So, shall I show Jeremy my studio? Get him on the wheel? Kids love the muck."

"No, we've got to go."

"So soon?"

"Mom was making lunch." I stood. "I'll help Jeremy pick up the Lego."

"I'll take care of it."

I retrieved the box from the coffee table. "Jeremy," I called. "Time to go."

"I don't want to."

"Now, honey."

"Okay, okay!"

Jeremy came out carrying a turret made of Lego blocks. "That stays here," I said, and he slumped back into Andy's room with it.

Jude and I both looked out the window at Valentine's unfinished house as we waited. One of my parents' cows stood at the doorway of the old house, like a vacationer stepping out to admire the view.

"It was Gus's uncle who started building that place, right?" Jude asked. "It must have been. He homesteaded the property, didn't he?"

"Yes. Valentine began building it when he got engaged to Mary Peterson. Do you remember old Mrs. Samuels, Mary Samuels?"

He shook his head. When I was a child, I had visited Mrs. Samuels with my mother. She offered me ginger cookies, and brought out her autoharp for me to play with. The weight of the harp in my lap, the pick in my fingers, the thrill of strings thrummed.

"Evidently she broke the engagement with Valentine and married Charlie Samuels and that was that; my great-uncle stopped working on the house. I suppose he might have finished the thing if he'd found someone else to share it with. But he was one of those men, like my father, who never seemed to need much. He was happy in his occupations and his own company. Like you."

Jude grinned.

"I found a newspaper clipping last night that says Valentine led a search for my grandfather when he went missing. Mom and Dad never talked about that with you, did they?"

"No. Never."

"The clipping was in my grandmother's wallet, wrapped around a picture of Uncle Valentine."

"Ah-hah! There's got to be a story behind that. You're going to write about it, of course."

"I don't know." I hadn't written much in the way of fiction in the six years since Ezra's stroke. There simply wasn't the time or energy for it. Instead I jotted down ideas in the notebook I carried in my purse, whenever I had a spare moment.

When this notebook was full I would squirrel it away with the others in a shoebox in my closet, thinking that one day I would lower a bucket into this reservoir and from it another novel would emerge.

"Jeremy," I called. "Come on. Time to go."

"When are you heading back to Alberta? I'd like to see you again."

"It depends on what happens with this fire."

"Mind if I pop over to the farm for a cup of tea?"

"It would be uncomfortable," I said, "with Ezra."

He nodded. "Then bring Jeremy over here, to see the studio. I'll show him how to throw a pot on the wheel."

"I don't know if I can get away."

"Try."

AS JEREMY AND I HEADED back across the field, I saw Ezra walking the trail toward us, carrying what at first looked like two olive green dinner plates, one overturned to keep the other warm. "Now what the heck is your daddy doing?" I said, and laughed.

It was a painted turtle he carried, its head and legs tucked within its shell. The creature was mature, about a foot long, and painted, as its name suggested, with bright red on its belly shell. Ezra grinned at me as he squatted to put the turtle down on the ground to show Jeremy, and the turtle ventured out of its shell to reveal the brilliant yellow stripes on its head, neck, legs, and tail. I wanted to take Ezra's hand, to let him know he was a dear man, but I didn't, thinking of the bacteria the turtle undoubtedly harboured. "I suppose we shouldn't let Jeremy touch it," I said.

"It's just a turtle. He can purify his hands."

"Please, Mom?"

I squatted down in front of Jeremy. "They carry salmonella. That's a nasty bug. It could make you very sick."

Ezra stared down at me a moment, the muscles in his jaw tensing, then turned to Jeremy. "I'll find it a good home," he said and started to walk away with it.

"Mom will have lunch ready," I said, raising my voice into the wind as I stood.

"I'm going to close that tree first."

"Can't you finish it later? Your lunch will get cold."

"Fuck!" he said, turning. "Can't you just get off my back?"

"Fuck!" said Jeremy. He laughed. "Fuckity-fuck! Fuck-a-duck!"

I shot a look at Ezra, warning him to watch his language around our son, and took Jeremy's hand. "All right, that's enough. Let's go back inside."

"Can I draw some pictures?"

"Sure."

"I'll draw you a duck, Mommy."

From inside the house I watched Ezra prune branches from the tree, feeling my frustration and anger dissolve like a lozenge on my tongue. He was beautiful. His long torso and legs, his shoulders moving under the fabric of his black T-shirt as he tended that dying plum. From this distance I could almost believe that nothing about him had changed.

5.

DAD SAT FORWARD IN HIS CHAIR at the kitchen table to look out the window at Ezra with me. His cards were spread out in front of him in a game of solitaire; they were the same pack of cards he'd used for nearly fifty years. Jeremy sat beside him, drawing with crayons. "Now what the heck is Ezra doing?" Dad said.

"Pruning that dying plum."

"Is he planning on butchering that calf today or not?"

I held out my hands and shrugged. What could I do?

"There isn't time for screwing around. They were just saying on the radio how the wind we got today spread the fire from just under a couple of hundred acres to more than seven hundred."

He nodded at the windsock blowing over the barn. "What if the wind turned like it does this time of year and pushed the fire down that slope? The fire could be on us in minutes."

"I told him."

Dad collected his cards to shuffle them before laying them out for a new game. "You're going to have to take the lead with him," he said.

"He would disagree. He thinks I try to control him too much."

"Doesn't matter what he thinks. You won't get nothing done around that farm of yours letting him run things like you do."

I glanced at Jeremy, then back at my father, to caution him not to say anything more about Ezra in front of our son. "He's a good man, Dad."

He shook his head. "I just hate seeing you dealing with him all the time. It's wearing you down."

"Where's Mom?" I asked, to change the subject.

"Out getting some eggs. She got lost in her writing and burned the hamburgers, so she's going to make us fried eggs instead."

"She's getting worse, isn't she?"

"It's those damn sleeping pills she's been taking. Makes her groggy and forgetful. Anyway, your mother's always been a little squirrelly."

"Not this squirrelly."

"You don't think so, eh?" He reached for his wallet, which sat on the table, and pulled out a yellowed newspaper clipping. "You take a look at that."

"What's this?"

"Our shivaree. Your mother wrote that and sent it into the paper, like she did all the community news for the valley."

"What's a shivaree?" said Jeremy.

"A kind of party," I said.

"Can I see?" he asked.

"I'll read it to you."

NEWLYWEDS FETED

A merry time was had on Saturday evening when a large number of friends and relatives resident in the Turtle Valley district gathered at the new home of Mr. and Mrs. Gustave Svensson. The party was a complete surprise to the young couple who had recently returned from a honeymoon in Vancouver. The evening was enjoyably spent with singing and old-time dancing. After the refreshment period the merrymakers circled Mr. and Mrs. Svensson and sang "For They Are Jolly Good Fellows."

"I remember Mom telling me about this."

"Well, she may have told you that version, but I bet she didn't tell you what really happened. We were living in the hired hand's cabin on Valentine's place at the time. Burned down the year you were born. I kept promising her I'd get around to finishing that house of Valentine's for her. But I never did." He pointed at the newspaper clipping. "We were just back from Vancouver that day, and came home to a yard full of cars. All those folks thought we were already back and had planned to bang on pans outside, to make a ruckus so we'd come out. But then we weren't home so they just went on inside to wait. They were dancing when we got there."

"Dancing?"

"There was always dancing. Sometimes we'd scratch up a platform and dance under the stars if the weather was good. I never went to anyone's house without my harmonica in my pocket. You had to make your own entertainment then. Wasn't like there was television. That night Dennis found my mouth organ, Rodney Nicoll found my fiddle, and my Uncle Valentine played his banjo. That cabin of ours had nothing but a rough lumber floor, uneven, full of cracks, so when we danced, dust billowed up from the ground underneath." He paused to catch his breath. "Beth was no housekeeper even then and the place was a muddle from us moving her things in. No place to boil coffee for that many people, so they'd just gone ahead and cleaned out a crock of pickled cabbage and boiled coffee in that. Tasted like the devil. Somebody brought matrimonial cake and ham sandwiches, but it wasn't enough to feed that troop, so I cooked up a mess of bannock on a fire outside. Served it up with Valentine's lingonberry jam."

My father's bannock was nothing but lard, flour, salt, and baking powder patted into big rounds and cooked on sticks over a campfire. I'd tried to duplicate the stuff in my kitchen, but it was a disappointing bread when made in the oven. Taken with coffee over an open campfire, though, it was something else altogether: an event, a communion that inspired storytelling.

"All the while I'm making bannock and entertaining those folks, your mother was hiding in the outhouse. I told them she wasn't feeling well and Dennis joked that she was already pregnant and it was a shotgun wedding, which got a pile of laughs as everyone knew John Weeks, the times he threatened God knows how many neighbours with a gun. But the truth was,

Beth couldn't face all those people. She thought they'd judge her for the jumble in the house, like any of them dancing fools cared. When it came down to it, it wasn't the mess that bothered her. She was just scared."

"Of what?"

"Doubt she knew herself. But it kept her from enjoying herself."

I handed my father the clipping. "Sounds like she came out of that outhouse eventually."

"Not until everybody left."

"But it says everyone circled around and sang."

"They circled around the outhouse singing while I tapped on the door and tried to convince her to come out. Never did get her to open that damn door. Eventually everyone left and I went to bed, and when I woke up I found her on her knees in the kitchen cleaning those dusty floorboards, as if all that scrubbing was ever going to get them clean."

The screen door opened and my mother set her egg basket on the kitchen counter. She heated up a pan as she washed her hands. "What did Ezra find out there?" she asked. "I saw him carrying something."

"A turtle."

"Wonderful! When I was a girl, the turtles crossed that road to lay their eggs in such numbers you couldn't drive without running over them. Mona Moses told me that this was how Blood Road got its name: it was stained with the blood of turtles. My father wouldn't drive over them. He'd stop the buggy and have us lift the turtles out of the way. He could be terribly kind, at times." She dried her hands on a dishtowel. "Now there are so few turtles."

Jeremy handed me a sheet of paper scrawled with crayon. "I drew you a picture, Mommy!"

"It's beautiful. Thank you." Two people, both of them looking rather unhappy, stood in front of a rough red square with a triangle on top scratched all about with red lines, a house on fire. Above it a zigzag in black.

"Grandma and Grandpa," he said, pointing. "They don't like their house."

"Oh? How come?"

"It's a bad house."

"Why is it bad?"

"I don't know."

I pointed at the zigzag. "What's this?"

"Lightning. The boom makes Grandpa mad so he runs away."

"I was struck by lightning," Mom told him.

"Wow! Really?"

"I was bringing in the cows when I saw it hit the ground, and then it rolled toward me. When it hit, my right arm went numb. I couldn't use it properly for some time after that, and even when I got better, my arm would fly off and do things by itself."

"Grandma calls it her lightning arm," I said. "Isn't that funny?" A story I never knew whether to believe or not.

"Is Grandpa afraid of lightning?" Mom asked Jeremy.

"*I'm* not scared," said Jeremy. "*Grandpa's* scared. Grandpa doesn't like big noises. Noises bug him, like they bug Daddy."

"Only when he's wearing a hearing aid," I smiled at my mother. "Most of the time he doesn't bother to wear it."

"Not live Grandpa," said Jeremy. "*Dead* Grandpa." He pointed out the window. "Loud noises scare Dead Grandpa." He clapped his hands. "Boom!"

I looked out the window in the direction Jeremy pointed. The patch of bush surrounding the old well. The fields of alfalfa beyond. Jude's home. Valentine's cabin and the unfinished house. "Where, honey?"

"Boom!"

But there was only Ezra. He came in the house and took his shoes off.

"You finished pruning?" I asked him.

He bent over and undid his runners but said nothing.

"Looks like you did a good job."

"We'll have fruit on it next year," Mom said.

Dad scratched his cheek and glanced at me. "If it survives the fire."

Ezra looked at me and away, and I felt my throat tighten as I anticipated another argument. But as Ezra sat at the table, something bashed against the kitchen window and we all startled. I saw a tumble of feathers and a flash of red as a bird fluttered backward and then dropped from view. "Oh, Kat, see if that bird is all right, will you?" my mother said.

"Sure. Jeremy, let's go outside." I led my son by the hand to hunt through the grass by the house, remembering the many times I had joined my mother in her search for birds that had crashed into the windows. She had cradled them in her warm hands until they fluttered to the lilac bushes, where they sat, dozy, until fully revived. I could walk right up to these dazed birds and stroke them and they would only nip drowsily at my fingers. My mother guarded them from the cats until they rose high enough in consciousness to fend for themselves. She knew about sick things, was at her best, most confident, with sick things.

I found the bird, a male house finch with red cap and breast, suspended on a lower branch of a lilac, unconscious but still alive. Its quick Timex heartbeat, the unbelievable lightness of its body. I cradled it in my hands to show Jeremy, waiting for the moment when it would begin to revive, when I could let it loose among the lilac boughs, but instead the bird arched in seizure, giving a last spread of its wings.

"That bird's flying," said Jeremy.

"I think it's dying."

"We'll feed that bird some birthday cake. That will make it happy."

"Once it's dead it won't eat anymore. Or fly."

Before I could stop him he touched the belly of the bird, and I lifted the finch out of his reach, fearing—what? Lice? The germs wild things carried.

"Grandpa's dead," he said.

"He'll be with us for a while yet."

"No, that Grandpa." He pointed at the bush that marked the site of the old well. The old man was there again, turned toward the house, looking our way, though I couldn't make out his face at that distance.

Ezra opened the kitchen window. "Something's unhinged with Gus," he said. Inside, my mother stood with an arm around my father. He was doubled over in his chair, coughing and moaning, with both hands clasped across his chest. His face was grey. Many of the cards he had been playing solitaire with were now on the floor. "I'll phone for a hospital truck," said Ezra.

"An ambulance will take half an hour to get here. It's quicker if we drive him ourselves. Can you start getting Mom organized? She'll need her pills."

Ezra nodded and closed the window.

"That bird's dead?" said Jeremy.

"Just about." I held the bird a moment longer, as I suspected no other creature would mourn its passing. Its heartbeat slowed until I could feel a pause after each beat. I waited for the next tick. And then the next. But the bird's chest was still.

6.

MY FATHER GROANED, AND TURNED as best he could in the hospital bed to vomit on the emergency-room floor. I knelt with my mother to clean up the mess with paper towelling. "What am I going to do if he dies?" Mom whispered.

"He isn't going to die," I said.

"How do you know?" She looked up, hopeful, as if I had some prescient knowledge. When I didn't answer, she yanked the paper towel from my hand and pushed me away. I sat back in the chair next to Ezra and watched her as she wiped the floor. I remembered this rage; when Ezra was in hospital in the days following his stroke, I told the nurse that I would be the one to wash my husband's body, and not her. He was *my* husband. I had to do *something*.

That nurse. Jamaican. Always in pink. Pink tunics, pale pink crepe-soled shoes. She kept an Okanagan McIntosh in the pocket of her tunic, and cursed the avocados I brought Ezra as ugly fruit. *A joke,* she told me. *They grow on trees in pairs, like testicles. We feed them to the pigs.* She left the basin of warm water and the washcloth by Ezra's bed, and when she was gone I tugged the curtains around us. The sun shining through the windows lit up the cloth of the curtains so they seemed to glow from within. I had the sensation that I was alone within this noon-filled room, that Ezra was no longer with me, that I was washing my beloved's dead body. I smoothed the cloth over his nearly hairless chest, the soft skin of his belly, and washed the line of silky, innocent skin between his thigh and scrotum, lifting the pouch to wash beneath, taking note of the details of his skin, making them mine, as if I were touching him for the last time.

This was not mere remembrance. I was *there,* in that Chilliwack hospital room. I could feel the warmth of the water, the rough texture of the hospital washcloth in my hand as I wrung it out.

Then I was here, in this emergency room in Salmon Arm, surrounded by curtain, sitting beside my father's bed. I was, for a brief moment, disoriented. How had I gotten here? How could so much time have elapsed? What had I been doing?

My mother tossed the soiled paper towels in the garbage, wiped her hands with an antiseptic wipe, and sat back in an orange plastic chair, squeezing the handles of her handbag with both fists. Ezra leaned against the wall beside her, holding Jeremy.

"I'm bored," said Jeremy.

"I know," I said. "We just have to wait a little longer." I rummaged through my purse and handed him the tiny flap book I kept there for times when we had to wait.

My father was hooked up to a heart monitor. I realized at that moment that I had rarely seen him without a shirt. I had never seen him swim, or go shirtless on a hot day as other men might. When he changed from the work clothes he wore around the farm into a clean shirt and pants for town, he did so behind the closed door of my parents' bedroom. The skin on his chest and arms, kept from the sun all those years, was shockingly white and youthful, as if his elderly head, hands, and forearms had been affixed to this young body. His nipples were tiny, just dots. There was a large scar on his left arm. The skin around it puckered when he moved.

"You got that scar in a hunting accident, right, Dad?"

"I was cleaning my gun in the toolshed when I dropped it and it went off."

"Boom!" said Jeremy.

I shushed him and turned back to my father. "Weren't you carrying it over a fence when it discharged?"

He looked over at my mother. "Yes, of course, that's right."

I didn't pursue the story. There was so much pain in my father's face. He winced and exhaled a jagged breath. "I don't understand why it has to hurt so bad," he said.

"It doesn't," said Ezra, and he handed me Jeremy before disappearing behind the curtain. "I'll be right back."

"Where's Daddy going?"

"I don't know, honey. I'm sure he'll be right back." I gave him my notepad and a pen. "Here, draw Mommy a picture."

Mom took out her writing pad. "Did I do something to offend him?" she asked.

"Ezra? No. Why?"

"He was so angry with Jeremy this morning, when he banged his glass for more lemonade. That was this morning, wasn't it?"

I nodded.

"I thought maybe I'd done something to annoy him. That he was taking it out on Jeremy."

"He wasn't angry with you, or even with Jeremy. He was just overwhelmed." In fact, he might not even have felt the anger he demonstrated. The counsellor I had talked to at the hospital following Ezra's stroke had told me that very often a stroke victim would not feel sad when he cried, or angry when he shouted; rather, he was stuck in a behaviour and couldn't get himself out.

"He hasn't ever hurt you or Jeremy, has he?" my mother asked.

"No."

She scribbled the word *Emergency* on the top of her writing pad and underlined it. "Are you still thinking about having another child?"

"We've been trying to conceive. I've been hoping to, in any case."

"I was wondering, after this morning, do you think Ezra could cope with another child?"

"I don't know."

"It would be hard on him. But harder on Jeremy and the new baby to have to deal with those outbursts of his, to have to be quiet all the time. My mother was forever telling my brother and me, *Do be quiet. Daddy's not well today.* We were made to feel it was our job to keep him calm. Most of the time my brother and

I hardly dared talk, unless our father was off the property. It left its mark on me, I think."

I nodded. I had never known her to yell, though when I was a child, she was quick to anger. Instead, as if growing up quiet had stolen her voice, she whispered her rage.

She turned back to her pad and wrote down the events of the morning, the bird that bashed into the window, the flight into town with my father, the wait in the emergency room. I glanced down at her writing now and again, curious about her take on things, but it was little more than a factual account, and held no revelations.

Ezra returned carrying heated blankets. He uncovered my father and laid the warm blankets over him, then packed the others on top, to keep the heat in. "When I felt pain, the hot was good," he said.

My father eased a bit, relaxing into the pillows. His breathing was less laboured. "It's nice."

I took Ezra's hand. "Thank you," I said. He nodded and lifted Jeremy from my lap.

A doctor pulled back the curtain. "Hello again, Gus. Just couldn't stay away, eh?"

"This is our daughter Kat," Mom said. "And her husband, Ezra."

"Yes, the writer. We've met before." He held out his hand to us both. "Michael Ellis," he said, and he turned back to my father. "So, let's take a look at you, Gus. You've been having some chest pain?"

My father touched his ribs. "Here."

The doctor gently probed my father's ribs and my father flinched.

"The doctor's hurting Grandpa!" Jeremy said.

I reached over to hold his hand. "No, he's taking care of Grandpa."

"Can you describe the pain?" Dr. Ellis asked. "Sharp? Intense?"

Dad sucked in air and nodded. "It's worse when I move."

"He was coughing when it started," I said.

"I wonder if this rib isn't broken." Dr. Ellis pulled the covers back up over my father's chest. "We'll get you X-rayed right away." He smiled and was gone through the curtains.

"How long will that take?" Dad asked.

"I'm sure someone will be here right away," I said.

My father coughed and then grunted. "It hurts so bad," he said.

"They've got to give him something for the pain," Mom said, and she was off through the curtains, limping between the beds of the emergency room, in search of a nurse.

"Mom, wait." I caught up with her just as she reached the nurses' station.

"Do something!" my mother told the nurse standing there. An elderly man in a wheelchair looked up to watch her. "He's in such terrible pain that he can't breathe!"

I expected the nurse to calm my mother, to lay a hand on her arm and soothe her as she would a distraught child, but instead she was set in motion by my mother's panic. "We'll get him to X-ray," she said, and followed my mother with a wheelchair. As the nurse and I helped my father up from the bed, Dad's knees buckled under him and he nearly fell. He winced and held his ribs, grunting and moaning as he settled into the chair.

"You can come with him if you'd like," the nurse said to my mother.

"Never thought I'd be carted around in one of these things," Dad said.

"Think of it as a spa," I told him. "Beautiful women pushing you around."

"Nothing new about that." He held my mother's hand as the nurse wheeled him off.

"I'm hungry," said Jeremy.

Ezra put him down and took his hand. "I'll cart him to the eating place. You want anything?"

I shook my head and watched them leave. Then I was left alone in the little cubicle, surrounded by the curtain, staring at the empty hospital bed. The pillow dented with the impression of my father's head. The poster declaring this a No Scent Zone. The turquoise urinal on the side table. The urinal could have been a vase standing there, awaiting a cheerful bundle of daffodils, if it hadn't been for the handle. During that first week in the hospital after his stroke, Ezra wanted home so badly that he put one of these urine bottles on his foot, thinking it was his shoe. We laughed over it afterward, that he had mixed up these two parts of himself. His feet were size 13.

He still spoke in sentences then, but his words were garbled and misplaced. He pointed to his right leg and said, "My skin is brass," to explain the numbness he felt there. When I asked if he knew my name, he said, "Marigold!" Wonderful to be thought of as a flower, by your lover. And there was recognition in his eyes. Even in his thickest dreaming, when he couldn't remember my name, he still knew who I was; that is to say, he knew we were comfortable lovers, husband and wife.

The nurses had tied Ezra to his bed at night so I could leave to get some sleep, so they wouldn't have to watch him constantly, because he wandered. But he found his way out of the confines, tugging at the knots beneath the bed, even before I had left the hallway of the ward, and when I turned back I saw him heading out the door of the private room they had given him, in that ridiculous short gown, holding the IV stand, wheeling it down the hall. Earlier in the evening, when I'd asked if he knew where he was, he'd muttered that he was sleeping on the washer and dryer at home, his feet somehow extended miraculously through the wall, and yet, in this dream state, he was still able to navigate his way out of his bed and down the hall, dragging the IV stand that some part of him understood was necessary.

I strode the length of the hallway as a nurse intercepted him and made him sit in a wheelchair. She confined him there too, strapping him in as she might strap a child into a stroller, and wheeled him into position across from the nurses' station so they could all keep an eye on him.

I crouched by his chair, talking to him quietly, hoping to calm him before I left. But he smiled at me in invitation. In his sickness, as in other men's drunkenness, his inhibitions were let loose to the wind like ribbons. He leaned into me to kiss my neck, tugged at the arm of my sweater, and began to undress me under the fluorescent lights of the intensive care ward of the Chilliwack General Hospital.

Despite my embarrassment, I desired him. I desired his child. I wanted that echo of him. I understood, then, the story an acquaintance had once told me of rushing home from her mother's funeral to rut with her husband. They made it as far as the living-room carpet. A neighbour came by with a casserole and saw them at it, through the window of the front door. During that time Ezra was in hospital, I was driven by grief to take that kind of risk of being caught. I helped Ezra sit on the toilet and mounted him like a lap dancer. In the shower I stroked him with conditioner until he came. They should have had rooms for this on the critical wards, rooms for the dying and their lovers to join. Even in prisons there were places where couples could come together; lovemaking was recognized as a force that would unite a husband and wife separated by steel and cement. Ezra and I faced the prospect of being torn apart by death, and yet here in the hospital we were made to feel ashamed. When I sat on the bed to lean into him for a kiss, the Jamaican nurse ripped open the curtain and said, *Come on guys, get a hotel,* as she groped my husband's arm for a vein.

THE CURTAIN PARTED AND VAL swept in. She leaned down to hug me. "So, what's the word?"

"Nothing yet. Dad's off getting X-rayed. Mom went with him."

Val's hair was wet. She dyed her hair to cover the grey, the same golden blond she'd naturally had in the pictures I had seen of her as a young woman. With the age difference between us, she had sometimes been mistaken for my mother, rather than my sister. But without makeup she had a little girl's face, freckled, vulnerable, nearly unrecognizable as I had so rarely seen her without a full face of makeup. In that moment she resembled our great-uncle Valentine, whom she had been named after. She put a hand to her cheek. "I'd just got out of the shower when you phoned."

"You look fine."

She rummaged in her purse, then squirted Oil of Olay into the palm of her hand, rubbed it onto her face, and smoothed it down her throat. "Where's Jeremy?"

"Ezra took him to the cafeteria."

I hugged my arms as I watched Val pour foundation into a clean sponge and pat it on her nose, her chin, and her forehead. "You look tired," she said.

"I'm okay." Although I realized at that moment that I was rocking myself back and forth.

"I imagine it's so hard for you," she said. "Being here, in the hospital."

"It comes back to me in flashes, so real, like I'm in that Chilliwack hospital, like I never left."

"It was around this time of year, too, wasn't it?"

I stopped to think of the date. In the rush to get down here to help my parents, all other considerations had been forgotten. But it would be six years this week. Ezra at the kitchen table. He complained of numbness in the right side of his face and his speech became slurred. I asked him to repeat a sentence after me and he couldn't. Then he fell to the floor.

"Be careful of those anniversaries," she said. "They'll jump up and bite you, years after, even when you think you're over it." She applied eyeliner and a coat of mascara as she squinted into her pocket mirror. "How was Mom when you brought Dad in?"

"Flustered. Panicked. As you'd expect."

"We're going to have to think about getting her into some kind of assisted living situation after Dad passes."

"It's not time for that yet."

"Last week I found the iron plugged in and scorching her nightgown in a basket of clean laundry. I'm sure it would have set the house on fire if I hadn't found it. When I pointed it out, she blamed me, said I must have done it. I think she actually believed it, too; I doubt she had any memory of plugging that iron in or putting it in the laundry basket."

"I came in late last night and all the burners were on. Mom was asleep so I didn't think it could have been her."

"The burners have been on a number of times when I've stopped in lately. I'm going to have to talk to Dr. Ellis about weaning her off those sleeping pills, or trying something else. She's been getting increasingly forgetful since she's been taking them."

"If it's just the pills, then there's no need to think about moving her into some kind of care facility."

Val shook her head. "It's not just the pills. She was growing more forgetful before she started taking them. Strange, isn't it? She remembers a story from fifty years ago in detail, but she'll phone me up three times within an hour with the same question: when is her doctor's appointment, or when am I going to pick her up?"

"So we put up a whiteboard near the door and write her appointments down. I had to do that for Ezra."

"But so much of her behaviour makes no sense. This past spring she kept buying macaroni, boxes and boxes of the stuff. I didn't think anything of it at first, but then I started finding dry macaroni all over the house, in the weirdest places. I asked her about it and she made out like it was a big mystery to her. Then I was over here for supper one night. Dad and I were watching the news, and I happened to glance over at Mom. She was wolfing down a handful of uncooked macaroni."

I could picture this, my mother with one eye set keenly on Dad and Val, to see that they were absorbed in the television, as she gobbled crackling bits of pasta, half-moons of dry macaroni clattering to the floor. "So what was that about?"

"Hell if I know. When I confronted her, she denied she was eating it. She said she'd dropped the box and was just picking the bits up."

Val looked into her purse mirror as she applied her lipstick. "I ran into Jude in the Safeway parking lot Saturday. He said he had a box of yours."

"I picked it up this morning."

"So you saw him. Already." She put her index finger in her mouth, withdrawing it through puckered lips. A trick she had taught me when I was a child: the excess lipstick came off on her finger and not on her teeth. She wiped lipstick from her finger with a Kleenex. "Are you going to see him again?"

"I don't know."

"You think seeing him again would be . . . dangerous?" When I didn't answer, she grinned. Her front teeth were short, in need of caps, because she ground her teeth in her sleep. On those nights when Ezra was in the hospital, when she had come down to stay and we had shared my bed, I had lain awake, staring at the ceiling, listening to the crunch of her teeth as if she had a mouthful of rock candy.

The nurse opened the curtain and wheeled my father back to the bed, then helped him into it, as I gave up my seat to Mom. The nurse set Dad up on a morphine drip and he settled back into the bed, more comfortable now.

Ezra returned and stood next to me holding our son. He nodded at Val. "We got one truckload piled up, at least."

"You can drop it off at my place before you head back this evening. I've left the garage open."

"Don't forget to take those boxes you stored in the barn," Dad said.

"I imagine that'll be the last of what we pack out," I said. During our move to Alberta that past spring, Ezra and I had left a number of boxes at my parents' farm in order to make room in the U-Haul for a last-minute gift from my mother, the table and chairs that had once sat in my grandmother's parlour. I had no idea what was in the boxes we had left behind. I hadn't yet unpacked the many stacked in the basement of the house we rented in Cochrane.

"What about the cattle?" Ezra said.

"It's all arranged," said Val. "I phoned Uncle Dan this morning and he said he'd take them. He'll be bringing the trailer around as soon as he can get away from the dairy."

Dad ran a hand over his mouth. "He's got enough to worry about without us bothering him."

"What will we do with the cats?" Mom asked.

"The SPCA has set up an animal shelter on the fairgrounds. We'll have to round them up and take them there for now."

"No!" Mom said. "They'll be terrified."

"I can't keep them at my place, Mom, there's just too many."

Jeremy clapped in excitement. "Are we going to chase the kitties?"

"Wouldn't that be fun?" I said. I looked up at Val. "How about the chickens? I doubt we can catch all those wild bantams."

"Oh, we must!" my mother said. "Imagine what it would be like for them, caught in a fire. I so love my chickens." She turned to me. "My favourite, of course, was Lady Barred Rock." This

GAIL ANDERSON-DARGATZ

was a bird Ezra and I had years before, not long after we were married, at the small farm we owned in Chilliwack. The bird would hear our movements in the house and run to the front or back door as we exited, looking for leftovers that she'd peck from our hands. One day I noticed the bird's comb was pale, and the next I found her dead within the roost. I buried her under the maple and planted tulips over her body. Mourning a chicken.

Dr. Ellis pulled back the curtain. "Well, Gus, the rib is broken. A cough could have done it. I'm afraid the bone was eaten through."

"The cancer?" Dad asked.

Dr. Ellis nodded. "It will take us a few days, as the room is currently in use, but I suggest we admit you to our palliative care room. It's a suite, really. Beth or one of your daughters can stay with you around the clock."

"I don't want to stay another night in this hospital," Dad said to Val. "All my life with your mother, we hardly ever slept in separate beds, except for these damn hospital stays. I can never sleep."

"You will need more care than your family is able to provide at home." Dr. Ellis looked down at the clipboard he carried. "Beth says you've been having trouble swallowing. I suggest we stop giving you the medications, and switch the morphine from pills to injections."

"You're giving up on me then?"

"Nobody's giving up on you, Dad," Val said.

"But I am dying, aren't I?"

"At this point the treatments will have little if any effect," said Dr. Ellis.

"How long?"

74

"I don't know."

"A matter of weeks?"

"Maybe less."

"I don't want Grandpa to die," said Jeremy.

I took him from Ezra and held him, rocking him back and forth, trying to think of something to say to comfort him, to comfort us all.

"I want to go home," Dad said. "Now."

"We can't, Dad," I said. "We may have to evacuate at a moment's notice."

"And the smoke from the fire will continue to be a problem," said Dr. Ellis.

"Put me on oxygen if you want. I don't want to die in some damn hospital with a bunch of strange women watching over every bodily function. I want to go home."

"The decision is entirely up to you, but I don't advise it," Dr. Ellis said. "Why don't you discuss it further with your family and I'll check in later."

After he left we all looked at the floor for a time, saying nothing.

"How long will it take to get Dad into that palliative care room?" I finally asked Val.

My father slapped the table beside him, upsetting the urinal and his glass. Water slid off the laminate to the floor. "I'm not going to die in a damn hospital! I want to go home."

"All right, Dad," said Val. "If that's what you want, I'll make it happen."

"Nobody's asking me what I want," said Mom. "I want him to live! He won't get better at home."

Dad took my mother's hand in both of his. "You remember how Valentine went?"

I had visited Uncle Valentine in the hospital with Mom during his final illness. He was curled into himself, his body as thin and out of proportion with his head as a fetus's. My mother pulled the blanket back up to my uncle's chest and we stood for a time at his bedside, listening to him whisper in Swedish. "What's he saying?" I asked.

"I don't know." She picked up his round brush from the bedside table and brushed his hair in the way she so often brushed mine, not to preen, but to comfort; to comfort herself as much as me. Valentine's hair had grown long in his illness; his white locks fell about his shoulders as she brushed them. "People often return to their pasts when they're dying," she said. "I imagine he's in his childhood, talking with his family."

Valentine had told me stories about his childhood in Lapland, of the Sami in their richly ornamented blue, yellow, and red costumes who herded reindeer through his father's farm in winter, camping out in tents on the snow-covered fields and buying hay from his father to feed the reindeer. These families travelled on skis and on *pulka*s, sleds pulled behind *hark*s, castrated reindeer. "They went like the dickens," Valentine told me.

As a child I had imagined myself as one of these Sami on a sled, hanging onto the reins of a reindeer as it snorted in the effort to run through snow, its breath clouding the night air under crystal stars and northern lights. I liked the idea that Valentine had returned to these winter fields and was flying over snow with the Sami into an endless, starry night.

"I hate the thought of drifting away slowly like that," Dad said, "spending months in hospital drugged up because of the pain. I want it to be over fast."

"I'll arrange for a hospital bed," said Val, "and for the nurses to come in to back me up. But I can give you most of the care you need."

"And if the fire does threaten the place?" I asked.

"Then we'll wheel Dad out to the truck and get him the hell out of there."

"You have to work."

"I'll take time off." Val put a hand on Dad's shoulder. "I'll need a day to get things set up. Make some room for a hospital bed. But I'll get you home. All right?"

Dad, still grasping Mom's hand, lay back into the pillows. "All right."

7.

AS WE HEADED TO SALMON ARM after dropping the load off at Val's place in Canoe, Ezra nodded at the SUV riding our tail. "They should hammer together signs that you can bolt to your truck," he said. "So you can flash messages at the car behind you, like *Back off asshole!*"

I glanced at Jeremy and then at my mother, to see if they had heard, then looked away. Ezra acted like this when he was tired. I knew he shouldn't be driving now, that we were courting disaster, but I'm ashamed to say I was afraid to take the wheel. There had been a time when I would drive off by myself with no particular destination in mind; I was just out for the pleasure of the drive. But after Ezra had the stroke it became important to us both that there was some aspect of our lives together where he took the lead. So when he was allowed to drive again, he became the driver. I still did all right on country roads and on side roads in town, but highway driving threw me. The thought of driving in a city like Calgary terrified me.

Ezra stopped for a yellow light at the intersection next to the McDonald's, and the driver in the SUV honked for him to keep going. "Fucking asshole!" said Ezra. When the light turned green and Ezra started off again, the SUV stormed past over a solid line. Ezra swerved into it, nearly hitting the vehicle. Both my mother and Jeremy cried out.

"Ezra!" I said. "What the hell are you doing?"

Ezra fingered the driver and the man fingered him back. The sticker on the window of the SUV read: *Know Fear.* "He's the asshole, not me."

The rage in his face. I took a breath and mentally paged through the responses the counsellor had offered me to deflect his anger in situations such as this, when his judgment was compromised. "How about I take a turn at the wheel?" I asked him, as cheerfully as I could.

"You don't like city driving."

"It's my hometown. I'm sure I can manage."

"You think I'm a shitty driver?"

"You're a very skilled driver, but you sometimes drive differently when you're exhausted. You often help me out. I'd like to help you here."

"Don't give me that patronizing therapist shit."

I turned away, blinking back the sting of tears, to look out the passenger window. A couple walked along the side of the road, carrying a branch between them from which a jack terrier dangled, its jaws locked around the stick.

Below us, the town followed the curve of this arm of Shuswap Lake. The town of Salmon Arm was named for the fish that were once so abundant that farmers pitchforked them from the lake, and the river that fed into it, to slash into the land for fertilizer. Now the highway cut the city lengthwise, drawing curve-nervous Albertans down to Shuswap Lake and into houseboats. A tourist town. A town I didn't leave until I was twenty-five, when I was jerked from these comfortable waters like those salmon caught silver and pink in surprise. I both thank and blame Jude for this. When I left the area, I left him.

As we came down the hill near McGuire Lake, our truck began to slow and drift toward the centre lane. Ezra smacked his lips and his right hand circled in his lap. Seizure.

I grabbed the steering wheel. "Put your foot on the brake!" I said. "Your foot on the brake!"

His foot was off the gas, sitting loose against the floor. I couldn't reach over the console between us to brake the truck myself. "Ezra! Your foot on the brake!"

My mother leaned forward. "What's happening?"

I honked the horn, keeping it pressed to warn other drivers as we passed through an intersection. Ezra turned to me, his tongue still pushing against the inside of his lip. His eyes were yellowed and glazed and his cheeks drawn. "Your foot!" I cried. "On the brake!"

He kept looking at me, and not the road, but he did brake slowly. I finally steered us to the side of the highway near the Dairy Queen and put the truck in park.

"Daddy, put your foot on the brake!"

"It's okay. We're okay now. Daddy had a seizure."

"A seizure!" Mom said. "Good God! We could have been killed."

A semi barrelled by, shaking our truck as it passed.

"Are you all right?" I asked Ezra.

He nodded. "Silly," he said, struggling to find the word *sorry*. He said it again and again, "Silly. Silly." Caressing my arm. Trying to let me know that he was okay, that everything was okay. As if either of us could believe that now.

"Sorry," he said at last.

I led him by the hand to the passenger side and buckled him into his seat. Then I got behind the wheel and signalled to get back on the road. I waited too long, unsure now how to merge with the stream of traffic. After a time a hole opened and I pulled quickly into the right lane. Too late I saw that I was nearing an intersection.

"You just scurried through a red light!" Ezra said.

"I know, I know. I didn't see it!"

When I finally parked in the Safeway lot, I sat a moment staring at my hands on the wheel. They were trembling.

Ezra put his hand on my thigh. "I'm so sorry I got into flames at you when you offered to drive. I should have listened."

"You're always sorry. After."

"When I'm stuck in it, I can't see. It feels like it's your fault. I think, if you'd just be hushed. But you keep talking and I can't keep up, can't think. I can't get myself out of it. My head is clay; my words come out all balled up. I feel like I'm in the middle of a lake." He waved his arms as if swimming, or thrashing.

"Like you're floundering," I said.

"Yes. That's the word. Floundering. I see myself acting

badly, but its not *me*. It's something else up here." He tapped his head and for that moment, at least, I understood what it was like for him, to be inside his skull, watching, helpless, as anger drove him.

"I expect this means you won't be driving for awhile then?" Mom asked him.

"Not until we get the seizures back under control," I said.

He rubbed his face with both hands. "Each time this happens I feel like my wings are pinholed."

"Why don't you stay in the truck and rest while we go into Safeway?" I said to Ezra. "Would you like me to pick up anything for you?"

"I'm okay," he said. "I'll go in with you."

I pulled a package of earplugs from my purse and held them out. "Sweetheart, you just had a seizure. I really think you need to take a break."

He wouldn't take the earplugs and I could see him struggling to keep his anger at bay. "I'm not sick like you think."

I glanced back at Jeremy but he was looking out the window. Beside him my mother fretted with a Kleenex, rolling it over and over between her fingers.

I got out of the truck. "Okay. Fine. Let's just go." I slammed the door and stood a moment to allow the palpitations in my chest to pass. The heat and smoke clung to my face, leaving me breathless and panicky, and yet others in this parking lot relaxed into the warmth as if into a hot bath. Ice-cream cones and cheerful faces, even as the mountains above us burned.

I led Jeremy over to the shopping carts, with my mother and Ezra trailing behind, but when I slid a quarter into a Safeway cart it just popped back out. I tried a second time but couldn't get the carts apart. A young man in his twenties, wearing a base-ball cap and a fluorescent safety vest, pushed a line of carts toward us. He stopped and mumbled something to Ezra as he and my mother approached the store. "Pardon me?" Ezra asked.

"I know you, don't I?" the boy said.

"I don't think so," said Ezra.

"Yes I do." Saliva foamed at the corner of his mouth. His voice was cracked and his speech was garbled. When he turned I saw a seam of skin in the close-shaved hair at the back of his neck.

"People don't always understand me," he said. "I have a brain injury."

"Huh," said Ezra. "I had a stroke."

"How long were you in the hospital?"

"A couple of weeks."

"I was in a coma for seven months," the boy said. "Na, na, na-na, na. Beat you." He waved as he pushed the carts toward the store at the far end of the parking lot. "It was nice to meet *me*," he called out. Too late, I thought of asking him for one of his carts.

"What's the matter with that guy?" Jeremy asked. "He talks funny."

"He had a brain injury, sweetie," I said.

"What's a injury?"

"His brain was hurt." I glanced at Ezra. "I'll explain later."

Ezra took several steps away from us, and leaned against the entranceway to watch the boy rattle away. He wiped tears out of his eyes. I should have walked over to him, and held him. I should have told him that everything would be all right, that we would find a way through this as we had through everything else. Instead I tried inserting the quarter again, and when it still didn't work, I read the instructions, which didn't make sense. The panic rose up, the feeling of being alone in a strange city and not knowing where I was. A feeling I'd had many times since Ezra's stroke. Then the skipping, rapid-fire heartbeat. I gave the cart a good, swift shake.

My mother put a hand on my arm. "Oh, honey, what is it?"

I tried jamming the quarter in the cart again, and lowered my voice. "I just don't know what else to do! How to deal with him."

"You haven't been driving much lately, have you?" she asked.

On the sidewalk just ahead of us a woman, beautifully dressed in an indigo jacket and skirt, rifled through the garbage can. A plastic bag filled with pop cans was slung over her arm. A widow, I imagined, in her early sixties, reduced by her husband's passing to cashing in returnables.

I looked up at her. "Not much, no."

"For years your father drove to town, and I didn't. Gus liked driving, and he always got into the truck first, to wait for me, because I was always late getting ready. So when I came out, I just got into the passenger side. I never really thought anything of it. I just assumed that I would drive again. But then he got sick and when I tried to drive I found I couldn't anymore."

"I suppose it was the same with Ezra and me. Just habit. I've never much liked driving." I looked over at Ezra and he turned away. He knew as well as I that this wasn't true. "Why can't I figure this thing out?"

The woman with the bag of pop cans turned to us and tapped the coin slot on my cart. "You push the key against the quarter," she said, and showed me. "The key on the next cart pops out, see?"

"Ah," I said. "Thanks."

She patted my hand. "I'm forever helping people with these stupid carts. I don't know why they don't just get some ordinary ones and hire somebody like Marshall there to collect them." She pointed at the brain-injured boy. "God knows there's lots like him who need the work."

Marshall waved at her and she waved back. A man driving a Volkswagen Beetle honked at him. So Marshall had become a fixture in the town, a character everyone knew, a mascot.

I lifted Jeremy into the cart and pushed him into the store as my mother held onto the side to steady herself. Ezra followed behind.

"I'm going to gather a few things on my own," he said. He put a coin in one of the carts inside the store and pulled it smoothly from the stack.

My mother stood next to me as I watched him head down the aisle. "He's not shopping with us?"

"Where's Daddy going?"

I turned my cart to push it in the opposite direction. "I don't know what he's doing."

Mom followed Jeremy and me. "There were times when my father couldn't drive," she said, "and either my mother or I had to drive him to town. He hated that. He said it made him feel useless. A woman didn't drive then if there was a man in the car." She nodded back at Ezra. "I imagine this is all so very hard for him."

I turned the cart down the baking aisle and Mom picked up a small bag of pastry flour for the pie she wanted to make for Dad. "In any case, in a year or two none of this will seem so bad," she said. "My mother always said that time was like a great flour sifter."

"Flour sifter?" I thought of my grandmother's flour sifter that my mother still used, the handle that turned the flour over the screen.

"You sift flour not only to get rid of lumps and impurities," said Mom, "but to aerate the flour as well, so you can measure it accurately. Measure unsifted flour and you'll have a dense cake indeed. My mother used to say that time works like that: it not only sifts out the lumps—takes the sting out of events that seemed so painful at the time—but it allows you to measure those events properly, with some perspective."

"I keep thinking if I just did things differently, handled Ezra differently, then we wouldn't argue."

She shook her head. "I remember a day when my mother and I took tea and scones out to my father. He was working on a well near that stand of cottonwood, yet another site where he said he was going to build a house for my mother. As he climbed out of that hole to have his lunch he was grey and shaky, but he wouldn't stop digging. 'You need to rest,' my mother told him, just like you told Ezra he needed rest just now. That's all she said. But he yelled at her. 'You just don't want me to finish,' he said. 'You want me to look bad in front of the neighbours, so it proves what you've been saying about me all along, that I'll never build this house. You think I'm useless.' It was a thing she would never say, of course, even if she thought it. As I picked wildflowers in the grasses next to her, she reassured him that yes, she knew he'd finish the house, that yes, she loved him for it, using the tone of voice a mother uses when her child has an upset."

As she told this story, I saw my grandparents in my mind's eye, as if from a distance, their hands gesturing in argument. My grandfather's hands were clenched mountain cliffs, and my grandmother's were at first trees, outspread, imploring, and then two trays, palms open as if serving a way forward. My grandfather took both her hands in his, and it was within those prayerful hands that the whole of my own future was contained.

Those hands as rough as wood, the desperation with which they clung to her, a drowning man's.

"What was wrong with him?" I asked.

She didn't say anything for a time and then, "There were a lot of things wrong."

"Daddy!" Jeremy called out and we both turned.

Ezra stood between bins heaped with green peppers and bananas, caught at an intersection where a man was filling a water jug from a dispenser. The man blocked the aisle to the dairy section, causing a traffic jam, and my husband, stalled by indecision, was unable to navigate his cart through those other shoppers. Women with children in their buggies and old men with baskets over their arms passed him. I lifted Jeremy onto my hip, to leave the cart with my mother, and slipped through the congestion to come up behind Ezra. "Why don't you just go?" I asked.

"Go, go, go!" Jeremy said.

"I'm waiting for the passengers to scurry out of my way."

"You'll wait forever. Just say *Excuse me,* then step out in front of someone." I demonstrated with Jeremy in my arms. But Ezra didn't follow; he stood where he was, watching the other shoppers march by. Bombarded and confused by the terrific business of the store, he turned his head to every sound. I felt my irritation slip into resignation, and I took the lead, as I did every day in the dance that was our lives. I put Jeremy in Ezra's cart and headed through the store with Ezra following behind. "How about you sit on the bench by the door with your cart while we finish shopping?" I said, knowing that he wouldn't argue now, and he didn't. He shuffled beside Jeremy and me like a dutiful sentry through the maze of carts, shoppers, and grocery displays, to the bench by the door.

MY MOTHER WAS IN THE pet-food aisle when I found her, instructing a pimpled young man on which flat of cat food to take down from the shelf. The clerk set the flat under the shopping cart and reached for another. "You must have a lot of cats," he said.

"Five," said my mother. Not exactly the truth of the matter; more than a dozen had greeted me that morning when I stepped outside.

I smiled to allow the clerk to leave. "You have quite a bit of cat food at home already, Mom." Her cupboards were full of the stuff.

"I'm just stocking up. It was on sale."

"Why don't we pick out some fruit for Dad and head home? I think we're all getting tired."

I hooked my mother's arm within my own and pushed my son in the cart to the produce aisle, and together we paraded among the oranges, chose fragrant Fuji apples, and squeezed avocados until my mother came across a plastic one that squeaked in protest. The produce manager had put it there, evidently, to stop customers from bruising his merchandise. "These grow in pairs," I told her, holding two ripe avocados. "On trees they call testicle trees." We laughed and for that moment, at least, my father's illness, Ezra's seizure and confusion, and the fire on the mountain were all but forgotten.

8.

MY SON CRIED OUT and I listened from my parents' room a moment to see if he would fall back to sleep, but when he let out a frightened howl, I ran into Val's old room and found him thrashing in the bed as if frantically trying to find something, or to escape. I left the door open so I would have enough light to see what was going on. He was sweating and his eyes were wide open, terrified. "Mommy! Mommy!" In the second single bed my mother whistled in her sleep, her eyes half open and moving eerily within dream, apparently deaf to his cries.

"What is it?" I said, and I wrapped my arms around him, but he pushed me away.

"Make him go away!" he cried.

"Who? Who's scaring you?"

"Mommy! Make him go away!"

"I'm right here." I held his face. "Look at me, I'm right here!"

But he was lost in some dark place and couldn't find me. He slid from the bed to the floor and tossed about there, in the shadows, calling for me. "Go away!" he yelled.

I sat on the floor beside him, not trying to touch him any more because I knew from what I had read that holding him would only agitate him further. He had experienced night terrors here in this house during previous visits, though never at home. I assumed that the excitement and wear of travel triggered them. I knew that in the morning he would remember nothing of it. But that knowledge offered little comfort as he thrashed about beside me. He was so afraid and there was nothing I could do for him. He pushed himself backward into the corner of the room, trying to flee whatever chased him, and I followed him there, staying close, murmuring over and over, *I'm here, I'm here,* even though I knew he couldn't hear me.

After a time Ezra shuffled into the room in his underwear and T-shirt. "You need a stop?" he asked.

"I'm okay."

"You don't think I'm capable of gentling him?"

I threw up my hands. "I can't reach him," I said. "I can't pull him out of it!"

He put a hand to his temple. "I'm sorry," he said. "I came here to help, not to add to your load."

I squeezed his hand to say it was all right, and let go.

"How about I dawdle with you awhile?" He sat on the floor

and wrapped an arm around me and I felt myself relax a little into him.

"Do you remember," I said, "in the hospital, just after your stroke, when you couldn't quite wake up?" I had to talk him up to the surface; he was like a spider trapped in a bathtub, the sides too shiny to climb. "One night you told me, *I'm drowning in mushroom soup.*" I laughed, a little, but Ezra didn't laugh with me. We had both laughed at the time. It *had* to be funny then, otherwise it would have scared us both to death.

Ezra nodded at my mother. "I don't know how she can gather her slumber." She startled in her sleep as Jeremy called out, her eyes fluttering, but she didn't wake.

"I imagine it's the sleeping pills she's taking. It worries me that they knock her out like that."

"Weird," Ezra said, pointing at my mother and then at Jeremy. "It's like they're singing the same dream."

Indeed, just a moment before Jeremy's cries rose back up to screams, my mother's face tensed as if in pain and her arms and legs jerked repeatedly—as dogs do when they run in their dreams—as if she was trying to escape. "Go away!" Jeremy cried.

Ezra rubbed his forehead. "The racket's too hard," he said. "I need to go back to bed."

"I understand. It's okay."

I wished that he had chosen to stay despite my protests, that he had continued to hold me as we waited out this storm. But he touched my shoulder and left the room.

From my corner next to Jeremy, I watched my mother for a few minutes, the fear in her brow, her half-open eyes moving in dream. I glanced into the shadows where she looked, almost expecting to see what frightened her so. Then her face relaxed and her eyes closed, and just like that, Jeremy's screams ended as well. I carried him to the bed, covered him with a sheet, and smoothed his sweaty forehead until I was sure he was fast asleep. So like the barn cats, terrorized by a chasing coyote one minute, snoozing on the porch the next.

I closed the bedroom door behind me and went into the kitchen to look out the window at the fire. As I watched, trees ignited and candled, flaring in the night, as the fire progressed along the ridge and down the slope. A U-Haul van and truck and trailer passed by the farm in the night, neighbours from up the valley rushing the contents of their homes out of the path of the fire. I ached for these uprooted souls as I ached for myself. Since our move to Cochrane, I had felt disoriented; it was the feeling of waking in a strange hotel and not knowing where I was. I had in fact awoken from sleep in our rented house thinking I was in my home in Chilliwack. I soon figured out where I was, but the odd feeling that accompanied this experience lingered. It was as if my soul hadn't caught up with me yet, as if it had stalwartly refused to leave what had been home for more than a decade and, its leash now pulled taut, was forced to follow me in this venture. There were those stories of pets that had found their way home over great distances despite outrageous odds. I thought of my soul in this way, as a lost cat struggling through unfamiliar territory to find its owner, and I tried to help it along. I unpacked boxes in that tiny rented house, searching for those dear possessions that defined who I was: the originals of the cartoons I had drawn for the *Salmon Arm Observer* when I worked there as a junior reporter; the tiny yellow cap Jeremy had worn in the hospital the day he was born, before the nurse had bathed him; the little heart-shaped silver pin with a pink rhinestone at its centre that had belonged to my grandmother; the raku vase that held my pens on my writing desk, the only vestige of Jude that I kept in my house. I foraged through the litter of moving, hunting for the familiar, searching for my lost self.

"Jeremy okay?" Val said from my parents' room, and I joined her there.

"Night terrors," I said. "He's back to sleep."

"I remember you having those on occasion when I came home for visits. Awful to watch."

I picked up a garbage bag as Val swept a pile of debris into the dustpan. "Those sleeping pills really knock Mom out," I said. "She slept through all of Jeremy's crying."

She nodded. "They worry me as well. I was thinking that we should set Mom up in the parlour for the duration. Make it easier on her, and you." She yawned. "We should get some sleep ourselves. What is it, eleven o'clock?"

"Twelve-thirty."

I stuffed yet another handful of mouldering paper into the bag. In order to make room for the hospital bed, Val and I had been sorting through the contents of this room for most of the day and into the night, ever since I had driven my mother, Ezra, and Jeremy home from town, and yet all around us bags of my mother's writings were stacked higgledy-piggledy to waist level. Both Val and I stopped our sorting from time to time to scan the letters, but there was nothing scandalous in what I read. One letter described one of my father's visits to the hospital, and my mother's fears as she waited in the emergency room with him. Another letter, all seven pages of it, chronicled the birthing of a litter of kittens.

"Ezra had a room like this in our house in Chilliwack," I said. "After his stroke his office was a complete disaster; he just couldn't keep it organized. But then as he got better, his office grew more ordered by degrees. It was like watching one of those films of a teacup being dropped on the floor and breaking, but in reverse, and in slow motion." The bits of teacup pulling themselves together and the teacup returning itself, whole, to the table.

"In Mom's case the room is getting worse," Val said. She reached to the floor and picked up a teddy bear dressed in a bright red hoodie with BEAR written across the front. "I found this under the bed. She stole it from the toy box I keep at home for Kerry and Samantha when Jennifer comes to visit. Can you imagine? A woman her age snitching her great-grandkids' toys for herself."

I shook my head, but I could imagine it. I had taken over one of my son's bears as my own, and had even brought it with me on this trip. It sat on the night table in my old bedroom now, and watched over me as I slept. I was shamed by this little totem of mine, this tiny pink bear, only two inches high, that I had found at the thrift shop a couple of months before, thinking I was buying it for Jeremy. It was an old thing, with movable arms joined to its body by wires. I felt the same need to care for it as I used to when I fussed over my dolls as a child, tucking it into the tissue box on my night table at bedtime. When I worried over this compulsion aloud to Ezra he said, "Maybe it's hormones. Like that cow we had that lost its baby and tried to take over that other cow's calf."

"I have a child to care for," I said.

"People bustle over their dogs. What's the trouble in taking care of a teddy bear?"

He was reassuring. Still, I worried about myself.

"Did you see this?" Val said. She handed me a photograph, a picture of Val and myself, a formal portrait. She was already nearly a woman, and I was just a baby in her arms.

I took it from her. "You were still living here, on this place, when this was taken, right?"

"Our place over at Valentine's had burned down that spring, so you and I and Mom and Dad were all crowded into that cabin by the barn." She nodded toward the window in the direction of the cabin that had once housed my grandfather's hired hands.

"So you were living here when Grandpa went missing."

She took the photo back and put it in the box she had found it in. "I was here."

"So what happened?"

"He went squirrelly and got himself lost."

"What do you mean he went squirrelly?"

"He'd stand at the kitchen window shaking, scared shitless of something out there, though he'd never tell us what. If I dropped a cup, he jumped and screamed at me. He grabbed me by the shoulders once and shook me until Dad pulled him off. My big crime was banging the dishes together in the sink as I washed them. I got really wary, you know, careful, waiting for the next blowup. It got so waiting for one of his rages was worse than the outburst itself. You see it in Mom, right? You can't walk up to her from behind without her startling."

"What was wrong with him? Was it shell shock?"

"Hang on a minute and I'll show you." She opened a box and swept away some dust before sifting through a stack of writings, my mother's flowery, elderly script on stationery rimmed with cats, seagulls, or roses. "I was vacuuming in here last fall and that cat freaked and knocked a stack of papers to the floor. As I was picking them up I found this." She pulled out a large manila envelope. "Grandpa's files from the psychiatric hospital at Essondale, and his military files. It looks like Grandma requested them at some point."

"He was in a mental institution?"

"Many times."

I took the envelope into the kitchen and slid the contents onto the table beside Jeremy's drawings from earlier that day. My grandfather's files from Essondale Mental Hospital, his military files and medals, a razor, a pair of glasses in a case. A photograph of a man landed on top; he was pale, his cheeks were drawn, and his eyes were wide, staring, empty, as if they were not seeing what was in front of him. Like a man just roused from sleep but still engaged in a dream, or a nightmare. This was the face of a sleepwalker.

"Spooky, isn't it?" said Val. "His eyes seem, I don't know, dead."

"I've never seen a picture of him."

"There weren't many to begin with. Mom took them all down after Grandma passed away, including Grandma and Grandpa's wedding photo. She threw them in the burn can and burned them."

"You know why?"

Val didn't answer. She picked up the medals, the glasses. "All these things were in the envelope when I first found it. I assume they were all his. The glasses certainly were. I remember him putting them on when he was about to go out hunting." She picked up the ancient razor. "God, I remember him shaving with this, leaning over the kitchen sink, peering into a tiny mirror that he hung there for that purpose. I hated being in the house when he shaved. I was always afraid he'd nick himself and yell at me for it."

"Why would he blame you?"

"That's what he did. If I made a noise, distracted him. Noise of nearly any kind set him off."

I inspected the medals as she rifled through the pages in the military file. She handed me a photocopy. "You see this? *Discharged by new disease supervening—n.y.d. shell shock.* Shell shock was a new disease. They still didn't know what the hell they were dealing with."

I read out loud. "*Hesitation in speech. Marked tremor of hands. Trembles and shivers while talking to strangers. Speech is halting. Memory very poor for retention and impressibility for recent events.*"

"He was in several hospitals, over the course of a year," said Val. "Here it says he is in Victoria, then Kamloops."

"Why would they send him all the way to British Columbia?" I asked. "He was British."

"He'd already been living in B.C. for some time before the war, so he joined the Canadian army. They were shipping him home." She handed me another sheet. "Look at this. *Cause of disability: shell concussion—buried.* The guy's buried alive and that's all they have to say about it."

"He was buried alive?"

"Evidently a shell hit close by, burying him within a foxhole, and then a second shell uncovered him but sprayed him with shrapnel. I remember Grandpa and Grandma talking about it when I was a kid. I imagine he was just one of thousands, hundreds of thousands, injured in that way."

"Or killed."

"He had some kind of plate in his head, to replace part of his skull that was destroyed during that second explosion."

I looked up at her. "He was brain-injured?"

"Brain-injured. Shell-shocked. Whatever the case, he was nuts." She picked up the razor and stared at it for a time, then stuffed it back in the envelope along with the medals and glasses, and closed the flap. "A kid should be sad when her grandfather dies," she said. "When he disappeared on that mountain, I was just glad he was gone."

"He died on that mountain?"

"His body was never found."

"Mom said he died of a heart attack."

"Like I said, she's getting more and more forgetful."

"Dad didn't correct her."

"Likely he didn't hear."

"It was the story she always told me," I said. "Why would she lie? Why didn't you or Dad ever tell me about it?"

She laid the envelope on the table. "Look, it wasn't like we were hiding anything from you. It was pretty clear from the start that Mom didn't want any of us talking about it. The story of Grandpa's disappearance was spread all over the papers. And of course the neighbours all pulled out their stories about Grandpa, what a crazy bastard he was. I took a lot of crap for it at school. After it was all over I think Mom just wanted to shut it out of her mind. I know I did."

I picked up the photo of my grandfather and stared at it a moment.

"I should get home, get some sleep," said Val. "We've got a lot to pull together tomorrow before we bring Dad home." She headed for the door, then turned to me. "Don't go stirring this up for Mom and Dad, all right? God knows they've already got enough to worry about right now."

I watched from the window as Val got in her truck and started the engine. The truck's lights shone two paths down the road through the smoky night.

Across the way, fire flared up in Jude's kiln shed as he removed glowing pots and vases from the kiln with tongs, and placed them into the metal garbage cans filled with newspaper; the pots themselves set the newspaper on fire before he jammed the lid on to starve the fire of oxygen. It was a process called reduction, and the result of this, and the raku firing itself, would be the glorious red, purple, blue, metallic, black, and crackled finishes of raku ware. But just one of those scraps of burning newspaper drifting from the garbage cans could set the dry grass of the surrounding field alight. I stood by the window and watched him for a time as he moved back and forth from the kiln to the cans in a practised dance, fire and smoke billowing around him. Then I spread John Weeks's Essondale files across the kitchen table and, with Harrison sleeping on my feet and the face of my dead grandfather staring up at me, I read them.

9.

TO: Mrs. Maud Weeks
Turtle Valley, B.C.
May 4, 1945

FROM: John Weeks
Mental Hospital
Essondale, B.C.

My dear Girl

This is Sunday & Iam so lonely & continually
thinking of home & you dearie. I ate the box of

fudge you sent already. it reached me, the staff here didnt eat it as I thought they would & each piece made me think of you, how you test the fudge rolling it between your fingers in a bowl of water & how you feed it to me in the kitchen if Beth isnt there. how you let me lick that sweetness from your fingers. there! let the staff here read that & be scandalized!

How is Beth keeping and yourself, donot work too hard, & if you wish it why not put on music for yourself it will cheer you anyway, but not for the neighbours, for you donot know just how rotten they are, say nothing to them ignore anything they may say & be careful of the new man. keep him out of the house.

You shouldnot have let Valentine build that greenhouse I said I would get to it & I would have if these headaches hadnot set me low. you donot think Iam capable of finishing things but Iam if you give me the chance. now Valentine's gone and built that greenhouse and I cannot do it for you he had no right. don't invite him in for tea any more you might be innocent to his intentions, but I am not.

Listen to me, my dearest: stay out of the bush & at very least carry the .22 with you when you bring in the cows, you don't know the terrible things that will catch you out there unawares.

Things are not too bad, its quiet here and Iam left alone & Iam able to write to you, last year I could not do that much for the Bromide the doctors filled me with took away what sight I have & made me like a drunken fool.

Well, sweetheart I must draw this to a close, so bye bye my dear Girl, ever your lover

"J. Weeks"

Ward Notes

REG. NO. XX,XXX

NAME

J. Weeks

DATE OF ADMISSION

March 17th, 1945

1945

March 17th This patient was admitted from Promise, B.C., March 17. He was given a bath and allowed up and about the ward. He seems apprehensive and nervous, continually shaking and trembling and starts violently at the least unusual sound. Complains of severe headache. Keeps his eyes closed and strokes head continually. He resists questioning, asking "to be left alone." He is very irritable. Disoriented as to time and place. He seems to feel that he is still fighting in the Great War.

March 18th This patient was today transferred to the Infirmary.

March 28th Since admission, this patient is showing some improvement. He is very nervous and apprehensive and has apparently been this way for some considerable length of time. He believes that the neighbours are all against him and, as a result, was threatening to shoot a neighbour named Valentine and was accordingly admitted to this institution. Evidently this Valentine was trying to intervene when Weeks threatened his wife and daughter with a gun. His wife is understandably afraid of him. His delusions of persecution against his neighbours are firmly fixed. When asked if any of his neighbours had actually harmed him, his family or his property, he said, "If they did I'd kill the sons o' bitches."

April 15th This man continues to show a slow improvement. He says that he likes the quietness of the ward and feels better. He claims that he was continually hounded by someone or something that followed him about the farm, threatening him harm, and that here he is "left alone." When questioned further about the nature of this person or thing that was following him, the patient refused to answer.

May 4th In a letter to his wife today, this patient shows marked persecutory ideas in regard to the people in their vicinity. He asks her not to associate with them as they are all rotten. He also warns her to stay out of the bush, that there is something out there that might harm her. His physical condition remains fairly good.

June 15th This patient was again brought to the attention of the Clinic today. DIAGNOSIS: TRAUMATIC PSYCHOSIS. For verbatim, see separate sheets.

Ward Notes

REG. NO XX,XXX

NAME

J. Weeks

DATE OF ADMISSION

March 17th, 1945

Verbatim taken by Dr. Spears

1945

June 15th

Q. Where were you born?

A. In England. Nottingham, Nottinghamshire.

Q. Is your father dead or alive?

A. I never knew him.

Q. And your mother?

A. She died giving birth to me. My grandmother raised me.

Q. Any siblings?

A. No.

Q. What is your wife's name?

A. Maudie. Maud.

Q. How many children have you?

A. Two. Beth and Dan. Dan joined up last year.

Q. Is Beth still in school?

A. No. She's seventeen. She works with me on the farm.

Q. How long did you go to school?

A. I was taken home to work when I was twelve. I was milking morning and night. Then my grandfather died when I was fourteen and the farm was sold to pay debts so I went to Eastwood Collieries and served my time there.

Q. What for?

A. No, no, not jail! I was in the mines, driving the ponies down into the bloody dark. You had to force the ponies down, you see, anyway you could. Kick them, poke them, whip them down. But I had one named Charlie that would only go down for me, and not for the other drivers. I kept sugar cubes in my pocket for him. But then a runaway dram got him. The both of us heard it rumbling at us but there was only time enough for me to press myself up against the rock before it rammed past me; I couldn't get Charlie out of the way. The dram flung away the oil lamp I was holding and thundered right into Charlie. I could hear him groaning in the dark until they found us. After that I came to Canada.

Q. Where did you go to first?

A. I went to a place called Toronto. But I couldn't find work that paid so I came west to work in the mines. Then I got it in my head to go back home to find a wife, so I joined up here and they sent me over.

Q. You were injured in the war?

A. A shell hit close by, and buried me. There was dirt in my mouth, in my nose. I thought I was dead. But then a second shell exploded and tossed me out of that hole and shot me through with shrapnel. There were a lot of men buried that way.

Q. You say shrapnel hit you?

A. Tore open my head. They put a metal plate in. Here, you can see the scar.

Q. And you convalesced in England?

A. At first, yes. That was how I met my wife. She was an ambulance driver, you see. Drove me from one hospital to another.

Q. I gather that was the end of the war for you.

A. They sent me back here to convalesce. My wife joined me some time later, after the war ended. She's had to look after me ever since. We got this farm at Turtle Valley—

Q. Turtle Valley?

A. It's a valley between Salmon Arm and the village of Promise, where I would be out of the way, where I wouldn't cause trouble. It's been hard for her, you know, to care for me all these years. I wish to God I'd been blown to bits in the war and been done with it.

Q. You don't mean that.

A. Yes, I do! What use am I to anyone? What use am I to Maud? I can't even build her that damn greenhouse, much less a decent house. If I could just get that house done for her.

Q. You're building her a house?

A. I had the plans drawn up, you see. But we need a good well. I keep digging on the place. If I could just find a good well, then I could start building the house for Maudie. For Maudie and me. And Beth, and Dan if he comes home. He'd come home, I think, if we had a decent house. Something I could leave him. That Maud could be proud of. She'd see I was worthwhile then.

Q. You don't think she sees that now?

A. The whole problem is that the people who live near me are such ignoramuses. They do things to make me look bad in front of my wife, to make me look incapable.

Q. How so?

A. Like Valentine. He knows Maudie wants a greenhouse. So he takes advantage of this situation, me being in here, to build it for her. I was going to build it for Maudie. I was getting to it. I just have all these headaches, and then I have to spend the day in bed. But I can do it. I would have done it. Now he's gone and built the thing and made me look bad in front of Maudie, made it look like I can't ever finish things.

Q. I understand you've been quite frightened; that you felt someone was following you. This neighbour perhaps?

A. No, not him.

Q. Then who?

A. I don't know. It's something, in the bush, always watching me, following me, coming after me. Never letting me get a moment's peace. I just can't stand it. I get so I don't want to go outside. I don't want Maudie going outside either, but she does. The cows have to be brought down, you see, for milking. I don't want her going into the bush.

Q. So, was that what frightened you this time?

A. Well, there was that thing in the bush.

Q. The thing you just mentioned? Following you?

A. No, no. It was one of them Japanese balloons. A spy balloon, come to watch me.

Q. To watch you?

A. And it crashed, I guess, before it could report back with whatever it found out about me. Then some men came and blew it up, to hide the evidence.

Q. Men came to blow the balloon up. That was spying on you.

A. Yes! It made a terrible noise. I don't remember much after that.

Q. Your daughter and your wife are frightened of you . . . Mr. Weeks? I said your wife is frightened of you.

A. I heard you.

Q. That comes as a surprise?

A. Why would Maud be scared of me?

Q. I understand you threatened her and your daughter with a gun.

A. No!

Q. The police report says they were frightened of you and tried to leave and that you threatened them with a gun.

A. I wouldn't hurt Maudie! She knows I wouldn't hurt her! Why would she be scared of me?

Q. Evidently you also threatened your neighbour.

A. Valentine came at me and I thought he was going to shoot me and I just lost control of myself.

Q. What did you do?

A. I don't know. That's what I would like to find out.

10.

I READ MY GRANDFATHER'S LETTER to my grandmother again: *. . . each piece made me think of you, how you test the fudge rolling it between your fingers in a bowl of water & how you feed it to me in the kitchen if Beth isnt there. how you let me lick that sweetness from your fingers.* It seemed so unlikely that my grandmother would do this; these weren't the actions of the reserved woman my mother had painted in her stories.

I tucked my grandfather's files back in the envelope, then retrieved the carpetbag from the box and turned it upside down so the contents spilled to the table. The little pot of rouge. The wallet. The photo of Valentine. The newspaper clipping. A tube of lipstick. A makeup compact. A comb. Her glasses case. A handkerchief with her initials, M.W. Her coin purse and a handful of coins. A water-warped copy of *The Prophet*, by Kahlil Gibran, landed on top of it all. When I leafed through it, the book fell open to a yellowed envelope tucked into the chapter *On Marriage*, to a page where a section was underlined: *You shall be together when the white wings of death scatter your days.* Inside the envelope was a tattered Christmas advent card from my grandmother's sister, dated April 6, 1932:

Dearest Maud,

Here is a teddy bear to replace the one John dispensed with. I can't imagine a father doing such a thing! Perhaps, at the very least, the lost little fellow will watch over your treasures. Tell me, if you can sometime dear sister, just why it is that you stay? I mean no disrespect. My concern is genuine. I worry for your well-being, and that of your sweet daughter and son. We all have our reasons for the things we do. I simply wish to understand. In any case I hope this finds you well, and I do hope little Elizabeth Ann makes grand friends with this new teddy.

Your loving sister, Sara

I closed my great-aunt's card. On the front Santa, dressed in green and not red, stood beside a Christmas tree lit with candles. Tiny numbered flaps covered the whole of the card; each lifted to

reveal a picture—of a reindeer, a soldier, a horn, a spinning top—
one for each day of December leading up to Christmas. Why
would Sara suggest that my grandmother leave her husband? My
grandfather's illness would have been a difficult load for her to
bear, but I wouldn't have expected a woman of that time to leave a
sick husband. In any case, with two young children to care for,
where would she go? What would she do? Yet here was this card
from her sister, a woman of her own time, who had assumed
differently, that she had a choice. I opened the makeup compact
and looked in its mirror. Had she contemplated leaving?

Sweet, I wanted something sweet. I went through my mother's
pantry. A yellow tin of Colman's Prepared Mustard. Heinz sand-
wich spread. Marmite. Bird's custard. I shifted the cans around
and found a bag of brown sugar. That was what I wanted, penuche,
brown-sugar fudge. Searching for the recipe that I knew it contained, I tugged my grandmother's scrapbook from the top of the
fridge and found the page with the tortoiseshell butterfly pressed
between its pages, its wings tattered and torn away. The penuche
recipe called for:

> 2 cups brown sugar
>
> 1/2 cup heavy cream
>
> 1 1/2 teaspoons vanilla
>
> 4 tablespoons butter
>
> 1 1/2 cups walnuts or pecans

I buttered the sides of a saucepan near the top, to stop the
penuche from sticking as it boiled, and put the sugar and cream
into it, stirring with a wooden spoon until the sugar dissolved.
Fudge-making was always a finicky process. I never bothered to

make it during rainy weather as it would simply soak up the moisture and wouldn't set properly. But even in hot, dry weather like this, I couldn't predict how the candy would turn out until it was done, and often found making it frustrating. And yet, perversely, I was compelled to make the stuff, and to eat it. Eating was now an instinctive act. I ate quickly, mindlessly, and when I was done, I looked down at my plate and thought, *When did I eat this?* I wasn't present in the act of eating, even when I ate the things I loved, though my body was there, reaching out to plate and fork, to the sweets I made myself, to cooked chicken and buttered bread, to salad greens fresh from our garden, to skinned peaches bathed in their own juices.

In my late teens, walking beside the boy I loved then, I found myself stooping for soil and licking the dirt from my fingers, just as I had seen deer licking the soil on roadsides, for the salt. On the farm our cows ate dirt looking for the minerals they lacked. Lyle asked, "What are you doing?"

I said, "I don't know," and from then on hid this strange craving from him and everyone else. When I finally took my compulsion to the doctor I found I was anemic; I ate the red dirt of Blood Road because my blood was thin. It was horrific to find my body so driven, to find that my mind was not at the helm, to discover that an animal instinct for nourishment took precedence over will. To see my own hand reaching out, not in my control, possessed as if by another entity, even if that entity was saner than me, wiser in its fleshly understanding of my needs. Now I craved penuche, brown-sugar fudge. Just as it was when I hungered for dirt to find iron, my body was on a search. What I lacked now I could only guess at.

Across the field a light blinked, and I turned off the kitchen light so I could better see. In his kiln shed, Jude flicked his fluorescent lights on and off. His figure was silhouetted in the open garage door, waving me over.

I switched the light back on, aware, now, that he was watching me move about the kitchen, and turned up the heat to bring the penuche to a boil. Then I waited by the stove, staring out the window at the kiln shed lighting up the night, resisting the urge to test the fudge too soon. I had ruined candy in the past by taking it from the pot too early. I had to guard against this tendency within myself to rush things, both small and large. I had rushed into Ezra, despite both Val's and my father's objections that we were moving too fast. I had moved in with him less than a month after I met him, and we married only five months after my affair with Jude had ended, long before my feelings for Jude had dissipated. And before Ezra I had rushed into Jude, disregarding the fact that he was another woman's husband. I hardly knew him that evening I saw him walking a few yards past his own gate on his way to the dance, carrying his wife's ornately carved, thickly upholstered chair over his shoulders, his body thrust forward with the weight of it. The chair was the only one Lillian could comfortably sit in, and I often saw Jude carrying it past my parents' farm on his way to functions at the Memorial Hall; he and Lillian drove the Impala and the chair wouldn't fit inside. He was just a neighbour then, another city artisan who'd bought himself a bit of cheap acreage in Turtle Valley, and a riddle for my young mind: a handsome man so bound to a heavy and handicapped woman that he would carry her chair nearly a mile down the road.

I stopped the Chevy and leaned across the cab to open the door after he'd hoisted the chair into the truck bed. "Should we go back for Lillian?" I asked.

"No, she's already there. She took the Impala."

I drove off. "Your seatbelt's to the side," I said.

"I don't wear them."

I raised my brows to him but he wouldn't allow me to catch his eye; he stared out the windshield. It wasn't yet ten o'clock and it was still light, though the sun had set behind the steep valley walls long before. The poplars by the road rattled as the wild valley winds blew a thunderhead toward us. Peterson's horses, excited by the coming storm, raced along the fenceline, nearly keeping pace with the truck.

"Kat is short for Katherine, I take it."

"No, Katrine. I don't like being called Kat."

"But your mom—"

"Everyone calls me Kat. I just don't like it." My mother had called me Katrine, I'm sure, so she could give me the pet name Kat. I hated it, but disliked the alternative—Katie—even more. And in any case it was useless to try to make my family call me anything but my childhood name. Jude was the only one who ever called me by my name. In return I never called him Jujube, as members of his family did.

"Katrine." I looked over at Jude, expecting him to ask me something, before I realized he was rolling my name over his tongue. "Pretty," he said. He nudged my camera bag with the toe of his work boot. "Planning on taking pictures at the dance?"

"I keep my camera in the truck in case I come across something, even on my days off. We're always looking for photos to fill the paper on a slow week."

"Cute kids, pretty horses, that sort of thing?"

"Yeah, I guess." I looked back in the rearview mirror at Peterson's horses. I had in fact considered stopping to take a photo of them.

"What the hell?" Jude said, and pointed.

A moose and its calf launched through the bushes beside us, leapt onto the gravel road, and galloped in their ungainly way in front of us, nearly matching, then exceeding the speed of the truck. "Grab my camera," I said. He pulled it from the bag and I took it from him. "Here, take the wheel."

"What?" he said.

"Take the wheel!"

I accelerated to catch up to the animals and snapped a couple of photos through the windshield before unwinding the side window. "Put your foot on the gas for me, will you?" I said. "This is great!"

He pressed his foot on the gas against mine and leaned into me in order to drive as I hung out the window to get my shots. "Look at them go!" I let out a whoop.

"There's a truck coming," Jude said.

"Huh?"

"Truck coming! Behind us!"

I took the wheel and handed him the camera, and he slid back across the seat as the truck passed us. The moose charged through an open gate and fled across a field, disappearing into a patch of bush.

Jude shook his head. "You're one crazy mama, aren't you?"

"Why?"

He laughed.

I turned into the Memorial Hall driveway and parked next to my father's Ford, but when I unfastened my seatbelt, Jude didn't immediately get out of the truck. He put his arm over the back of the seat, filling the air with the smell of Ivory soap and cumin. "I didn't mean to offend you earlier," he said. "You do some good work for the paper."

"I'd take more care with the photos if I had the time, but when you're a reporter on a small paper like the *Observer*, you've got to do everything. Tomorrow morning I cover a baseball tournament. Tuesday I sit in court. Wednesday afternoon I've got to take photos up at the pool. I'd like to see *you* get a good shot of seniors' aquatic square dancing."

Jude laughed and I watched his mouth as his smile faded. "Well," he said. "I guess I'd better get this chair inside and head back home before it gets dark."

"You're not staying?"

"Lillian can't dance, and I don't like sitting around, shouting over the music. That's her thing."

"I won't be staying long either, but I promised my father a polka or two. Mom never goes to these dances."

"Maybe I'll have a beer then, and drive back with you. Unless I'm taking you away . . . unless you're meeting someone."

"No, no."

Tables filled with people lined each side of the old hall. The place smelled of cedar and cigarette smoke and its hardwood floorboards were deeply scarred by decades of dancing. After repairing damage from countless acts of vandalism, the hall committee, of which my dad was a member, had elected to remove the glass and board up the windows permanently. There was a small stage at one end where a band played: a drummer, a guitarist, and a singer on a keyboard. They were all young men about my age, but I didn't recognize any of them. On this stage many years before, my father had played the fiddle and harmonica and my Uncle Valentine had played the banjo. I had read all about it in the Turtle Valley community notes my mother had written for the Promise paper and collected as clippings in her scrapbooks. My

My father was on the dance floor with Mrs. Simms, bounding out a polka to the band's rendition of Blondie's "Call Me." The younger dancers boogied listlessly around them, stepping out of the way as my father and his dance partner swung through the room.

"We saw a moose and her calf on the way here," I said.

"I've never seen moose in this valley," said Lillian.

"Katrine got some photos of them, for the paper."

"At least now I've got something for the front page."

"You should do a story on Jude," said Lillian. "He's got a show coming up in a couple of weeks. You could get some photos of him during the next raku firing. High drama. Lots of smoke and fire."

"I can't work with people watching me."

"You are trying to sell these pots, aren't you?"

"I'll do a story," I said. "When are you firing next?"

"You said Sunday, right?" said Lillian.

"I usually drive out from Salmon Arm on Sunday nights to have supper with Mom and Dad," I said. "I could stop in at your place on my way by."

Jude made a face.

Lillian reached up to pat his cheek. "Think publicity. Think mortgage payments. You'd think with a gorgeous mug like that he wouldn't mind having his picture taken."

Jude put his hands up. "Okay! Okay! But not until late in the day, when I'm in the flow. When distraction is less of an issue."

We all watched the dancers for a moment.

"So, you want a beer?" Jude asked me. "Or may I have the honour of this dance?"

"Is that all right?" I asked Lillian.

"Go! Dance! God knows I can't."

Jude gave an exaggerated bow and held out his arm to escort me to the floor, and, following my father's lead, he charged me around the room in a polka, forcing other dancers to jump out of the way. When the song ended, the band began to play the Red River Waltz, a tune I knew my father must have requested. Jude and I stood facing each other for a few moments, breathless, with our hands hanging at our sides, watching my father and Mrs. Simms dance. Then Jude held out his arms for a waltzer's embrace. "Shall we?" he said.

I glanced over at Lillian. She was turned the other way, chatting with Ruth Samuels, who ran the organic carrot farm near the reserve. "Lillian won't mind?"

He shrugged and placed a hand on my waist to guide me around the floor. As we circled, I looked over his shoulder at the neighbours I had known all my life, drinking beer from cans and wine from plastic cups and shouting at each other across the tables. Mr. Simms, who could no longer dance comfortably because of his arthritis. Sandra Henderson, who had once taped a note on my back that read *Wide Load* when we were in grade five. Uncle Dan, my mother's brother, red-faced and tipsy on Kokanee, flirting over a table with Mrs. Randalls. He winked a conspirator's wink at me when he caught me looking his way.

Jude's cheek brushed against mine. "You smell like cookies," he said. "Vanilla."

The back of his shoulder where I held him was damp from sweat. His hand was hot in mine. I felt him begin to grow against my thigh before he stepped back to put a space between us.

11.

THIS WAS WHAT I MADE FUDGE FOR: the feel of the little ball between my fingers in the cold water as I tested it, the chewy texture of it between my teeth. That first sweet taste. When I was sure it was ready, I set the pan into a sink partly filled with cold water, then added the butter and vanilla before stirring it. When it suddenly thickened, became lighter in colour and lost its sheen, I poured the penuche into a greased pan.

I checked Jeremy, and then Ezra, to make sure they were both sleeping soundly, then I picked up Jude's box, the tray of penuche, and the manila envelope containing my grandfather's files, and slipped outside to follow the path across the field. A water bomber that had just been put on night duty droned low overhead. But still the fire marched on, breaking through the fire guards that ground crews had built, advancing ever farther across the top of the range.

Jude's kiln shed stood adjacent to his studio and had an open floor plan that made me think of the cookhouses at some government parks. Large garage doors could be opened on three sides to allow the air to flow through. Shelves all around the kiln held glazed pots and vases, ready for the raku firing. A few finished pieces sat here and there on the top shelves.

Inside the open kiln, pots appeared translucent as the glazes swam on their surfaces. Jude lifted one of these vases with a pair of blackened tongs and carried it to a galvanized garbage can. He wore a red flame-resistant Nomex workshirt, and heavy Kevlar gloves that extended up his arms. A cloth smoke mask was strung around his neck, but he didn't wear it as he worked. His hair was as unruly as ever, but peppered now with grey.

"Anyone ever tell you that you bear a striking resemblance to Harrison Ford?"

He swung around and grinned. "Only you." He pulled out another pot and placed it in a garbage can and arranged newsprint around it as flames shot up over his gloved hands. "I didn't think you were coming. I mean, I was just thinking, why would I imagine that you would come? But here you are."

"It took me a little while to get organized. I was making fudge."

"You were making fudge in the middle of the night?"

"You're firing raku when we could be evacuated at any moment?"

"What are we supposed to do? Put our lives on hold? My sister phoned from Vancouver last night, and I told her I was making linguini and she said, you're *cooking?* As if that wasn't the thing to do when the mountain above you is on fire. But you've got to eat, right?" He went back to the kiln for another pot. "And I've got a show in Vernon next week."

I leaned against the doorframe to watch him work.

"How can you get away with a firing during this evacuation alert?" I asked him.

"I'm working in a contained area. It's legal."

"But is it wise? You could start another fire."

He grinned at me. "Haven't yet."

He closed the kiln to bring it back up to temperature, then lifted each of the garbage-can lids one by one, to let more air in, to stuff more newspaper around the pots, to spritz some with salt water and vegetable oil to further crackle their glazes. Flames blasted up from the garbage cans as he opened them, and bits of burning newspaper swirled up and drifted down to the concrete floor. The insides of the garbage cans were black from countless fires.

"You and Val were working pretty late tonight," he said.

"We're still hauling out Mom's things, and now we've got to make room for a hospital bed for Dad. The cancer has spread to his bones. It looks like a matter of weeks."

He stood straight to face me. "Oh, Katrine."

"He refuses to stay in the hospital. We hope to bring him home tomorrow. I don't think it's a good idea, but it's what he wants."

"I'd want to die at home." His eyes were glistening. I had forgotten this, his ability to feel so passionately, to tear up so readily over another's heartache. Years before, I had watched him wipe his eyes over newscasts describing the plight of earthquake victims, or those who had lost their homes to floods. In my ungenerous moments his sentimentality had annoyed me. But now it had the effect of making me weep as well. I wiped the corner of my eye with the heel of my hand and turned away.

"Here," he said. "Let me put in my next load so we can talk."

I watched him stack his glazed pots and plates, cups and teapots into the kiln. He closed the lid with gloved hands and flames shot up out of the hole at the top of the kiln.

"So, that story I was telling you about?" I said. "How my grandfather went missing on the mountain? Val told me tonight that he was never found."

Jude flicked his hot gloves to the ground in one practised motion. His hands were dirty with soot and newspaper ink. "He died up there? Why would they keep that from you?"

"I don't know. Val made noises about how Mom didn't want to talk about it, that it was all too painful. And it would have been." I pulled the manila envelope off the box. "Val found my grandfather's military files, and his files from Essondale."

"Essondale?"

"A mental hospital. Evidently he was institutionalized a number of times. He was shell-shocked, but he'd also sustained a brain injury during the First World War."

Jude rubbed his hands on his pants before taking the files from me.

"It looks like he had paranoid delusions," I said, "and thought something was following him, out to get him. He didn't trust his neighbours, Uncle Valentine in particular. Look at this letter he wrote my grandmother. He thought Valentine was sweet on her. But even with all they had to deal with, there was still passion between my grandparents. He talks here about how she fed him fudge from her fingers."

I watched his face as he read through the letter and then paged through the Essondale file. "This letter from the doctor who admitted him is pretty interesting," he said, and he read it aloud: "*Nearly a year ago I considered him insane, but a second certificate was not forthcoming and he was treated at Shaughnessey Hospital and later allowed to go home. He is not safe (in my opinion) to be at liberty at home. He was brought in today by the provincial police after he fired on a neighbour who tried to intervene when Weeks threatened his own family with a gun. His wife had evidently been trying to escape the farm along with her daughter when the incident occurred. His wife is understandably frightened of him. Last year when he was brought in the police—*"

I took the letter from him. "*—informed us that he had attempted to kill a hired hand and was nearly successful, though I fancy this was an exaggeration.*" I tapped the letter. "Dad was his hired hand. I wonder if that's how he got the scar, why Mom and Dad wouldn't talk about it."

"What scar?"

"He has a nasty scar on his arm. He and Mom always said it was from a hunting accident, but when I asked about it in the hospital, Dad got the story wrong. Both he and Mom seemed flustered, as if they were hiding something."

"But why would they lie about any of this?"

"I don't know."

He handed me the files. "So, are you going to offer me some of that fudge, or what?"

"I don't know why I brought it over. It won't set in this heat. I'll have to put it in the fridge."

"I'd like a taste anyway."

"I don't have anything to cut it with."

He handed me a knife that had sat on a plate with a half-eaten apple. "Don't worry, it's clean," he said, when he saw me inspecting it.

I cut into the penuche, wishing I had a spoon instead, and offered him a limp piece. He held up his blackened hands and pointed to his mouth. "You mind?"

As I held it out for him, he grasped the fudge with his lips, taking in my finger as well. The thrill of his teeth on my skin. He held up his hands again. "Let me wash up."

I watched him pull his T-shirt over his head and drop it to the floor. The slick of sweat over skin, his muscles in motion as he hoisted a bucket up from the floor and spilled water into a white enamelware washbasin. Then he washed, splashing water over his face and hair. He flicked the basin with the nail of his index finger, setting it ringing. "I found this in your uncle's cabin years ago," he said.

"It was Valentine's?"

He picked up a towel to dry his hands and face. "I imagine I should have offered it to your parents, but I liked it."

I ran my fingers around the rim of the basin until I became aware that he was watching me. His bare chest: the moles like constellations, the dark nipples.

"So, what's with the box?" he said.

"The stuff in it isn't mine. Or it's not all mine in any case." I opened the flaps, pushed aside the cards and letters Jude had given me, and showed him the sketchbook. On the cover, in Jude's handwriting, was my name, Katrine. On the first page was a drawing of me, sitting at the table in my mother's kitchen, holding a small makeup mirror in my hand. Below the sketch were Jude's notes:

> I spent the evening at Gus and Beth Svensson's
> along with Lillian and a handful of Beth's other
> friends and neighbours, a birthday party for their
> daughter Kat, though Kat didn't seem too happy
> about it. Something her mother had forced on her,
> I think, as she was surrounded by her mother's
> friends and not her own. I refilled Lillian's coffee
> from the pot on the stove and saw the birthday girl
> sitting as if by herself at the kitchen table, ignor-
> ing the others at the table around her, with her
> cake in front of her, drawing the late evening sun
> into the room with her purse mirror, playing with
> the light as a child might. I thought that scene
> would stay with me forever, but when I started to
> sketch at home, this was as much as I could
> remember. Can't get her expression right. She
> looked so lonely. Likely she was only bored. She's
> so lovely. I'm thinking of asking her to sit for me.

I didn't remember the moment he wrote of. I had lost so much of my life. Was I ever capable of that kind of rudeness, playing with my purse mirror and ignoring the guests at my own party, to make my unhappiness with my mother perfectly clear?

She's so lovely.

"I didn't know you had noticed me that early on," I said.

"How could I admit to that? You were just a girl. And I was married."

I turned the pages in the sketchbook. After that drawing there was a flurry of sketches of me that Jude had done in his studio as Lillian chatted with friends in her kitchen. Under one sketch, he had written, *The smell of her! Vanilla, I think. I'm not sure if it's perfume or the scent of apple pie or coffeecake she might have eaten. Or even her natural smell. She said she wasn't seeing anyone. I hope she's not seeing anyone.*

I tapped the note. "Do you think I would have let you kiss me that night if I had had someone?"

"I kissed you and I had Lillian."

"You startled me, you know, with that first kiss. You had me sitting there, just so, all arranged like you wanted—"

"No. Like I always saw you sitting, with one knee up, and the other foot tucked under."

"Then you jumped up all of a sudden and marched over to me, still carrying your sketchbook, so I thought you were about to rearrange my hair or my clothing again. But you leaned down and kissed me. Surprised the hell out of me. Your beard stubble tickled my upper lip."

"I remember thinking, *Her lips are so soft.*"

"You were so, I don't know . . . determined."

"I was scared shitless. I figured if I didn't make myself kiss you then, that night, while I had the opportunity, I wasn't going to."

"Scared?" I said. "Of me?"

"I wanted to kiss you from that first time we got together, when you dropped me and Lillian's bloody great gothic chair off at the Turtle Valley hall for that dance. Don't you remember? When I apologized for being such an ass, about what I said about your photographs in the *Observer*. I put my arm over the seat behind you. Right there, I wanted to kiss you. But there was a hall full of people in front of us. And Lillian."

I looked down at the sketchbook, and leafed through it, feeling shy. There was sketch after sketch of me. At first I was clothed, then naked, and then my belly was as round and ripe as a pumpkin. Then the sketches ended. I paged through the remainder of the sketchbook, following a progressively thinning trail of my life: a grin-and-grab photo of me flanked by smiling arts council members holding a scholarship cheque to help me on my way back to university, a mug shot next to a little story that said I was leaving, an invitation to my wedding at the Turtle Valley Memorial Hall only a few months later that my mother must have sent Jude, against my wishes. Then many empty pages; more than half the book was left unfilled.

"I had no idea you kept a sketchbook, a scrapbook really, about me, as if I was a subject you were studying."

"Muse," said Jude. "You were my muse."

"I'm not angry. I make similar notes about people myself. It just unsettled me. It's strange to see yourself through another's eyes." I put the sketchbook back in the box and pushed the box toward him. "In any case, this is yours."

He picked up one of the cards he had given me and read what he had written: "*There were a couple of hot air balloons hovering just above the highway as I got close to Kamloops this afternoon. They looked so peaceful, just hanging there, weightless, at the mercy of the winds, or their lack, able to rise or fall, but nothing more. This is how I am, weightless in your love, and at your mercy. . . .* God, did I really write this drivel?"

I laughed. "I liked it at the time."

"I don't understand how all these cards I gave you got in here."

"I had stored that stuff at Mom's. The day after my wedding I left an envelope full of the things you had given me on your doorstep."

"Why?"

"I don't know. After I saw you at my wedding, I guess I just wanted to say—"

"That you still thought of me too."

I smoothed a hand over the wedding invitation in the scrapbook. "Why did you come to my wedding?"

"It was a community event; the whole valley was there. Lillian would have wondered why I refused to go. Obviously she had her suspicions."

"I half hoped Lillian would find that envelope of your cards first."

"I imagine she did, and stuck them in this box. I never heard anything about it. But then she wouldn't have said anything. She would have hoped that I would stumble across it myself. Jesus, that woman, she would never just come out and talk to me. It was all cat and mouse." He waved the card. "But you weren't much better, leaving those cards on the doorstep for Lillian. I didn't think you had it in you."

I grinned. "I guess I did at one time."

"That explains why you never came over to visit Lillian and me in all those years."

"Well, how could I?" I said. "After everything we'd been through? I never understood how you got away with coming over to see me when I was back home. How you found the nerve."

"Ezra was always there, and your parents. We were chaperoned." He shrugged. "I had to see you."

I stared up at the fire glowing on the mountainside, not sure how to respond. After a time he ran a hand down my spine to the small of my back. "Mosquito," he said.

I raised my eyebrows to him but he didn't remove his hand. Instead he doodled on my back with his finger, as the girl sitting behind me had in elementary school, as I had doodled on the back of the girl seated ahead of me, to tickle and shudder the senses: *Criss-cross, apple sauce, spiders crawling up your back. Spiders here, spiders there, spiders crawling in your hair.* Jude's was the same seductive, agonizing tickle. I wanted him to stop. I wanted him to go on.

"Guess what I'm writing," he said. A game we used to play during those afternoons we spent in bed in my apartment.

"I don't know."

"Guess."

I shook my head and drew away. "I've got to go."

"I'm sorry."

"No, I shouldn't have come over. I don't know what I was thinking. What if Jeremy wakes and I'm not there?"

"Won't Ezra get up with him? Or your mother?"

"Mom's not up to taking care of Jeremy anymore. And what if Ezra did wake? How would I explain coming over here? I shouldn't be here."

He took my hand. "Please stay a few more minutes, Katrine."

"I've got to go."

I WALKED THROUGH THE DRY GRASS back home, carrying the pan of fudge and the manila envelope, breathing smoke. Someone in the valley was playing the old tune "If You Were the Only Girl in the World" on a piano. Was it Mom? It sounded as if it was coming from the farm. The tune was something she often played, a quaint choice at odds with the war that raged in the hills above us. But there were no lights on at the house. Perhaps, then, the sound originated elsewhere, at a neighbour's, and was bouncing off the steep valley walls. When I was a child Mom warned me not to talk about the neighbours outdoors, in case our gossip drifted over the hayfield to their ears.

A figure emerged from the dark, standing by the bush surrounding the old well.

"Hello?" I said. The man stood completely still and said nothing. I saw no face, no hands, only his outline as a shadow in the black, a glint of light reflecting off his glasses. "Can I help you?" I said. He stepped back against the bush so I couldn't see where he was anymore. I stood a moment, my heart beating against my throat. Then I ran, and once I passed the well, I heard footsteps running after me. I dropped the pan of fudge and fled toward the house, my ears filled with the sound of my own breath and the thump of blood. The heavy footsteps gaining on me. The jingle of keys in a pocket.

The piano was clearly coming from my parents' house. I reached the porch out of breath and coughing, the footsteps behind me crunching gravel. As I slammed the kitchen door shut behind me, and locked it, the music stopped abruptly.

"Mommy!" said Jeremy. "Look! Look!" I turned to find Jeremy standing in the dark of the kitchen, his face lit up in the red glow from the stove. All the burners were on again.

12.

MOM OPENED AND CLOSED her hand as she read what she had written, then shook the hand to loosen the accumulated ache of decades of writing. I knew this ache, the electric jolts to my fingers, the fright of waking in the night to find my hand dead, then tingling as I shook the feeling back into it. In bed each night I wore what Ezra, searching for the right word, once called my "evening gloves," my night splints. As a small joke between us, I now called them my "industrial-strength evening gloves," clumsy plastic things that discouraged touch between Ezra and me in the precious morning hour before Jeremy woke. I suffered from the ubiquitous carpal tunnel syndrome, a symptom of the writing life. That's not how my mother saw her condition, though; she blamed that lightning strike for the shocks that buzzed up her arm and made her fingers tingle or go numb.

"You want anything, Mom?" I asked her. "It's coffee time."

"Just a cup of tea."

I plugged in the new kettle that sat next to my mother's. I had bought this one for her but, though she left it sitting on the kitchen counter, she never used it, preferring the old one that had witnessed countless conversations, arguments, and celebrations. My mother made cup after cup of tea throughout the day, and served it, without fail, at the kitchen table with the beautiful Noritake creamer and sugar bowl that had belonged to my grandmother, the set Maud had used when she entertained Valentine. Both the creamer and the sugar bowl were hand-painted with the stylized eyes of peacock feathers, and stared up at us as we drank our tea, just as they would have stared up at Maud and Valentine. My mother was married to these familiar objects of her past as much as to her habits.

"I want cinnamon toast please!" said Jeremy.

"We don't have any brown sugar," I told him.

"I've got a bag in the cupboard," Mom said. "Don't I?"

"I used it up making a batch of Grandma's penuche last night." And I hadn't had a piece of it. When I had gone outside to retrieve the pan earlier that morning, my fudge had been a lump on the ground licked and eaten by Mom's cats.

"If you wanted sweets, I have a box of chocolates on the fridge," she said.

"Chocolate!" said Jeremy. "Can I have a chocolate?"

"No, but you can have apple and peanut butter," I said, and

I started cutting an apple for him. "I had a craving for fudge," I said to Mom.

"Something your body needs, I imagine." When I raised an eyebrow she said, "This past spring I had a craving for uncooked macaroni. I ate handfuls of the stuff. Couldn't get enough. I suppose Val told you."

I glanced at the parlour, where Val was stacking boxes, trying to make room for Mom's bed. "She mentioned something about it."

"I thought I was loony too. I'd buy a month's supply at a time and hide it all over the place. I ate it in bed, and while I sat watching television with your father, I'd hide handfuls of macaroni in my lap under the crochet blanket I was making for Jeremy. Your dad asked me, 'Where does all this damn macaroni come from?' I told him a box had broke open, that I must have missed some when I swept it up. I thought I was losing my mind, so I told my doctor. She had me tested for anemia."

"Anemia?"

"Most pastas are fortified with iron. I didn't know that. Did you know that?"

I shook my head. "Why didn't you tell Val?"

"She's convinced her old mother has lost it. She thinks I go around leaving all the burners on and flinging hot irons into the laundry. If she wants to believe that, she can go right ahead."

As I handed Jeremy his plate, I looked over at the parlour to catch Val's eye, but she hadn't heard. "All the burners *were* on again last night," I said. "Although I did wonder if we'd had an intruder in the house. I saw somebody out by the well. Then I heard footsteps, and keys jingling in the man's pocket."

"That was one of my father's habits," Mom said. "He'd come up behind me, *jingle, jingle.* I hated that sound."

I poured water from the kettle into the teapot. "And I heard the piano being played," I said, and I hummed "If You Were the Only Girl in the World."

My mother picked up the tune and sang it, though her elderly voice was a wisp that I strained to hear. "My mother loved that old song."

Val came out dusting off her jeans. "Okay, so I've made some room. Now we can move that single bed out of my old room and into the parlour for you, Mom. Kat, can you give me a hand?"

My mother started up from her rocker. "Can't you do it later?"

"I'm just about to pick up Dad," said Val. "In fact I'm late. I said I'd be there by ten."

"Then just leave the bed in there. Jeremy doesn't bother me."

I glanced at Val. "It'll only take a few minutes to get things organized," I said, and I followed my sister into the room, where we immediately spotted what Mom didn't want us to see—the kitten among the bedclothes, a tiny tabby, too young, surely, to be taken from its mother. She must have intended to feed it milk by dropper, as she once fed the wild hares I found in a burrow and brought home, hares that died after two weeks of exhausting care. She would have known the kitten was too young, of course— she knew about the needs of young things—but had forced her mother urge on this kitten, to ensure its affections.

"Oh, Mom," I said.

She picked up the kitten. "I was going to take it out to the barn before Jeremy's nap. I know you don't like cats."

"I like cats," I said. "I have three at home." But our cats were barn cats, working cats, and earned their salary of dry cat food and the occasional scratch behind the ear by keeping the rodent population down. I had inherited this attitude toward cats from my eminently practical father, who had neutered the toms himself: he placed them head first in a gumboot, cut them open with a jackknife, and sterilized the wound with Dettol. Once he had quickly accomplished this task, he immediately released the cats and they staggered off from their ordeal, shaking one hind leg and then the other, to lick their humiliation beneath the potting shed.

"It's just—the last thing you need is another cat," I said.

She cuddled the kitten to her cheek. "What's going to happen to her if I don't take her?" She didn't wait for an answer. She headed back to her rocker in the kitchen, talking to the kitten as she went.

From the kitchen Jeremy called out, "Kitty!"

"Ruth Samuels was just leaving when I got up," I said to Val. "She must have brought it over."

Val began stripping the mattress of its bedclothes. "Don't make a fuss over it, Kat. It doesn't matter."

"But you keep on finding these cats homes for her," I said, "and she just keeps on taking in more strays. She must spend nearly three hundred bucks a month in cat food alone, and then there are all those 'treats' she buys them."

"She's been doing it for years," said Val, "decades. You saw those photo albums we dug out of her room. She's got more pictures of her cats than of us. Giving her hell isn't going to change anything." She tossed the sheets to the floor. "In any case, why does it bother you? I'm the one who has to deal with them."

"I don't know." The screen door in the kitchen opened and a chair scraped on the floor as Ezra, presumably, came in for coffee. I picked up one sheet and then the other, to fold them, as Val folded the blankets. "When I was a kid I'd come home from

school and find Mom sitting in that rocker, writing, lost in it,"
I said. "You know how she gets. No *Hello, how was your day?* It was
like I wasn't there, like she didn't give a shit about me or anything else. But then one of her cats would come yowling around
her legs and she'd pick it up and coo at it like it was a baby."

"You can't tell me you're jealous of the cats."

"It wasn't the cats," I said. "It was that she wasn't *here*.
I remember wandering around the house when I was, I don't
know, three? Screaming, thinking that I was in the house
alone. I was terrified. Then I found Mom curled up in bed, a cat
at her feet, writing away like she hadn't heard me crying. I pulled
at her pen and said, *Mommy, stop!* But she wouldn't."

"Or couldn't."

"Other times she really did leave me alone in the house, or in
public places. I had a tantrum on the grocery floor once, and she
just left. I wandered around crying until I found her looking out
the front window of the store. Another time at that same grocery
she left me sitting, crying, in the shopping cart and walked off.
God knows what would have happened if I had decided to climb
out. Eventually another shopper took me to the checkout
counter. The clerk and I found Mom sitting on the bench outside, crying."

Val sat on the mattress. "I didn't know she'd done that."

I tossed the folded sheets on the second bed and sat beside
her. "Every single time she left, I thought it was for good. Then
there was this day when I was maybe six or seven. I'd taken one
of Grandma's vases outside to collect lilacs as a gift for Mom—it
was that lovely blue and white vase—and I tripped and dropped
it and chipped the rim. When Mom saw what I'd done she burst
into tears. I guess the vase had been a favourite of Grandma's.

She stood there for a minute just shaking, clenching her fists, and then she walked off down the driveway, heading for Blood Road, like she had a hundred other times when I'd done something wrong. I started to follow, crying, thinking she was leaving and never coming back. Then as she was walking away, she stepped on a twig, and it was like something inside me snapped as well. I turned back and headed for the barn where Dad was working. I just unplugged myself from her."

Val rubbed her face and then turned to me. "I want to tell you something that might help explain Mom, something that happened to me. You were asking about Grandpa. After he disappeared I was so afraid that he hadn't actually died on that mountain, that he'd just turn up in the night. I slept with the light on, so he couldn't surprise me."

"Why would he surprise you?" Then I understood. "Oh, Val!"

"Most of the time he caught me out in the barn, or in the field, or in the bush when I was bringing in the cows. I'd hear his keys as he approached, you know, jingling in his pocket, and I'd hide, but he'd always find me." She looked down at her hands in her lap. "His hands were so huge, the size of dinner plates. Now they teach kids to say no, to tell. But how could I say no to a man with hands that big?"

She looked up at me, but in that moment I didn't know how to respond, what to say.

"One day Mom and Grandma were in Kamloops shopping, and I was feeding the calves over at Grandma's, and he caught me in the barn and pushed me down into the hay. I don't know what got into me, but this time I kicked him hard in the shin. I said, 'I'm going to tell Dad.' But he dragged me by the arm out to the yard and then into the greenhouse where one of the barn cats had just given birth to a litter. He held one of the kittens over a bucket of water and threatened to drown the whole batch if I didn't keep quiet. I struggled to get away, but he made me watch as he drowned that kitten. It squirmed in his hand, trying to get breath. Then he picked up another kitten and was about to drown that one too when Uncle Valentine came running across the field and into the greenhouse; Valentine held a rake like it was a gun and told him, 'Put the cat down, John, and let the girl go, or I'll tell Maud all about this.' Like he knew, you know, like he knew everything. The next morning I found all those kittens in that bucket, dead."

"Jesus, Val."

"Given how much energy Mom puts into her cats, I imagine he must have done exactly the same kind of thing to her. You understand now, don't you? Why I don't make a fuss about her cats, why I try to find them homes, why I don't want you to make an issue of them?"

I nodded.

She patted my thigh. "Speaking of which—can you and Ezra get those barn cats rounded up into cages this afternoon? Then maybe Ezra can drive them to the SPCA shelter at the fairgrounds. I'll need to stay here with Dad."

"I'll have to do it myself. Ezra won't be able to drive for some time."

"Yes, of course."

"I doubt I could keep him focused on the job long enough to help me in any case. He still hasn't gotten around to butchering that calf."

A chair scraped against the floor in the kitchen and then Ezra was at the doorway. "Your mother heard every saying," he said. "She heard every goddamned word." He turned on his heel and left the house; I heard the screen door slap shut.

I rubbed my face. "Shit."

"You should talk to Mom," Val said. "About what you told me." When I looked up at her, she said, "Nothing I said was new to her." She glanced at her watch. "I told the nursing staff at the hospital I'd be picking up Dad about now, so I'd better run. Maybe you can get Ezra to help you move Mom's bed?" I followed her into the kitchen and she started for the door before turning back. "Mom, you want anything?"

Mom sat within her rocker, fussing with the collar on her blouse as if arranging it for a photograph. Jeremy played with the kitten at her feet.

"Mom?"

"I don't want anything."

Val stood a moment fiddling with her keys, then walked up to Mom and kissed her on the forehead. "I'll pick something up for supper," she said.

13.

I STOOD AT THE KITCHEN WINDOW with my back to my mother as I watched Val drive off in her truck. Ezra walked toward the house, dragging a green garden hose behind him. He set up a sprinkler near the house and turned it on, to saturate the cedar-shake siding and shrubs around the house as Jude had, I presumed, so embers drifting down from the hills wouldn't take root.

"What you told Val," said Mom, "how I walked off on you, it wasn't like that. I never would have left you."

When I turned to her, she kept her gaze on Jeremy who played with the kitten at her feet. I handed the cat to my mother,

149

and took my son's hand to lead him to the door. "You go help Daddy set up that sprinkler, okay?"

"Sprinkler!" he shouted, and bounded down the steps.

I watched from the window to see that Ezra had taken him in hand before replying to my mother. "I know, now, that you wouldn't have left me," I said. "But I didn't know that then."

She stroked the kitten within her lap for a moment. "You didn't like that I wrote."

"I didn't like that you disappeared into it. That I couldn't reach you. But I have the same desire to write everything down, so I'll remember it."

She shook her head. "That's not it at all. When I write my mind is *here*, in the present. I don't remember the past. I can forget, then. And there's so much that I want to forget."

"I don't understand."

A bantam hen fluttered up to reclaim its fragrant nest among the sweet alyssum growing in the window box, and my mother carried the kitten to the window to watch the chicken with me. "You remember that rooster we had when you were in your teens," she said, "the one that stabbed its claws into my thighs every time I tried to feed the chickens? Nasty creature. It got so I dreaded going into the henhouse to get the eggs, and you know how much I love collecting eggs."

Yes, I knew. The warmth of a chicken's body beneath her feathery skirt, the smooth weight of a warm egg. The deep satisfaction of a basket of eggs, a treasure sought and found.

"Every day it was a battle with that rooster. I had to carry a bucket ahead of me, like a shield, so he wouldn't gouge my thighs. When he lunged after me, I tossed the bucket over his head."

I nodded. I had also carried buckets into the chicken coop to protect myself from roosters, from one in particular, a bird I had named Christmas for his glorious red and green feathers. After he set his talons into my legs I learned to capture him with an upturned bucket. Strange how he sat there under that pail, never trying to move. When I finished setting out the grain and collecting the eggs, and took the bucket away, Christmas just went on sitting there, eyes fixed on a distant horizon. I had to throw a rock at him to get him to move. He had a short life. Tiring of the daily battle with him, I butchered him for soup stock and found his testicles were as large as a man's. So much luck in such a small body.

"Dealing with my father was like dealing with that bloody awful rooster. I never knew when he might attack. I was so frightened of him, but that's no excuse. I should have protected myself, and Val, much sooner than I did."

She put a hand to the window and the chicken pecked at her fingers through the warped glass. "I did my best to make sure Val was never alone with him, and I asked Valentine to watch her if I had to go into town and couldn't be there when she got home from school. I didn't tell Gus why until years later, though both he and Valentine guessed, I think. But I didn't know that my father had gone after Val, not until Valentine told me he had caught my father forcing Val to watch as he drowned those kittens."

My mother held the kitten close and I reached out to pet its head. "So Val was right?" I asked. "He did hurt you, in that way?"

"One of my earliest memories is finding my teddy bear on my bed with its head cut off just after I had run away from him. I hid the bear under my bed, but my mother found it. She never asked me what happened; she just sewed the head back on."

"Oh, Mom." I felt the jag of a long forgotten childhood pain pierce my belly. When I was very young I found my beloved plastic elephant on my bed, similarly destroyed. My mother had yanked the wheels, ears, and three of the legs from it, as punishment for some misdemeanour. I didn't remember what I had done to enrage her so, but the elephant still existed; it was packed away in a box of toys in my old room.

"He was a terribly wounded man," Mom said. "Brain-injured. Shell-shocked.

When I visited him during his stays at Shaughnessey—the big veterans' hospital in Vancouver—I saw men who'd been in hospital since the Great War. Some had only their eyes and fore-head left; their lower faces had been blown away. I remember thinking my father was like these men, with bits of himself missing, though you couldn't see the damage from the outside, not until he started raging, or until the fear took hold of him.

My mother kept a light on in their room at night; if it was dark, even the scurry of a mouse would wake him. He very often woke screaming. Night terrors, my mother told me, memories of the war replaying in his mind. She would never come up behind him without clearing her throat, a little cough, an *ahem*, quite proper, mind you, but loud enough to let him know she was there. If she hadn't, he would have startled and turned on her. Any loud noise would set him off, like a neighbour blasting stumps. He went wild that day they blew up the Japanese balloon."

"That was real? The doctor who interviewed him in the Essondale files seemed to think it was a delusion."

"You read them?"

I nodded.

"Oh, it was real, all right. Your father was the one who found it, early in March 1945. He and Valentine and your grandfather were out logging with the horses when Gus saw a big white blob in the trees up on the hill. Valentine and John hiked up with Gus to investigate. It turned out to be a mat of papery stuff draped over tree branches. The balloon itself, inflated, would have been twenty-five, maybe thirty feet across. Wires all around the bottom, like what you'd see in a truck motor. There'd been rumours about balloons that had been found or had exploded, so we had a pretty good idea what it was. One came down near Squilax that same year. It still had the bomb attached and I guess it blew quite a hole. The Japanese had sent thousands of those balloons loaded with bombs, trying to start fires all over North America. They had to send them in winter, to take advantage of winds that would carry them all the way from Japan. The thing is, that time of year, the balloons landed in snow, and if the bomb did go off, any fire that started just fizzled out. And because the military managed to keep things pretty quiet, and next to nothing was ever reported in the papers, the Japanese figured the plan had failed, and didn't try again."

"So did Dad blow it up then?"

"No, no. They all hiked back down to the road, then Valentine and your father drove into town and told the RCMP officer we had around here at the time, DeWitt, and he phoned the army base at Vernon. Then we went back home for lunch. That afternoon three army fellows turned up at the place and Valentine, Gus, my father, and I all led them back up the mountain. One of the men was heavy, must have been an office man. He got across the creek and only about a quarter way up before he played out and just sat. The other two yanked the balloon out of the tree and took it apart. They kept the metal ring from the bottom, with all the wires. One of the fellows called it a chandelier, I imagine because it had dangled down from the balloon when it was up in the air. Then they stacked the rest of it into a pile and set it off. Good Lord, it made a racket. The blast shook buildings miles away. My father fell to the ground holding his head, crying."

My mother looked up at me. The ghostly white rims in her eyes. "Oh, Kat, it was so terrible to watch. My father thought he was back in the war, in the thick of fighting all over again; he couldn't walk, he was shaking so hard. But those wretched army fellows just laughed at him. Valentine and your father and I had to drag him down off that mountain, kicking and screaming, without their help. When we finally got him back to the house, my mother made a pot of penuche for him, as she often did when he was upset, and that settled him down a bit, as it almost always did. That man loved his sweets. Once he was quiet, Valentine walked across the field back home and Gus went back to my father's hired hand's cabin, where he was living at the time, to get some sleep."

She looked up at the mountain. "But then later in the evening I came up behind my father to fill his cup, surprising him, I guess, and he whacked the teapot out of my hand. Scalding tea went down my dress and all over the floor. His face was so pale and his eyes bugged out, in terror. He was shaking so hard. Then he grabbed the 3030 from the gun rack over the door and aimed it at me. I'm sure that at that moment he had no idea who I was.

"Mom stepped in between me and the gun and told me, 'Keep quiet, walk very slowly into your room, and gather your things.' While I did as she told me, I could hear her talking to him, very quietly, soothing him like she always did. By the time I came out with my carpetbag, she had hers packed as well. My father was lying on his bed. She said, 'Let's go,' and she led me down the road. But we didn't get to the gate before my father came out, levelled that gun at us, and shouted at us to stop."

She turned to me. "That was what awaited my mother if she ever thought to leave. That gun. When my mother didn't immediately stop, my father fired over her head. Gus came running out in his long johns to see what was going on, and then Valentine ran across the field from his cabin. He knew what my father was capable of. So he saw my father turn that gun on Gus. Oh! I can remember that night so clearly. *If you're going to shoot someone, then shoot me,* Valentine told him. So my father turned the gun on Valentine next, and I could see him thinking about shooting him, you know. Valentine just kept on walking toward him with his hands out. That's when my mother slipped off behind the house and ran over to Petersons' to get help. I was just frozen, I was so terrified. I couldn't think what to do other than watch. Gus started walking toward my father too, with his hands out, just like Valentine, and my father swung that gun back on Gus, then on Valentine, back on Gus. All the time my father was backing away, toward the house, and they were getting closer and closer."

She brushed her face against the cat's fur. "It was stupid of them, cornering him like that. My father bumped into the porch and fired at Valentine but missed. Gus charged forward, slammed my father to the ground, and kicked the gun away. While Gus held Dad, Valentine picked up the rifle and kept it trained on him until the police came barrelling down the driveway with the siren blaring and the lights flashing. Then they bundled my father away for another one of his visits to Essondale. He was gone a year. By the time he got back, your father and I were married and Val was born and there was nothing he could do about any of it."

I watched Ezra a moment as he set up another sprinkler near the house and turned on the water at the tap by the steps. Jeremy tripping along behind him. "I just don't understand why your mother married your father in the first place. He was already injured when they met, right?"

She nodded. "Part of his skull had been blown away by the shells that first buried him and then unburied him. My mother told me bits of shrapnel from those explosions were still lodged in his brain. I thought of them as living things, eating away at him, like maggots."

"So why would she put herself in that position, having to care for this man her whole life, knowing how hard it would be?"

"Oh, I don't know how much they knew then. They didn't know much about brain injuries and they certainly didn't understand shell-shock. They were still tying men to posts in firing range of the enemy for it so they'd be shot; they treated them like deserters, traitors. But the situation was familiar for her, I think. Her own father and mother had been sick throughout much of her adolescence and Mom had nursed them both until their deaths. She'd been taking care of someone for so long that she didn't know anything else. So my father's illness gave her a kind of life's work. Even so, I'm sure there were a great many times when she wished she had never married him."

I looked up at the clouds of smoke sweeping across the Ptarmigan Hills. "Do you think it came as something of a relief for her then when your father finally died on that mountain?"

When my mother looked up at me, her eyes wide as if frightened, I said, "Val told me last night."

"What did Val tell you?"

"That he was lost up there, that he never came home." When she didn't respond I said, "I don't understand why you felt you needed to lie about it."

"I didn't want to remember that time. I knew you'd ask questions." The kitten squirmed in her hands and she put it down on the floor. "I wasn't well for a long time after my father disappeared. My lightning arm would do things, terrible things."

"I don't follow."

She crossed her arms and stared out the window for a time, at Jeremy running back and forth through the sprinkler. "One afternoon, Val came home from school and I asked her to do the dishes but she wouldn't. She said, 'Why don't you do them? You never do anything around here anymore.' And that's all it took. My lightning arm took hold of Val's hand and brought her to her knees; her fingers slid free from my grip one by one until I was holding her little finger and I watched myself bend it backwards, like it was someone else doing it. There was a terrible crack, and her screams, and then your cries as you woke, and Gus yanked me away. He had to hug me from behind, so I couldn't get at Val." She turned back to me. "I broke her finger, Kat. I would have done a lot worse if Gus hadn't stopped me."

I turned away, to look out the window, feeling queasy. "Jesus, Mom!"

"When I walked away from you, I wasn't leaving you. Those were the times I was afraid of what I might do."

In the yard Ezra excitedly pointed toward Jude's property in order to get Jeremy to look, and I searched the fields as well.

"There's deer," I said, pointing them out for my mother, relieved, at that moment, to have something else to focus on. Five does and a young buck in the alfalfa field, tails twitching.

We watched them together for a time. "Remember that night when my father couldn't bring himself to shoot those deer?" she asked me, as if I had been there when it happened, and so I had been, many times, when she told me this story. I followed her there again now, into the field where the wheat stooks stood silver against the moon, and I waited with her behind my grandfather as he levelled his gun, as he watched three does and a buck come into view. We waited as he waited, and breathed out in relief as he sighed and lowered the gun. The deer grazed for a time on the stooks and then, startled by a rustle in the grass, bounded back into the woods.

My grandfather's shoulders fell as he turned, and we followed him back to the house, listening to the jingle of his keys within in his pocket, the crunch of barley stubble under his feet. I could see the ridges in the bottom of his boots; the moon was that bright. He sat next to the stove to kick off his boots, and my mother took them outside to knock them against the side of the house to rid them of mud. Then she picked up a broom and dustpan, and swept his footprints from the kitchen floor.

14.

I LAID MY HEAD on Ezra's shoulder and breathed in his smell: sawdust and sandalwood, the whiff of coffee from beneath his arm. He pulled me close in his sleep, something he had always done, and I ran my hand down his stomach to touch his penis lying soft on his thigh, which he had once responded to no matter how deeply asleep. But not this time. I sighed, turned away, and curled into myself, and he rolled toward me and hugged me from behind. So he was awake. "It's not you," he said. "Kat, glimpse at me." When I didn't, he sat up on one elbow and turned my face toward him. "You're beautiful. It's not you. I'm tired. All the time I'm tired. And I'm not sure who I am to you anymore. I feel like I'm no use."

I sat up and put on my robe. "I'm going to get up for a while."

"Kat, wait."

As I left the room I heard him getting out of his side of the bed.

Mom was standing at the stove. The lights were out but her figure was clearly lit up by the red glow of the burners. They were all turned on and she held a dishtowel over them. One end of the cloth dangled against the burner and was blackened, smoking. Harrison and the kitten sat at her feet. The cats both looked up at me and meowed as I approached.

"Mom, what the hell are you doing?" I grabbed the dishtowel and threw it into the sink, where it sizzled out among the dishes soaking there. But she still stood at the stove, staring at the burners. I turned them off and took her by the arm. "Mom?" I said. Her eyes were wide open but unseeing. I gave her a little shake. "Mom!"

Then she looked at me. "Oh, hello, dear."

"Are you all right?"

"Yes, fine. A little tired."

"You were sleepwalking, I think."

"Sleepwalking?" She looked around the dark kitchen, at Ezra standing like a shadow behind me. "Oh!"

"Can I catch you both anything?" said Ezra.

"It's okay," I said. "I'll get her settled."

"I could gather some hot milk."

"We'll be fine."

He stood a moment, a dark silhouette in the kitchen, and then turned back to the bedroom. Mom leaned down to retrieve the little tabby.

"Let's get you back to bed," I said to Mom, and I led her by the arm to her bed in the parlour.

As she lay down, Mom looked up at me with those ghostly eyes. Without her glasses, she searched my face, unable to focus. "Ezra wanted to help you, to be with you," Mom said. She touched my cheek. "Let him help you."

"I'll try." But I didn't want to go back to the bed I shared with him. Not now. I ran a hand over her forehead, through her thick grey hair. "You get some sleep."

I KNOCKED LIGHTLY ON THE DOOR to my father's room and opened it. On the hospital bed my father lay in his pajamas, dreaming morphine dreams. His eyes were closed and his face was turned away—already he was distancing himself from us—and yet I could see his old face in the mirror of the bureau, surrounded by the family photos Val had placed there: Val and myself taken when I was two; the last photo of my grandmother as she carried that carpetbag down the streets of Kamloops; the one of Valentine in the garden; Uncle Dan, his face hidden behind a gas mask, taken during the Second World War; my own wedding photo, and my parents,' one that was obviously taken by a family member or a neighbour, not by a professional photographer. In this photo my father was thin and boyish, with a head of thick red hair, not the balding, corpulent man I had known my whole life, not this frail old man in the bed in front of me. In the photo, he held my mother's elbow as if to guide her. My mother wore a simple flowered frock, and she looked not up into the camera but down, to the tiny bouquet of yellow violets in her hand.

"How about I take a shift?" I said to Val.

Val yawned. "I'm okay."

"You need some sleep, and I haven't had a moment alone with him."

GAIL ANDERSON-DARGATZ

"All right." She stood. "He hasn't been sleeping well." She leaned into my father and raised her voice. "Kat's going to sit with you for a bit, all right?"

"Hmm? Kat?" He looked up at me, for a moment confused. "Oh, yes."

Val kissed him on the forehead and patted my arm as she left the room. Tonight my father's breath was shallow, erratic. "The smoke getting to you?" I asked.

"It's funny," he said. "I used to walk the trails on those hills with a loaded backpack and never got out of breath."

We both stared out the window for a time, at the fire blazing across the mountain in the night. "That fire isn't going to give me the luxury of hanging around," Dad said. "If I'm going to die at home, I better do it quick."

The fire was close. Throughout the late afternoon and evening, embers had drifted down, starting spot fires up and down the valley. I had put one fire out myself in our sawdust pile that evening, drowning it with water from a garden hose.

"You'll be with us for a while yet," I said.

He shook his head. "I wish I hadn't slept the whole way back from the hospital this afternoon. I wanted to take in as much as I could on the drive. I don't expect I'll come by that way again. Not alive, in any case."

I didn't reply. His voice was thin and whispery and there was a kind of transparency to the skin of his face, as if he wouldn't simply die, but grow more and more translucent until he disappeared.

I pointed at the wedding portrait of my parents. "Mom was telling me today that your romance with her all started the day the Japanese balloon blew up, when Grandpa threatened Mom and Grandma with a gun."

164

He turned to look at me. "She told you about that?"

I nodded.

"Huh. Well, I think she took notice of me there, all right, as the hero, you know. She started bringing little gifts to the cabin. The funniest things: a scrap of red velvet, a string of bells, little bouquets of violets."

I waited until he caught his breath again and then asked, "Was that the start of something between your Uncle Valentine and Grandma as well?"

"They were better friends after that, if that's what you mean. Valentine was over nearly every day, during those months John was in the hospital, helping Maud with the chores and in the garden. Helping in any way he could. Like I said, he built that greenhouse for her. But he made himself pretty scarce after John came back. He didn't come over much. Though he sent notes to her."

"He wrote Grandma letters?"

"I was the courier," he said, and his voice was wheezy, "carrying them back and forth, making very sure your grandfather never knew anything about it, of course. I didn't even tell your mother about it at the time."

"But they lived just across the field from each other."

"They couldn't see much of each other when John was home; he wouldn't have allowed it, or understood it. Lord knows Maud and Valentine should have got together. But Maud felt sorry for John, I think. She often wondered aloud how he would ever cope if anything were to happen to her."

I looked at my own wedding portrait, waiting until his breathing had settled before asking anything more. How would Ezra cope without me? "You think that's why she stayed with Grandpa?" I asked. "Because she felt sorry for him?"

"Who knows? I never understood why she stayed. I expect she and Valentine might have got together after John disappeared, even at the age they were then. But of course Maud passed away the day she heard the news that the search had been called off. The stress of it all, I imagine."

"Did you read any of the letters?"

"No, no. Maud must have burned them. What if John had found them?"

"And Valentine? Did he keep Grandma's letters?"

"Oh, girl, you have so many questions!"

"I'm sorry."

"No, it's all right. Just give me a moment." I held his hand as he laboured to catch his breath. "We never found any letters when we went through his things after his death," he said finally. "I expect he would have destroyed her letters or hid them. John was the kind of man who would have looked through Valentine's things if he had his suspicions. No one locked their doors then, except for John. He carried his keys with him everywhere he went."

"When I was a kid I came across one of Valentine's tobacco cans under the floorboards of that old house."

"Were there letters in it?"

"I don't know. It was rusted shut. I never thought to look for it again. Mom didn't like me going in that old house."

He nodded. "You said there was a man in there, a man in the wall. Scared the daylights out of your mother."

"Mom told me about that, but I don't remember much of it myself."

"I thought you were talking about shadows, your own shadow, or our shadows when we were with you. That's what

I told your mother, to reassure her. But you insisted there was a man in that old house. He came out of the wall and went back into it. You didn't like him. You called him a bad man. You said he was scared. Scared and sad."

I stared out the window, listening to the rasp of my father's breathing. Outside falling embers caught air and flared up, like disembodied spirits.

"You should take a look in case those letters are there," he said. "Be a shame if they were lost to this fire."

"If I can get away in the morning, I'll ask Jude if I can go in there to take a look for that can."

He closed his eyes and after a time his face tensed. I put a hand on his shoulder to comfort him but he opened his eyes looking confused, alarmed.

"I didn't think you were asleep," I said.

"The morphine. It makes me as fuzzy-headed as your mother."

"I shouldn't be keeping you awake."

"No, no, I want to talk."

I pointed at his arm, the old wound there. "So, how did you get that scar? It wasn't what you said, was it? A hunting accident. Was it Grandpa?"

"Your mother doesn't want me talking about it."

"I can always look it up, you know. If he did shoot you there's undoubtedly something about it in the papers. Files going back to the first edition of the *Observer* are on microfiche at the library."

"You'd do that?"

My father brought his hand to his mouth. "There's no need to go to the library. Your grandmother kept all those stories. She filled a scrapbook with them; it had a Valentine's Day card on the front. As I recall, the scrapbook is in that steamer trunk she brought over with her as a young bride. You've brought it down from the attic, I hope."

"I don't know if Val thought of it."

"Good Lord, get it down from there. Your mother couldn't bear it if that went up in smoke."

"So what happened?"

He lay back and closed his eyes. "You can read it for yourself."

"I'm sorry," I said. "I had no right to bug you about it, especially now."

"It's all right. We should have told you a long time ago." Then he held my hand and sat up a little, as best he could. "Listen, I want to say something to you. I think I better do it now." I waited as he coughed and caught his breath. "Things aren't so good between you and Ezra, are they?"

"No."

"He loves you, though, I think."

I nodded.

"It's a terrible thing to love a woman and not be able to reach her, to make her love you back in the same way. I don't think I ever reached your mother that way, not like I wanted to." He turned toward the bureau, to the wedding photo of him and my mother, and stared at it as he talked. "Earlier tonight I dreamed I was working on the railway in snowy open country, without a tree in sight—just one little bush sticking out of the snow. There were two of us working, me and a big man all dressed in black, with a big black hat like what your grandfather John used to wear. But I couldn't see his face so I don't know if it was him. We each had a small flat spade and we had to shovel sand the work train had dumped in between the tracks. The train was long gone, and it was getting dark when we finished, and there was nothing around us but snow and bush. That big man walked off into the night and I was left alone. I could see a house a long way off that had snow all over its roof but no lights on. It was that unfinished house on Valentine's place. I knew your mother was inside, so I started to walk toward it. There were no roads or fences, and the snow was thigh-deep and bitter cold and a labour to push through. I just kept thinking when I got to that house Beth would open the door and let me in. But as much as I walked, I never got any nearer to that place."

He turned to me. "I see you trying so bloody hard with Ezra, and I love you for it. But I hate that you're tired and unhappy all the time. It's not doing Ezra any good either, if you can't love him back the way he loves you."

He lifted an arm to the bureau and I leaned over the bed to hand him the photo he was reaching for. But he didn't take it from me. It was my own wedding portrait, a photo Val had taken of Ezra and me standing at the doorway of the Turtle Valley Memorial Hall. Strange how a camera captures truths those in the photograph might not admit to each other, or even to themselves. There was too much distance between Ezra and me. He was reaching toward me, about to put his arm around me, and smiling into the camera, and I was turned from him, putting space between us, looking away.

"You were still in love with Jude when you married Ezra, weren't you?"

I looked up at my father—his startling aqua-blue eyes—then back down at the photograph in my hands. "Yes," I said.

He tapped the glass on the portrait. "You remember what I said at the hall, at your wedding, just before I walked you down the aisle?"

I nodded. He didn't say anything more. He closed his eyes and appeared to drift off to sleep. I sat back in the chair, holding the wedding portrait in both hands. In that moment my father spoke of, Ezra had stood at the front of the hall next to the minister, waiting with his back to me, dressed in his black suit and tie, his thick, dark hair pulled back in a ponytail. We had both dressed in traditional wedding garb to please Ezra's parents, although I would have preferred much less formal wear, especially in that rustic setting. I was at the door with my father, about to make my entrance, wearing that white gown I had felt coerced into buying. And Jude was staring at me from across the room. It was the first time we had seen each other since our affair had ended less than five months before. He stood behind the table where Lillian sat holding her stomach; she was eight months along with Andy at the time. Jude had not dressed up for the occasion as Lillian had. He wore only a T-shirt and jeans. His arms were crossed and his biceps bulged defiantly as we held each other's gaze too long. I was the one who finally looked away.

I don't know if my father saw that exchange, if it was this that prompted him to whisper into my ear. Whatever the case, just before I walked down the aisle toward Ezra, he leaned into me so that only I could hear and said, "You can still get out of this, you know."

15.

TO REACH THE ATTIC, I had to climb up a stepladder and through a hatch in the ceiling of the hall. The ceiling in the tiny attic itself was so low that I had to shuffle through the room on my knees. With each move I made, there was a crunch like brittle leaves, from the dry bodies of thousands of ladybugs that littered the shiplap floor and the stacks of cardboard boxes. Scooping up a handful, I was surprised to find that among the dead were a few still alive, their legs reaching sluggishly to my fingers in order to right themselves. I slid open the window to toss ladybug confetti to the porch roof below, and some of the insects flew up into the circle of yard light before disappearing into the night.

Below the attic window my grandmother's trunk was heaped high with more of my mother's years of musings. I set these boxes and bags of her memories on the floor and opened the trunk. It smelled of naphtha flakes and was filled, as I remembered it, with the Cinderella things of another time that I'd so loved as a child: a fragile, painted paper fan; a pink-flowered china candleholder; a mother-of-pearl mirror, comb, and brush set that still held strands of Maud's black and silver hair; cut-glass trinket dishes with embossed brass lids; Peerless ink bottles, fountain pens, and nibs; a Bible and hymnbook.

I opened a Peek Frean cookie tin and found a rose sealed in wax. The wax had cracked and the flower within was dry and crumbling. It was the same rich red as the Bonica roses that bloomed around the unfinished house. Had Valentine given it to her? Would she have ever preserved a rose from John Weeks? Would he have thought to give her one?

There were stacks of scrapbooks, and letters and postcards that my grandfather had sent my grandmother after he was back in Canada from the Great War, before she had made the trek across an ocean, and across a continent, to reach this homestead in British Columbia. *Dear Girl,* he called her, and he signed each letter, *Your Affectionate Lover, J.W.* On top of it all there was a roll of blueprints, plans for a house that was never built.

I pulled out a scrapbook and leafed through it, then another and another, before finding what I was looking for. The cover of this scrapbook was adorned with a Valentine card. Two children climbing a ladder up to a harvest basket overflowing with hearts. *To My Valentine.* The scrapbook was almost entirely filled with newspaper clippings, something that had never interested me when I was a child. The first one read:

TURTLE VALLEY IS JARRED BY
SLIGHT TREMOR

Some claim it was an earthquake; some assert it was
an unusually heavy distant clap of thunder; others
suggest it may have been a large land or rock-
clearing blast, and still others, of an alarmist tem-
perament, query whether it might have been a Jap
balloon bomb.

Whatever the cause or origin, the valley was jarred
by some kind of an earth tremor last Thursday.

The Japanese balloon my father had found. The blast when
it was blown up. The blast that threw my grandfather back
into the war, and back into Essondale. It was here, recorded
in the newspaper. I looked at the date my grandmother had
scrawled on the edge of the clipping. *March 15, 1945.* The night
Valentine had stayed with her. I leafed quickly through the
scrapbook, scanning the stories, then turned back to the cover.
To My Valentine.

Across the field, light poured from Jude's home. I could
clearly see him moving from one window to the next as he
walked around the living room. The kiln shed was dark. Why
was he up so late?

"You up there, Kat?" Val called.

"Yeah."

The stepladder creaked as she climbed up into the attic. "No
change in Dad, eh?" she said.

"He was sleeping soundly so I thought I'd slip up here for a
few minutes and see what I could find."

Val reached into the trunk for a photo of our grandmother as a young woman, taken just shortly before she met my grandfather. She was dressed in her ambulance driver's uniform of long dark skirts and a heavy coat that appeared too big for her. Her hat, flipped up on one side, made her look jaunty and adventurous, but the shadow she cast was a man in a large black hat approaching ominously from the gloom in the corner, like the bad guy in a comic book. She stood gripping the back of a chair with one hand; the other was balled into a loose fist. She looked very much as I did now, though she had been more than a decade younger than me when this photo was taken. Her long nose and full mouth, her dark hair and brows, the sloping shoulders that made her neck appear longer—these were all traits I had inherited. There was a wide-eyed look of anticipation about her that I sometimes caught in the mirror and often saw in my son, a mix of wonder and embarrassment, as if she knew she was about to receive a birthday surprise.

"God, it could be a photo of you," Val said.

"Eerie, isn't it?"

She pointed at the scrapbook. "What have you got there?"

"Dad told me this was here, in the trunk. I think I've seen all of Grandma's scrapbooks before, but not this one. Mom never showed it to me, and she relegated this trunk to the attic when I got too curious about it. I'm beginning to see why." I patted it. "There are clippings in here from 1965, stories of Grandpa's disappearance and the search for him. But it starts in 1945, with the story about the explosion, when that Japanese balloon was blown up. All these stories except the first, about the explosion, are in some way about Valentine, and I think even that one was.

Look at the cover." The children, the harvest basket of hearts. *To My Valentine.*

Val took the scrapbook from me. "Why would Grandma keep a scrapbook about Dad's uncle?"

"That's the question, isn't it? They knew each other for a long time before the Japanese balloon was blown up, before that night when Grandpa went nuts and Valentine intervened." I reached over and opened the scrapbook to the first news story and tapped it. "But she started this scrapbook about him here, with this story.

"You're suggesting they were lovers?"

"I'm not sure what to think. But something started this night, for Uncle Valentine and Grandma, and it went on for twenty years. This scrapbook ends with the stories about Grandpa's disappearance in 1965."

I turned the pages to the back of the scrapbook to show Val the full front page of a *Kamloops Sentinel* from 1965. "This is the same story I found in Grandma's wallet, at the bottom of the page. It's just a tiny little story, but at least it made the front page."

"He'd only been missing a day, by the looks of it," said Val. "Nothing to compete with this." She tapped the lead article of the week:

"COUNTRY AT WAR?" CALLERS ASK RCMP AS BRILLIANT FLASH LIGHTS HEAVENS

Hysterical women asking if the country was at war telephoned Promise police station last night, following a brilliant flash and loud explosion in the night skies. RCMP Cpl. Ted Robinson, NCO in

charge of the Promise detachment, said shortly
after the flash and blast he received several calls
from women thinking the country was at war.

Immediately after the flash there was a loud
noise and all the buildings started to shake.
Promise streets immediately filled with people.

Meanwhile from over a wide area came reports
of sightings of a brilliantly lit object travelling
south to north, lighting up the landscape, and a
subsequent loud explosion.

"There were articles in the paper at the time to the effect
that it might have been a U.S. spy satellite falling back to earth.
But it was a meteor. Scientists sweeping with magnets found
tiny fragments of it on the shores of Shuswap Lake. And then
some hunter found a hunk of it in a burned-out area where it
had hit, up in those hills." She nodded at the Ptarmigan Hills.
"That meteor was what set Grandpa off that night he disappeared. When it hit the sky lit up and the whole house shook.
Grandpa thought we were being bombed."

"Looks like a lot of people thought that," I said. "I guess the
war was still pretty fresh in everyone's mind." I looked up at her.
"I don't remember any of you talking about this."

"The story of the meteor was all wrapped up with Grandpa's
disappearance. Mom didn't want us talking about it." She nodded at the hills. "He went up there to find it. Or rather, he went
up there to find the enemy. In his head that mountain was the
front and he was going up to root the enemy out."

I looked up to the hills, the fire blazing there, as Val paged
through the scrapbook.

"Here's the news story where they gave up the search for Grandpa," she said, and handed it to me.

GUNMAN PRESUMED DEAD AFTER SHOOTING
SON-IN-LAW

Turtle Valley resident John Weeks is presumed dead after an extensive week-long search throughout the Ptarmigan Range turned up no sign of him. Weeks became the object of an RCMP search after he shot and wounded his son-in-law, Gustave Svensson, in the arm. Svensson is now recovering in Kamloops General Hospital and is reported to be in stable condition.

At the time of the shooting, Gustave Svensson and his uncle, well-known area woodsman Valentine Svensson, were attempting to find Weeks within the Ptarmigan Range. Weeks initially went missing April 1 after sighting the meteor that lit up area skies. Evidently Weeks, who had been receiving ongoing psychiatric treatment and was apparently delusional at the time, saw the flash of the meteor and, in a state of confusion, felt that he and his family were under attack. Family members say he became determined to find the "enemy" that he felt was hiding in the Ptarmigan Range and headed up into the hills with his gun. He was improperly clothed for mountain conditions and carried no rations. His wife, Mrs. Maud Weeks, alerted Valentine Svensson of the situation and he and his nephew, Gustave

Svensson, attempted to track Mr. Weeks throughout the night and the next day.

When the two men continued the search the following night, they came upon Weeks and tried to talk him into coming down with them. However Weeks, still in a confused state, shot at them, hitting and wounding Gustave Svensson in the arm. Fearing further bloodshed, Valentine Svensson abandoned Weeks and brought his injured nephew back down the mountain trail.

The search for John Weeks over the following days has been hampered by rain mixed with snow that has continued to fall on the mountain since Weeks disappeared, washing away evidence of his whereabouts. Searchers have also been faced with steep and rocky slopes, as there are no logging roads to the area. Svensson says access to this rough terrain is limited to ancient and now largely unused Indian trails.

RCMP Cpl. Ted Robinson says he finally made the decision to give up the search for Weeks on the advice Valentine Svensson, who lead the search and is an expert tracker often used by the RCMP. Svensson says heavy rainfalls, high winds and the freezing temperatures overnight in the mountains have made it highly unlikely that Weeks survived. "The weather conditions and the difficult terrain have made the search treacherous," he says. "We can no longer justify putting the searchers in danger."

> Although Robinson says he can't rule out the pos-
> sibility that Weeks made it off the mountain himself
> and may have retreated to another area, he says the
> next search will be undertaken with the aim of recov-
> ering his body once weather conditions improve.

"So that's how Dad got that scar. Why would he and Mom lie about that? Why wouldn't you tell me?"

"Like I said, Mom didn't want us talking about it." She tapped a tiny newspaper clipping beside the story of my grand-father's disappearance, one of my mother's contributions to the paper. "I remember hearing these shots the night after he went missing," she said.

LARGE COUGAR SHOT ON
FARM AT TURTLE VALLEY

> Turtle Valley—A large cougar was shot by
> Valentine Svensson on his property midweek.
> The cat was approaching the barnyard where
> there were some newly arrived calves. Tracks of
> these animals and also of bobcats and lynx are
> frequently seen in the area.

"Uncle Valentine had just brought Dad down off the moun-tain," said Val, "after Grandpa shot him, and there was a cougar following too close, attracted by the scent of blood, I imagine. So Valentine shot the cat out by the unfinished house."

"Why would Mom write about this and not about how her father had gone missing? Or about Dad being shot?"

"All that was already in the papers."

"Why would she write anything at all during that terrible week?"

"It's what she does. She'd sit and write if the house was burning around her."

I rubbed my face. Even during the terrible weeks following Ezra's stroke, I had never felt so tired. "What are you doing up now anyway?" I said. "It's, what, twelve-thirty?"

"Just after one. Couldn't sleep. So I took a few more boxes out to the truck." She pulled a note from her jeans pocket and handed it to me. "I found this tucked into the doorjamb just now," she said. "I was hesitating over whether to give it to you. Good thing I found it and not Ezra."

The paper was folded in half and my name was written on the front, in Jude's handwriting. *I saw you were up and came by hoping you'd see me out the window, but I didn't want to knock. Please come over, any time. I'll wait up for you.*

"What are you doing, Kat?"

"I don't know." I looked up at her. "So much of what I've done this week makes no sense. I just waltzed over to Jude's in the middle of the night last night with a batch of fudge. Oh, God, Val, he makes me feel exactly like he made me feel back then. Desirable, you know? No, more than that. *Brave.*"

"So here you are, suddenly saddled with a choice: Ezra or Jude."

"It's not that simple." Or was it? I looked back down into my lap, to my grandmother's scrapbook about Valentine. What had she done? What choices had she made? There were clues here, in this scrapbook, I was sure of it. The warped and yellowed newsprint, the lines of Maud's handwriting where she had included recipes or remedies on the pages that surrounded the clippings. Something of my grandmother was sealed here in ink: in her careful, controlled penmanship, in the choices she made over what to set down. She had preferred a fountain pen over a ballpoint; the evidence was here, in the flow of ink from a fountain pen, as she wrote this recipe on how to preserve a rose: *Dip the whole blossom and stalk in melted wax, coating completely to seal from the action of air and the passage of time.* If memory were a colour, it would be this blue, the colour of the ink my grandmother used to preserve her treasured memories from the wasting effects of time.

So Valentine *had* given her that rose.

Val nodded Jude's way. "He's over there now, waiting for you," she said. "Are you going?"

16.

JEREMY PLAYED ON THE HAY BALES beside me as I rummaged through the boxes that we had left in the barn during our move to Alberta that past spring. That morning I had discovered that these boxes contained the better part of my married life: our wedding photos and certificate of marriage, birthday cards and photos from vacations, scraps of paper from Ezra's desk and mine, our tax records, and envelopes full of bills paid. In one box I had found my wedding dress and the baby dish that had been mine as a child, one that my mother had given me when I was pregnant with Jeremy. Jeremy had eaten his first solid food from it.

The box I looked at now was marked simply *Papers,* in Ezra's handwriting. My first Mother's Day card was in it, one Ezra had made for me less than a year after his stroke: Jeremy's hand-prints as a baby were in blue on the front and back of it. The card opened, like an accordion, to the length my son's arms were at the time. Inside Ezra had written, *I love you this much and my arms are still growing!* I had caught Ezra just after he made the card, trying to wash blue food colouring off Jeremy's hands in the bathroom sink. My son was naked except for his diapers and he was crooked under Ezra's arm; his little hands attempted to grip the stream of water from the tap. Ezra hadn't thought to use the water-soluble poster paint we had in the house, and Jeremy's hands were blue for a day afterwards. Blue under the half-moons of his tiny nails. Ezra had tried so hard to please me. He always tried so hard.

I held the card out to show Jeremy. "This was how long your arms were when you were a baby." He took the card from me and folded and unfolded it as I looked through the box. There I found a sheet of foolscap in Ezra's handwriting. It began with my name and I thought for a moment it was an old love letter:

> Kat. I wish I could make her grasp my story. A
> picture jumps into my skull in the day, or I dream
> it at night: a bird trapped in a glass box, thumping
> its wings against the sides. I'm that bird. I can
> glimpse where I need to go, but I can't reach there.
> Something shadowy blocks me and I can't grab why
> I can't get out. I don't have a long-ago because I can't
> learn by heart what happened this morning. I have
> no tomorrow because I can't plot it out, can't see it.

> I'm snared in this confusing present just as much
> as Kat is stuck in yesterday. She can't see me now.
> She only sees me then, when I was sick. I'm trou-
> ble to her, someone she's got to nurse, like a child,
> always scolding me what to do, what to say. I'm
> scared I've plummeted out of love with her.

I stared at the page. *I'm scared I've plummeted out of love with her.* I turned it over, looking for any indication of when Ezra had written it, but there was none. *A bird trapped in a glass box, thumping its wings against the sides.* I understood because an image popped into my head daily, during any quiet moment: I hung on a trapeze in the middle of a void, nothing but black above and below, and I had to figure out a way to stay on that swing and not fall off into oblivion.

"What's that, Mommy?" said Jeremy, pulling at Ezra's note.

"Nothing, honey."

"Is it a card from Daddy?"

"Yes, it's from Daddy."

I folded the sheet and put it in my pocket, then carried the box to the pickup along with the baby dish, with Jeremy follow-ing behind. "What's up?" Ezra asked. He had been loading the boxes as I chose them, as the fire was now only two miles away. We expected the evacuation order at any time.

I stood with the box in hand a moment, staring across the field at Jude's place. "Nothing," I said finally. I put the box down, but hung onto the baby dish. "I'm taking Jeremy inside. Snack time."

Jeremy held out the Mother's Day card to show him. "I love you this much!" he said.

Once inside, I slid off my sandals and put the dish down on the table. Mom immediately picked it up. "You found it!" she said.

I started to chop up an apple for Jeremy at the kitchen counter. "I didn't want it to get lost again in all those boxes."

"This was the first thing I bought for you." She turned it, admiring the figures painted around its edges. "I wanted you so much. I ached for you, before I knew for sure I was pregnant."

I knew that ache. I had felt it in my belly even before I had conceived Jeremy; it had begun in the hospital, immediately following Ezra's stroke. A desire unlike anything I'd ever felt before, to be with Ezra, to create a life with him. The scent of a child billowed around me like a sheet thrown over a clothesline on a March afternoon. Peach and powder, warm sun, it licked up one side of me and down the other, a dawning remembrance as if I had left something behind at a café, a glove or a pair of sunglasses. No, something far dearer than that: my grand-mother's wedding ring, left in the bunched paper in the waste-basket of the ladies' room.

"You all right, dear?" my mother asked.

I wiped my eyes and glanced out the window at Ezra. "Just not getting enough sleep."

I gave Jeremy the plate of apple slices. "I should see if Val needs a break," I said, and I joined my sister in my father's room. My father slept even as Val rolled him to slip a new Depends under his buttocks, and as she wiped him clean. I had changed Ezra's Depends in just this way when he was in the hos-pital. His moist, limp penis against his thigh, the smell of urine.

"Dad's breathing is so shallow," I said.

"That's to be expected."

"Did he wake?"

She shook her head. "He'll sleep much more from now on, and when he does wake he'll often be confused. There will be times when he won't recognize you, Kat. Be prepared for that."

I turned to the window to allow my father some privacy as Val finished changing him. When she was done, she joined me at the window, rubbing her hands with an antiseptic wipe.

"Thank you," I said.

"For what?"

"For everything you do for Mom and Dad."

"That's what I do, take care of people."

I looped my arm through hers. "But who takes care of you?"

"Oh I'm alright. I take care of myself. Every night I treat myself to a glass of wine and a hot bath." She nudged my shoulder with her own.

"But who takes care of you? Not Ezra, evidently. Tell me, when was the last time you let him do something for you?"

I hesitated a moment, fingering the note in my pocket that Ezra had written. "The other day, when we were in the store with Mom, Ezra wanted to pick up a few things by himself so he got his own shopping cart. I thought he was just being childish, you know, that he had to do things for himself again, to prove himself, like he does. But then he got tired, so I took him to the bench by the door to wait as we finished shopping. As he was sitting down I noticed a jar of lingonberry jam in his cart, like the jam Uncle Valentine used to give us when we went to his place, but in a wee little jar like what you might get with breakfast at a hotel. I thought, so that's why he wanted to shop by himself; he wanted to pick up a surprise for me. I said, 'Is this for me?'

"He said, 'You like that stuff, don't you?'

"I hugged him and kissed him and wept over it. It surprised me, you know, to be so very excited by this little gift. The feelings I had were way out of proportion to it. Then it occurred to me that I couldn't remember the last time Ezra had bought me a gift, or taken me out on a date without my urging, or even made me a cup of tea. The last time he remembered my birthday was before the stroke. Isn't that dumb? Getting all weepy over a stupid jar of jam."

"It's not dumb," Val said. "It's almost impossible to maintain romance when you're dealing with the symptoms of a stroke day in and day out."

"Ezra doesn't want me, you know, in that way."

"I imagine he's exhausted a good deal of the time, and he's reinventing himself. Most couples have difficulty in their sex lives after a stroke." But then her attention was directed past my shoulder, to the kitchen door behind me.

I turned and found Ezra silhouetted at the screen door. He thumped back down the porch stairs and I slid on my sandals to follow him outside to the truck, where he rearranged boxes. "Why did you have to tell her that?" he said. He was tearing up, and looked so very tired; at that moment I realized just how many years we had been together. The silver hairs at his temples that he had once insisted on plucking, until after the stroke when energy fled him. When I tried to take his hand he pulled his arm away from me and started to walk off. "I'm going to finish carting those boxes."

The screen door opened and Jeremy came out carrying the little plastic elephant that had been mine when I was a child. The one missing ears, wheels, and legs. "Mommy, all the toys here are broken," he said.

I wiped my eyes. "I'll find something for you to play with in a minute, Jeremy. I just need a moment."

He sat on the steps with me and looked down at the broken elephant. "Is Daddy going away?"

"He's just getting more boxes from the barn."

"There's fire in my head."

I held him and put my hand to his forehead. "You mean you're worried about the fire?" When he didn't respond, I hugged him close. "The fire is scary, but when we're told to go, I'll make sure we get out of here before the fire arrives. Okay?"

"Okay." He wrapped his arms around me, settling his head into my neck, and I rocked him. Jude stepped up to the door of the kiln shed and looked out across the field. When he saw Jeremy and me he waved. I held up my hand to him.

"Can I play with that guy's Lego?" Jeremy asked. "Can we go to his house?"

I stood and held out my hand to him. "Why don't we do that? There's something there I'd like to find. Will you help me?"

He nodded and I led him across the yard, heading for the trail to Jude's house. I glanced toward the barn once, searching for Ezra. But as soon as I caught sight of him watching us from the door, he turned away and disappeared into the darkness of the barn. The smell of the smoke in the air; a Christmas spruce burned after the holiday was over.

17.

I APPROACHED THE DOOR to Jude's studio holding Jeremy's hand. The inside walls were covered in posters from the many pottery shows he had participated in over the years, and clay dust caked everything: the turned pots and the shelves that held them; Jude's containers of brushes and tools; the television and VCR in front of his wheel. The shelf of mementoes, presumably from Andy's childhood, that were stacked one on top of the other: Thomas trains, a remote-control jeep, a porcelain baby cup that Jude had no doubt made himself, airplanes and Hot Wheels, and a black ouija board embossed with the alphabet in red.

Jude stood with his back to the door at one of the long worktables, dipping what appeared to be the base of a table lamp into a bucket of glaze that was thick and creamy-smooth, the consistency and colour of buttermilk. The lamp base had already been dipped and left to dry once. This was its final, decorative glaze. Years ago I had watched him paint the glazes on, twisting and manipulating the brush with the finesse of a Japanese calligrapher. "You're not using brushes anymore?" I asked.

He startled and turned, then grinned, before sponging off the bottom of the freshly glazed lamp base and putting it on a rack to dry. He picked up a vase and turned it upside down to dip it into the bucket. "Brushwork is too predictable. All my pots were looking the same. I like the chance happenings, the surprises I get at the end of a firing when I glaze like this."

"Another firing tonight?"

"The last before the show." He put the vase on the rack and grabbed a cloth to wipe his hands, then pulled a section of clay from a Rubbermaid plastic bin and handed it to Jeremy.

"Play dough!"

"It's clay," I said. "Isn't it wonderful stuff?"

"Play dough for grown-ups," said Jude. He lifted Jeremy onto a stool at the worktable so he could model it there.

"You still wedge the clay by hand?" I asked. Years ago he had shown me how to soften the clay into a state in which it could be worked, pushing it down, bringing it up, my whole body rocking; it was very much like kneading a stiff bread dough. My arms had ached for days afterwards.

"Got to do something to stay in shape," he said. "All that sitting at the wheel makes it hard to keep the weight off." He patted his belly. "I've put on a few pounds."

I smoothed a hand over my own stomach. "Haven't we all?"

"You're perfect," he said, and gave my hand a little shake for emphasis. "Perfect." When I looked away at Jeremy, he dropped my hand and said, "How's your dad?"

"He hardly spoke today." I rubbed the back of my neck. "He was still quite chatty yesterday, but he's suddenly withdrawn into himself. Val says she's worried because he's got it in his head that he wants to die before the fire forces us out. She says she's seen it over and over in the clients she works with. They'll just give up and be dead within days."

"I'm so sorry, Katrine." He waved at his potter's wheel. "Do you have a little time now? Why don't I set Jeremy up on the wheel so we can talk?"

"Actually, I wonder if I can borrow a hammer and snoop around that unfinished house."

"A hammer?"

"To pull up the floorboards."

"I doubt you'll need one. The cows have ravaged that place." But he pulled a hammer from a toolbox under the worktable. "What are you looking for?"

"A MacDonald's tobacco can. I found it there when I was a child. I'm hoping it contains some letters."

"Let me guess: you think they might be from your grand-mother to Valentine?"

When I smiled, he held out his hand to my son. "Well, Jeremy. Let's go investigate. We're archaeologists off on a dig."

Jeremy took Jude's hand and together they marched off toward the door. "I'm an archaeologist, Mommy!"

A huge pumpkin patch surrounded the bit of unruly pasture Jude kept about the old house. The plants still offered up their huge yellow flowers but the green pumpkins were already beginning to blush orange. Valentine had planted pumpkins decades before, as a contained garden at the back of his cabin, but after his death the pumpkins had propagated and gone wild, so they now crept over the ancient and rusting bits of farm machinery around the barns and grasped the frame of my old bicycle that leaned against the side of a granary. I had left the bike there just before getting a new one for my birthday when I was a child thirty years before, and it was still locked, wheel to wheel, to itself. I had licked those handlebars when I was a girl; they had tasted salty from my hands, then harsh, metallic.

Uncle Valentine's cabin was to the far right, nestled within what was now a pasture that bordered on the creek. The building was braced by a couple of posts so it wouldn't collapse. Much of the caulking between the logs had fallen away, so that at sunset the building was shot through with orange-red light, as if it were on fire from within. During my childhood my parents and I had spent many Sunday afternoons in that cabin with Valentine, eating Peek Frean cookies from the tin and drinking "cooked" coffee, as he called it, coffee grounds boiled right in the pot: gritty, thick stuff, so strong we had to suck it through a sugar cube held between our teeth. There were only two rooms in the place, and no door between them. In the back room the bed was always neatly made, and Valentine's few shirts and trousers were hung on nails pounded into the log walls. Open shelves over the sink held all that he might need: coffee and flour, sugar and canned milk, dried beans and peas and pastas, and preserves he'd canned himself: beets, pickles, and canned plums and peaches; strawberry, raspberry, saskatoon, and lingonberry jam. The place smelled of woodsmoke from the stove, and MacDonald's pipe tobacco, because my great-uncle was rarely without a pipe, and of canned milk and that thick coffee. He had resisted electricity and indoor plumbing, preferring to cart his water inside in a bucket to wash in an enamel basin, and to make use of the outhouse hidden within lilac bushes even into the 1970s. I thought him ancient, a man from another time entirely, my grandmother's time.

To the side of Valentine's cabin, the unfinished house was so weathered that it looked like a natural part of the landscape, as if it had grown from the earth. Valentine had never lived in it; no one had. The windows had long ago been broken by hail or thrown rocks. Jude's big lanky tabby sat on one windowsill, its colours blending with the wood of the wall; if it hadn't sung for my attention, I wouldn't have noticed it sitting there. The Bonica roses Valentine had planted here decades before had spread, growing wild and ragged, but still offered sweet red blossoms well into fall.

Inside, the subfloor was strewn with glass shards, torn clothing, and beer bottles. A hornet's nest was affixed to one corner of the hallway. Under this, graffiti were scrawled in black spray paint: *Death to Cows* and *This is where I live* and *You do not want to disturb me.* The stairwell to the upper story had been removed altogether. Jude was right; the cows had done so much damage to the floorboards that we hardly needed a hammer. There were great holes where they had stepped right through the shiplap boards, exposing the joists beneath.

"I shouldn't have Jeremy in here."

"I want to see!"

"We'll watch him," said Jude. "He'll be fine."

I took Jeremy's hand and led him over the holes in the floor and into what would have been the living room, where the floor was in better shape. A mouldy mattress lay under the window. On the far wall, in dripping red letters, was written *Too bad you found your keys.*

I pointed at the mattress. "You've had visitors, I see."

"Yeah, well, every so often I have to chase some local kid out of here. An empty house seems to attract them." We turned to look at the walls around us, at the graffiti there, the glass crunching beneath our feet. One wall read, *Danger!* Another read, *A gradual instant of destruction.* Low on this wall, over a series of knotholes, was written, *I can see you!*

We wandered through the house, to the room at the back that would have been the kitchen, and then to the small room off the downstairs bedroom that my father had roughed in, a room that would have become the bathroom. It smelled vaguely of skunk. Someone had spray-painted a "mirror" here, a woman's face within a frame. Over top of it was written *How much time have you spent here waiting?*

"I hope none of them found that can."

I led Jeremy back into the living room and Jude followed. "So, where was it?" he asked.

I tried to picture the house as I remembered it from my childhood. A floorboard. A marble hidden beneath a joist. A shadow on the wall. Bits of ragged memory. My childhood in tatters. I would lose this time with Jude in the same way. My recollections of the moment I was in now—which seemed so very sturdy—would shake and shift like this old building, and finally fall. In a decade or two I would remember only this plank under my feet, this nail, but not the whole structure, how it stood on this hot summer's day.

I knelt beside Jeremy, to get a child's-eye view of the cracks between the boards, the dust, the glittering glass. Then I found the moment I had been looking for. I gripped the loose floor-board and yanked it up, exposing the joists beneath.

"There it is!" Jude said. The MacDonald's tobacco tin; much of the paint was worn away and the tin was rusted badly around the lid. When I couldn't open it, Jude banged it with the hammer and pried it loose. There *were* letters inside. A few of the envelopes and the edges of the letters were water-stained, but for the most part they were in remarkably good shape.

"They *are* my grandmother's. It's her handwriting!" I opened one and then another and another. "They're all notes she wrote to Valentine. Most are just invitations to lunch or thank-you notes for something he helped her with during the times my grand-father was in hospital. Here, look! She's thanking him for building that greenhouse. Did I ever tell you my grandmother died in that greenhouse? My father found her there. A heart attack."

He nodded. "You did tell me. You mind if I read a few?"

I gave him a handful and we read.

"This one is curious," he said. "She writes, *As for your last note, there was no need for reminders. I think of such things daily, hourly. It is necessary to think of such things, in order to get through my day.* That suggests a lot."

"But what? What was she thinking of?"

"Him?"

"Or a Bible verse, for all I know. Some passage from Psalms she took comfort in."

"A lot of these look like they were written in response to something he wrote. So there must have been letters from him."

"There were. Dad told me last night that he carried letters back and forth between them."

"Did she keep them?"

"Mom says she's never found any."

"Huh. The way your grandmother talks to Valentine about your grandfather in this letter, as if your grandfather is a child they are both responsible for. She describes how she and your grandfather were out walking the property, divining for a well site. Then she writes: *You don't have to tell me again: I know this house will never be built. But if, for a time, with his dream of it he can believe that he is so much better able than he actually is, then it will be a peaceful time for him and for me as well. What he needs is for me to believe he is capable, so he can believe it himself.*"

I took the letter from him. "She felt sorry for him."

"Like you feel sorry for Ezra."

I looked up at him. "I'm not sure how he'd survive without me, if that's what you mean."

"Yes, but how do *you* survive?"

"I don't want to talk about Ezra in front of Jeremy."

Jude squatted down beside Jeremy. "Did you see that pumpkin patch? How about you go find the biggest, best pumpkin in the whole patch, and when it ripens, I'll help you make it into a jack-o'-lantern."

"Pumpkins!"

I watched from just outside the unfinished house as Jude lifted the barbed-wire fence to allow Jeremy to crawl through, and then led Jeremy through the field toward the vines of the wild pumpkin patch; monarch butterflies lifted from the milkweed as they approached and Jeremy jumped this way and that, chasing after them as they fluttered just out of his grasp.

Jude bent over a milkweed plant and showed Jeremy his prize: a monarch clutched his finger. He returned to the unfinished house with the butterfly, but it fluttered away as he held it out for me. His mouth as he smiled. I stepped forward and kissed him but he didn't respond. His stubble was prickly on my lips. I stepped back. "I'm sorry," I said.

"No. It's all right. You just surprised me."

"I can't believe some of the things I've done this week."

"You mean coming to see me."

"I feel, I don't know, possessed."

"Like those ants."

"Ants?"

"They're taken over by a fungus that eats into their brain and forces them to climb up to the top of a plant and impale themselves, so the fungus can grow in the ant's body and disperse its spores from up high."

I laughed. "You are so full of it."

"No, it's true. They really exist." He took my hand and led me back inside the unfinished house, where he ran his fingers through my hair and then pulled my chin up so I would look at him. "All those years ago I let you and me slip away," he said. "I have another chance here, I think." He waited a moment as if expecting an answer, and when I didn't say anything he moved forward, tentatively, to kiss me. His hand on my waist. His thigh against mine. But then I heard the sound of keys jingled within a pocket, a rustle in the grass outside. I stepped back. "Someone's coming."

We both listened.

"I didn't hear anything."

"I heard keys," I said.

"It's just Jeremy."

"No."

I turned within the unfinished house, looking from window to window as the rustle through grass moved around us, then stopped. An eye in a knothole. "I can see you!" Jeremy sang. The eye moved to another knothole. "Grandpa can see you!" There was again the jingle of keys as footsteps crunched through the undergrowth.

"Jeremy," I cried. "Jeremy, come here." But he hadn't left his pumpkin patch and the dancing monarchs.

"What is it?" said Jude.

"Didn't you see him?"

"Who?"

I started around one side of the old house. "Hello?" I said. "Can we help you?"

There was a shadow of a man cast on the ground at the other corner. As I stepped forward the shadow receded into the grasses. I turned this corner, and the next, certain each time that the man would be just around the corner—a trail opened through the grass in front of me and I could hear footsteps and the jingle of keys in a pocket—but when I reached Jude as he came around the opposite side of the house, there was no one else there.

"Did you see where he went?" I asked.

"There wasn't anyone."

I glanced at my parents' house. "Could it have been Ezra?"

He took my shoulders and turned me toward him. "Katrine, there was no one here."

Jeremy pointed to the side of the house where I had seen the eye in the knothole. He covered his eyes with both hands, then opened them wide. "Peekaboo!"

18.

AS I SEPARATED THE GIMPY CALF from its mother and herded it down the driveway to the small corral by the barn, a caravan of army trucks rumbled past the farm, heading up the valley. I had heard on the radio earlier that morning that a hundred members of the Canadian Forces had been called in to help fight the fire as, fueled by winds and the beetle-kill that littered the forest, it continued to rage uncontrolled. No doubt the troops were heading to the fire camp on the Jefferson ranch, which was close to one of the logging roads that led up to the mountain and the front lines of the fire. Private pickups loaded with boxes swerved out of the army trucks' way as they headed in the opposite direction.

As I locked the calf in the corral, a red Ford pickup pulling a stock trailer drove down the driveway and parked in our yard. It was Uncle Dan. He appeared to be younger than my mother, though he was several years older. He still ran his own dairy, but in recent years he'd relied more and more on hired help.

"Kat!" he said, and he hugged me. "Been a while, eh?"

"A couple of years. Thanks for doing this."

He waved at the Bombardier droning low overhead. "God, I don't know how you stand this. Drives my Lab nuts. When these bombers fly overhead on their way to the lake, he hides in the closet. You see Sarah Dalton got married Saturday outside at their folks' place like they planned? Water bombers and helicopters flying overhead, sprinklers going off all around them." He laughed. "Life goes on."

"Life goes on here too, I guess. Seems crazy, doesn't it, to bring Dad home to this?" I nodded at the haze of smoke around us, the ash fluttering down from the burning forest above, the bomber dropping its load on the fire—now more than halfway down the mountain—and the forestry trucks rumbling by.

"Gus in any kind of shape to take a visitor?"

"A nurse is checking him over now," I said. "He was in a lot of pain so she's putting him on a higher dose of morphine. He isn't talking much anymore, but he can still hear you if you want to sit and chat later." I nodded at the calf. "He was embarrassed about the calf, about not taking care of it himself. He didn't want you to see it."

"That's just dumb. Wish I could've been more help these last couple of years." He looked around the yard. "You got something I can use for a table, put my stuff on?"

"Sure." Together we carried the patio table over to the corral, the umbrella turning circles as we walked.

"I hear you and Ezra just bought a farm," Dan said.

"A quarter section without a house, close to my in-laws' place. We're using their equipment until we get on our feet."

"You're not living with your mother-in-law."

"No. We're renting a house a couple of miles down the road." A farmhouse just five hundred square feet in total, with a musty unfinished basement. A tiny, elderly woman named Alice owned the place. She couldn't be five feet tall, and her husband had built the house fifty years before to suit his petite wife. Ezra claimed he was now doing the same for me. He hoped to build a house with spacious bathrooms and high ceilings so we would never feel constrained to hunker down. For the time being, though, we lived in a rented house built for another, and my back ached with the effort of stooping to fit this little woman's world.

I helped Dan cart all he needed from his truck to the table: his .22-calibre rifle, a handsaw, chains, knives and a bread-board to cut the organs on, a sharpening stone, towels and rubber gloves, a bucket to wash his hands in, a pail for the liver and heart.

"Got something to ask you about," I said.

"What's that?"

"I just found out from Val that Grandpa died on that mountain." I nodded at the smoke-covered hills. "I came across some newspaper clippings about it last night, how he shot Dad."

Dan turned away with a pail, to fill it at the tap on the side of the house. I followed. "I was wondering if you could tell me what you remember."

He bent to turn on the tap, then stretched his back as the bucket filled. "Can't you ask Beth about that? She'd know more than me."

"Mom has been . . . reticent in talking to me about it. I understand that there was a manhunt for your father. That Uncle Valentine led the search."

He turned to look at me. "You know what I felt when I heard they'd given up the search? Relief. Isn't that terrible? I was relieved for myself, and for my mother and Beth as well, that none of us had to deal with him any more." He bent over to retrieve the bucket. "But then after they gave up the search, I wondered for a long time if Dad wasn't still alive, if he hadn't simply gotten it into his head to take off. I still wonder that—if he hadn't started up a whole new life somewhere else."

I followed him back to the patio table. "Where would he have gone?"

"Hell if I know. Nothing he did made sense. He was a psychotic bastard. I don't know how many times he beat the crap out of me with a razor strop. *There, there*, Mom always said. *Dad just can't help it!* I suppose he really couldn't help it, but I wish to God my mother had found a way to protect Beth and me from him. When I was five years old I dropped a tin my mother kept her loose change in—"

"Mom still has it," I said. "I saw it in one of the boxes Val packed. A Nabob tea canister full of coins."

"That's it. Dad was hanging a picture for Mom when I dropped the tin and it made a hell of a racket. Pennies all over the floor. He swung around and bashed me in the head with the hammer. It's a wonder he didn't kill me. As I got older I had bugger-awful headaches and I remember my mother giving my father this look when I had one, blaming him, you know, and Dad would turn away, and leave the house."

I watched as he wiped the sweat from his forehead with a handkerchief. The scar that was still visible there. "There are a few things about his disappearance that don't quite make sense to me," I said.

"There's a lot about that story that doesn't make sense. Like how'd he get lost in the first place? He knew those hills like the back of his hand."

"So you don't think he was ever actually lost?"

Dan shrugged. "Lots of people have gone missing in that bush over the years. During the war several kids on the reserve disappeared; there were stories about something in the bush picking them off one by one. A bear killed that girl—what was her name now?—Sarah Kemp, around that time. Plenty of others died of exposure up there. There was that herder who worked for old man Peterson. He just disappeared one day. I guess most of the men in the valley were out looking for him, including me, just like they all went out looking for my father. We finally gave up when the snows came. Next spring another herder found the guy's shirt and his bones scattered around a downed log. Looks like the guy had gotten lost and crawled into the space under this fallen tree to get some shelter and died there." He looked up at the mountain. "Yeah, plenty of folks have gone missing in those hills."

"But you don't think your father was one of them."

"There were so many things that didn't add up. There were shots that night after he disappeared, here on Valentine's place, when Dad was supposed to have shot Gus up in them hills. Valentine said he shot a cougar that was following him and Gus. But folks up and down the valley heard four shots and I never knew

Valentine to waste more than two bullets on an animal. He always went for a clean kill; he'd give up a hunt if he couldn't get it."

"It was dark."

"Sure. But then you tell me how Gus survived that trek down from the hills that night with a gunshot wound. When I was in school, there was that McPherson kid who was shot in the arm by Jimmy Walters. They were messing around, playing soldiers. Gun went off as Jimmy was lowering it. Bam, right in the arm. Severed an artery. That kid was dead in the time it took Jimmy to run from the field to the house for help."

"So—what? You think Valentine was covering things up with the story about the cougar? You think he killed your father?"

"I didn't say that. Your father was the one who took the shot to the arm." When he saw the look on my face he said, "It was just something folks wondered about at the time, that maybe Gus shot my father to protect himself. I'm not saying he did. Or they figured it was Valentine who shot Dad. There were rumours over the years of a thing going on between him and Mom. Valentine was forever walking over to Mom's while Dad was away on one of his little 'vacations.'"

"And nobody told your father?"

"Hell no. I imagine they were all glad Mom was getting a little pleasure out of life. Whatever form it took. I'm not saying there was any hanky-panky between her and Valentine, though there were plenty of folks in the valley who were sure that was going on too. Mom was such a dignified lady, always very polite and careful. She wouldn't have lowered herself to anything like that. Given what my father was capable of, she would have been terrified to. But she was friendly with Valentine. And she needed that, living with my father. Nobody faulted her for that."

"I don't understand. If things didn't add up the way you say, why would the RCMP believe Valentine?"

"Valentine had worked with the cops for years; any time somebody went missing in these hills, he led the search. He knew all the guys at this detachment. And nobody in the valley was going to say a word against him to the cops. Everybody liked Valentine. Most of the valley owed him for some favour. I remember when Mona Moses was sick with pleurisy, Valentine lent her enough to cover the hospital bills, and helped out with her field work besides. On the other hand, nobody missed my father when he disappeared. Mona Moses always said someone should take a gun to him and put him out of his misery, though you know, she still made Dennis and Billy drink all that milk they took from his cows."

"What do you mean, they took milk from his cows?"

"Beth never told you that story?" Uncle Dan laughed. "Dennis and Billy were a couple of Native boys Dad had working for him, both of them about my age. One night they got it into their heads to get up early, milk out his cows before Dad had a chance to milk them himself, so he'd wake to a bunch of dry udders and wonder what the hell was the matter with them. Jesus, the things they did just to drive him crazy."

"This Billy and Dennis you're talking about, was either of them the hired hand your father fired at?"

He nodded and pointed at the outbuildings, the old hired hand's cabin disintegrating into the ground. "You can still see the bullet hole where my father shot through the door, but he managed to miss Billy altogether." He scratched the back of his neck. "Yeah, I think he thought Billy and Beth were going at it in there."

"Was that a possibility?"

He laughed. "You'll have to ask your mother about that."

I glanced toward the kitchen where my mother sat. "I imagine Billy left at that point."

"Beth asked him to. She was afraid, for Billy and herself, of what Dad might do. So Billy joined up, got himself killed in the Netherlands instead. Good thing for Gus that Dad was away in the nuthouse for that whole year when he and Beth hooked up; they were married before Dad got back so he couldn't do a damn thing about it. My father would have driven any of Beth's suitors away."

I watched him for a time as he sharpened his butchering knives. I thought I knew my family, and yet here were all these stories I had never heard before. Hearing them now, from Uncle Dan, left me feeling like an outsider, uncertain of my place within my family.

"I understand from your father's files and what my Mom says that he was shell-shocked, and brain-injured."

"Yeah, well, those doctors they send you to like to complicate things, make you talk about your feelings and all that. But I figure what hit me after my war, what hit my father after his, was no more complicated than what hit this barn cat I got. He was a cocky tom, strutting around, terrorizing every other cat. Then he gets hit by a car in front of our place. So I take him inside the barn, put him in a cage. You know how cats are. They'll heal themselves if you keep them locked up. In a couple of months his bones mended. But the fear didn't; it stayed in that cat's bones. He wasn't cocky no more. Now he jumps when I go by him with the wheelbarrow. Fear like that stays inside you forever if you don't find a way to get rid of it." He looked up at a helicopter flying overhead. "I showed you that postcard that Dad took off the body of a young German soldier he killed, didn't I? It's still got the mud of the trenches on it."

"Did your mother ever say why she stayed with your father?"

"No, no. She never talked like that, how women do today, about their feelings. It would have been the best thing for all of us if she *had* left when we were still young. The best thing for my father too, I think. You use a crutch long enough, you never get rid of your limp, eh? He was like a child in so many ways. Mom made it worse by covering for him. I often think it would have been better for him if she'd just let him get himself into real trouble. Well, he did, of course. But then she was always there to clean things up for him, make things right."

"But what would he have done?" I asked. "If she'd left him?"

"I don't know. I should have done something to take care of her. Him too, I suppose." Dan looked down at his feet. "You know, I'd meet Mom in Kamloops or phone her every so often, but I only saw my father once in all those years after I left home, and that was by accident. I walked into a café in Kamloops with my boys—they were maybe eight and ten at the time—and there he was, standing at the counter with a cup in his hand, giving the waitress hell because she hadn't used a decent tea. Nabob tea was the only one he'd drink. The poor girl was just dumb-founded, of course. She didn't know why this man was yelling at her. I put my hand on his arm and he swung around with his fist up like he was going to punch me. I said, 'Whoa, Dad. Take it easy.' He looked at me like he was trying to figure out who the hell I was. Then I said, 'Thought you might want to meet your grandsons.' You know what he said? 'There's two things I hate: one is this dishwater they try to pass off as tea. The other is kids.' He threw change down on the counter, grabbed that big black hat of his from the rack, and stomped out of the café. That's the last I saw of my father."

Ezra had acted that badly with waitresses and service staff at times following his stroke. We had once planned a late lunch out together without Jeremy, but when we arrived the restaurant we had chosen was closed. A waiter who was sweeping the floor opened the door to tell us the place would open again at five p.m. "What the fuck kind of spot is this?" Ezra said to him. "What kind of shithouse eating place closes at two o'clock?" I dragged him away from the door, mumbling that it didn't matter, we could go to another place, but he swore on, kicking stones from the sidewalk as the waiter looked on.

"You're supposed to love your father," said Uncle Dan. "But how do you love a man who acts like that?"

19.

THE SCREEN DOOR SQUEAKED OPEN and Ezra followed my mother and Val outside carrying his coffee cup. I had asked Val to keep him inside while we butchered the calf. When I caught her eye, looking for an explanation, she glanced at Ezra and shrugged by way of apology. "Where's Jeremy?" I asked Ezra.

"He got groggy watching cartoons. I tucked him into bed." He pointed with his chin at the field. "What does he want?"

I turned to find Jude walking past the old well towards us. "I don't know." I watched him as he approached, hoping for some indication of what he was up to, but he kept his eyes to the ground.

GAIL ANDERSON-DARGATZ

My mother handed Dan a cup of coffee and took a sip from her tea. "Thanks for taking the cattle, Dan. I don't know what we would have done otherwise."

"No skin off my nose," he said. "Got to keep myself busy. Don't know what the hell I'm going to do when the dairy sells. You get attached to things, you know, your animals, or your farm or truck or whatever, even when you think you aren't, even when they've been a whole lot of trouble. You find that out when you try to get rid of them." He looked over my shoulder. "Looks like you got company."

When Jude reached us he nodded at Val and my mother, but didn't look at me or Ezra. Instead he directed his attention to Uncle Dan. "I saw the trailer. Figured you might need help loading the cattle."

"I'll butcher that calf first," Dan said. "Don't want to load the cows up too soon and have them all crowded in there on a hot day like this."

Ezra took my arm and held on too tight. "You jostled Dan into killing that calf?" Ezra said.

"Please don't make a scene."

My mother glanced at Ezra and away. "I hate butchering time," she said.

"Well, no wonder." Dan spoke to Jude as he loaded his rifle. "Our dad took the advice of an old German butcher not to stun a cow, but to cut its throat and let it bleed. He always said the animal bled cleaner that way, that the meat wouldn't be riddled with bloody cuts. The poor creature stumbled around, slowly bleeding to death, until it collapsed to its knees. Horrible to watch." He picked up a knife with a broken handle. "This was the knife he used. It's one of the few things of his that I've got. Best butchering knife I've ever found."

218

"I could never kill an animal," said Mom. "Even when my father ordered me to."

"Oh, I don't know," said Val. "Remember that time that turkey tom went after me? I was, what, four? There I was running with this bird chasing after me. Mom was chopping firewood at the time and she threw her axe, maybe just to scare the bird, but the axe hit it, cut its head clean off. The bird's head went one way and its body kept on running after me."

I laughed. "Mom, warrior princess."

"I did no such thing."

Dan took a last sip from his coffee and put the cup on the patio table. "Well, I better get at it."

"I'll do it," said Ezra. He turned to me. "I told you I would do it."

"Uncle Dan is here now. He's got the equipment set up."

"You muddled this up for me."

"We just had to get it done. It couldn't wait any longer."

"You're scrambling to make me look poor, in front of Jude."

Jude leaned against the fence with his head turned away as if he wasn't listening. I lowered my voice. "Does that really make sense to you? Why would I do that?"

"I know I'm a gimp. You don't have to keep telling me and everyone else about it."

"You're not a gimp. You've got a handicap, that's all. I wish you'd let me help you find a way to manage it."

"Manage it, or fix it?"

"What do you mean?"

"I'm never going to bustle the way you want. I'm never going to be how I was. Why don't you just shoot a gun to my head. That's what you do to gimps, isn't it?"

I put a hand to the back of my head. The pain there. Two hands squeezing a melon. I started to cry. "I can't do this! I can't do this anymore!"

My mother patted my shoulder to comfort me or caution me against further outbursts, but I pulled away, wiping my face. "Let's just get on with it."

My uncle put the gun down on the table and held both hands up. "I don't want to get in the middle of this."

I looked up at Ezra but his jaw was clenched and his face was mottled with rage. He shook his head and strode back to the house.

"Fine," I said. "Fuck! I'll do it." I picked up the gun and trained it on the calf as it stumbled this way and that, kicking up its legs haphazardly before falling. Its mother bawled for it from an adjacent field where I'd put it so it wouldn't have to watch, and I thought of the barn cat we'd had in Chilliwack, leaping around my legs as I held an armful of kittens I had just discovered, their tiny, tender bodies, their bones through fur, the tick of their heartbeats. I couldn't drown them in the bucket of water, though I had been certain that I could. The last thing we needed was more cats. But the insistence of the mother cat, its yowling. Its paws against my thighs, not its claws; it wasn't threatening. It was pleading.

I lowered the gun and set it back on the patio table. "Oh, for Christ's sake, this is so stupid," I said. "Somebody has got to do something about that calf."

The calf fell once again to its knees and bawled in pain. Then I heard the click of the gun. The blast. The calf fell and kicked. Blood at its forehead. I turned and my mother was there beside me at the patio table, with the gun at her shoulder.

"What the hell?" Dan said.

Val glanced at me and raised her eyebrows.

My uncle picked up the knife. "I guess I'll get to work, then." He slit the calf's throat with the knife my grandfather had used for that purpose, then jumped back to avoid the animal's kicking. The stunned calf's thrashing was the mindless reflex of a dying body, but could still break a man's leg.

Mom lowered the gun and placed it on the table. "There," she said. "Now, what was I doing?" She touched the hot barrel of the gun and caught sight of the calf kicking as the life wound out of its body. "Oh!" she said. Val took her arm to steady her. "I think I'll take a little nap before lunch," she said, and she turned to the house, holding onto Val's arm. I watched alongside Dan and Jude as my mother limped away, opening and then closing her right hand into fist, and shaking out the numbness from her lightning arm.

20.

THE FIRE WAS SO CLOSE that the valley outside the parlour window was white with smoke, as if a fog had settled in. Even now that I was inside, the smoke still stung my eyes and the taste of it was thick on my tongue. I could hear the helicopters flying back and forth overhead almost constantly, but I couldn't see them. I had heard on the radio earlier that evening that a total of twenty helicopters had now been assigned to this fire, as it continued to burn out of control.

"What the hell are we going to do if we have to evacuate and Dad is still with us?" I asked Val. She had been rifling through Mom's things in the parlour behind me, searching for any last items that we should salvage and spirit out of the fire's path. Jeremy sat beside her on my mother's bed, playing with the kitten. The smoke made him cough.

"We'll wheel him out on the bed and load him onto the back of the pickup if we have to," said Val. "Let's just hope it doesn't come to that."

"I've got to think about getting Jeremy out of this smoke."

"Can Ezra take him somewhere, while we wait this out with Dad?"

"He can't drive now."

"Of course. I keep forgetting."

She walked up to me carrying a box and glanced through the door into the kitchen before talking to me in a near whisper. "I'm sorry I didn't keep Ezra inside this afternoon, like you asked. I had no idea he would make such a fuss about the calf."

I shook my head. "I should have taken him into town and asked Uncle Dan to butcher while we were away."

"He still would have been angry."

"At me, yes, but in private."

"Is he like that often?"

I nodded and rubbed my neck. The tension there. "I am so tired of coming up with strategies and solutions for dealing with him. Trying this and trying that. I'm just so tired of it all."

Val was quiet for a moment; like my friends at home, she was uncertain what to say. Then she placed the box on the piano bench. "Here," Val said. "I have something that will cheer you up." She placed the box on the piano bench. My name was scrawled along the side of the box in black marker, and inside there were photos of me as a baby, and at church camp, my arm around a buddy in a cowboy hat. A photo of me at my sister's wedding, where I was dressed as a flower girl. In another I was dancing by the lilac bush outside the house, my face a swirl of white, my hand up in the air catching rain. I remembered this day. It was summer and Val was visiting, staying in her old room. She gave me one of her slips as a present, to play in, and I put it on and ran out into the summer rain and danced until I was wet through. The feel of the nylon against my legs, the rain on my arms, the movement of my body. I didn't know that Val watched through the window, and pulled my mother over to see, or that they took this picture. I wasn't quite five, still young enough that I only thought about the sense of things: the smell of the rain hitting the ground, the feel of moss under my feet, the sharp ping of rain hitting my arms as I swirled round and round.

I tucked the photos back in the box and reached down through the layers of the years to find a softness that I knew immediately.

"Huh," said Val as I pulled out the teddy. "Pooh Bear. I remember having to find it for you or you wouldn't go to sleep." She lowered her voice again. "Better not let Mom see it or she'll add it to her collection."

I smiled at her.

Ezra leaned into the doorway. "Kat, the oven music just went off."

"I'll be right there." I put the bear back in the box. "Can you leave this out for now?" I asked Val. "I'd like to take another look at it after supper."

"Sure."

The kitchen was bare except for the table and chairs—we had removed all the bags and boxes to Val's garage in Canoe—and my eye now found the peeling paint, and the lines beneath the wall-paper on the partition where the board underneath had begun to pull away. I had never been fond of this house. It was too dark and sullen, too small, too sad. I had often found excuses to avoid bringing childhood friends home, not only because of my mother's messes but also because of the odd layout of the house. Its haphazard arrangement of added-on rooms spoke of poverty, of a disordered mind.

"The house is so naked now," I said.

My mother looked around the kitchen with me and nodded. "I don't feel like myself without my clutter," she said. "Much of the time I think I'm in my mother's house, all those years ago."

I pulled the roast beef from the oven and found my mother's meat knife in the drawer, its blade so often sharpened that it was now only a slim crescent of steel.

"Every Sunday we had to have Yorkshire pudding with roast beef or there'd be hell to pay," she said. "My father had to have things just so. He couldn't bear to divert from his routine. This was his recipe." She tapped the scrapbook that was open on the counter in front of her. "He loved his Yorkshire pudding, but it had to be made just so. Flour to cover the bottom of the bowl." And she used my grandmother's old sifter. "Salt." She shook salt from the shaker into the palm of her hand and pinched some into the bowl, throwing the remainder over her shoulder to keep the devil at bay. "Milk to mix to pouring state. Then one egg, and beat."

I handed my mother the elderly eggbeater she used.

"No," she said. "With a spoon, never an eggbeater. There. Now add another egg. And beat, beat, beat!" She whisked with the spoon. "I think it pleased him to see my mother or myself so committed to beating this to suit him. Of course if he was away, in the fields or in the barn, then we'd use the eggbeater. One of us watched out the window in case he headed toward the house."

I wondered if she didn't half expect her father to walk up to the screen door now, and see her whisking with a spoon, not a beater, and throw her a bone of praise.

Jeremy came into the kitchen carrying my Pooh Bear under his arm, and holding a clutch of baby photos of me from the box we had just found. "Is that your baby?" he said.

"That's me when I was a baby," I said.

"Where are the pictures of your baby?"

I lowered my voice. "I don't have any." I took the photos from him and placed them up on the windowsill. "These aren't for playing with, honey. But you can hold the teddy for a few minutes if you're careful with it. Go sit at the table. We're about to have supper."

"What baby?" said Ezra.

I took plates down from the cupboard.

Ezra turned to our son. "Jeremy, what baby?"

"Mommy's baby. The one in her tummy in those pictures over at that guy's house." He pointed at Jude's.

"You fashioned a child with Jude?" Ezra asked me.

Val peeked around the corner of the parlour to look at me. I turned my back on her and put plates on the table. "I lost her," I said. "When she was four months along." Ezra lowered himself into his chair as I took a fistful of cutlery from the drawer. "We can talk about it later."

"I want to till it over now."

"There's really nothing to discuss." I laid down a fork, knife, and spoon in front of him. "I lost the baby. Lillian got pregnant. I lost Jude. End of story."

"Why didn't you tell me?"

"It was a long time ago."

"Would you be tied with Jude now if the baby had breathed?"

I paused. "I don't know."

"You still have feelings for him!"

I looked out the window at the darkening sky. The smoke boiling around us.

"Would it really matter to you if I did?"

"Of course! You're my wife. I love you!"

"Do you?" I pulled the note I had found in the barn from my purse and watched as he read his own handwriting. *I'm scared I've plummeted out of love with her.* "Do you mean this?" I asked.

He hesitated a moment. "It was what I was mulling at the time. We'd been butting horns."

"When was this?"

"As we were stacking our things for the move. You must have tumbled the same thinking some time in all our troubles."

"I've never stopped loving you. What else do I have to do to prove it to you? I carry earplugs in my purse for when you need a rest. I do your tractor work when you're tired. I keep house even though I'm the one bringing in a wage. For God's sake I even lay out your clothes so you don't have to decide what you're going to wear in the morning."

"That's exactly it. I'm not passion anymore. I'm work, something to worry about." When I didn't respond he said, "It's true, isn't it?"

"I'm just tired, Ezra."

He carefully folded the note and put it in his pocket.

My mother patted my arm. "This is something best discussed in private," she said and she turned to Jeremy. "What do you have there?"

"Mommy's funny bear."

"I had a bear like this once," Mom said. "It was the only real toy I had at the time, that was store-bought, at least. I don't know how many times Dan and I threw that teddy over the partition wall from my bedroom to the kitchen and back again. It was a game, back and forth, back and forth, over the wall. It never once fell in the gaps between the studs."

"You mean there's no top to that partition?" I asked.

"No, no. It was never meant to be a permanent wall, you see. My father put it up when I was born. Val's room was my old bedroom. He didn't put much effort into its construction. He always planned to build a whole new house for us." She looked back down at the bear. "I was sitting on my bedroom floor one day, singing, pretending the bear was singing. I don't know why I didn't hear my father come in. Maybe he'd taken his boots off outside for once. So I was singing, you see, when he came in the house, and he hated that, couldn't stand it. He snatched the bear from me and threw it up into the partition, inside, to the space between the studs. On purpose. He meant it to stay there." She handed the bear back to Jeremy. "I imagine it's still there."

I thought of this little bear slumped between the studs of that old wall all those years, coated with dust and cobwebs, its belly a nursery to mice. "*Watch over your treasures,*" I said, aloud.

"What was that?" said Mom.

I opened the junk drawer and rummaged for the flashlight and set it down on the table before bringing in the stepladder from the hall.

"What's going on?" said Val.

I set the ladder next to the partition wall and climbed. I could see into Val's old room through the foot-high space between the partition and the ceiling. "Can you hand me the flashlight, and that dishtowel?"

Val passed them up to me.

I cleaned away a thick layer of cobwebs, dust, and cat hairs that had accumulated at the top of the partition and shone the flashlight down into the wall. Strings were tied to nails on the studs, strings that dangled down into the dark. "I don't think your mother was dusting all those times you saw her up here," I said to Mom. I pulled up one of the strings and found a bundle of letters tied to the end. I wiped the dust from the bundle with the dishtowel before tossing them down to my mother, then pulled up another string and another, but whatever they had held had long since fallen to the bottom of the wall.

I got down from the ladder and slid my hand along the ridge under the wallpaper, where the board had come loose. "I'd like to open this up," I said.

"Whatever for?" said Ezra.

"There's more in here, much more." I turned to Mom. "Your mother's sister wrote in that card, *At the very least the lost little fellow will watch over your treasures.* I think your mother was leaving you a clue in that copy of *The Prophet.* She was telling you where to look for her treasures, should anything happen to her."

My mother stared at the wall a moment and then nodded.

I retrieved the hammer from the junk drawer and, after ripping away generations of wallpaper, I turned the hammer's claw into the board to yank it loose. Nails screeched and the board popped open and a wash of ladybugs spilled to the floor. Most were dead, but a few crawled up the wall, or took flight around our heads. "Good God!" said Val.

"Ladybug, ladybug, fly 'way home!" said Jeremy.

"Let's get this cleaned out." I reached under the sink for the dustpan and broom and began the task of scooping lady-bugs and decades of dust and debris into the brown paper bag that Val set before me. When the bag was nearly full, Ezra took it outside and tossed ladybugs across the driveway. Many lifted up and flew away, spiraling over his head.

"Jesus," said Ezra. "How many bugs are there?"

"I don't know," I said, and then I hit something with the edge of the dustpan.

"What is it?" said my mother.

I lifted a crumbling teddy from the wall. Covered in dust and cobwebs, its stomach had indeed been nested by mice. Its head lolled to the side, attached by just a few remaining threads. "Oh, God!" said Val. She sneezed. "Let's get it into a garbage bag."

"No!" said my mother.

"It's filthy."

"She hasn't seen it for nearly seventy years," I said.

Val handed her the bear and Mom sat in her mother's chair and rocked, playing with the bear as a child might. Harrison jumped onto her lap.

"There a bear for me?" said Jeremy.

"No. Only for Grandma."

I turned back to my mother. "Are those letters from Valentine?"

"No, from her sister."

"Why would she hide letters from her sister?"

"My father was jealous of anything that didn't involve him."

"Valentine's letters must be here," I said. "I know they're here."

I sifted through my grandmother's treasures at the bottom of the partition. A 1931 Butterick pattern for a peplum frock. A tube of lipstick. A little bottle of lilac perfume. A *Chatelaine* magazine from 1953 with a string threaded through a hole punched in one corner. On the cover was a photograph of Prince Philip ("in colour for framing"), but the contents were much the same as in the modern version of the magazine. The cover promised a story on how to "Eat all you want and reduce," "Bargains in glamour vacations," and "A new complete romantic novelette." Inside there were advertisements for Sunbeam coffeemakers, Birks, General Electric refrigerators, Gerber's baby foods.

And then I found the Peek Frean cookie tin. I popped open the lid and there they were: Valentine's letters to Maud, from 1945 right through until my grandfather's disappearance.

My mother rose to join me, and her chair went on rocking behind her. We all stood at the table for several minutes, leafing through the letters, scanning them.

"There's a letter in here that she wrote to *him,*" I said. "She wrote it the day Valentine told her they had given up the search for Grandpa's body." I handed my mother the letter.

"My mother died that evening. A heart attack. Gus found her lying on the greenhouse floor."

"Can I see that again?" I said. My mother handed the letter back to me and I glanced at it before tucking it and all of Valentine's letters into my grandmother's carpetbag, where I had put her letters to him. I kissed Jeremy on the forehead. "Jeremy, you stay here with Daddy and Auntie. I won't be long." I turned to Val. "Can you keep an eye on him for a few minutes? I'll be right back."

"Where are you going?" said Ezra. But I had already closed the screen door behind me and stepped into the night, and I was far enough away to pretend that I hadn't heard him.

21.

April 2, 1965

Dearest Mrs.,

Forgive me for calling you Mrs. again, Maud, but
that's what you'll always be to me, my darling, my
Mrs. I feel I must apologize for what happened
tonight. I know the kiss was stolen, and I know
you must feel that you have betrayed your husband
again. Please forgive me. But if I do in fact have
a second chance with you, then I must know. You

only have to say the word and I'm yours. But of course now is not the time to talk of such things.

Gus is saddling up Star and Pride right now, and Beth just arrived with lunch, so I'll send this note back with her. We'll take short trips up the mountain again tonight as we did last night, following the old Indian trails, and keep checking back at the farm. I hate to leave you and Beth and the girls alone here for long, as John's mental state has likely deteriorated further. But the cops won't let the other searchers hunt for him in the night, and I don't want to search for him alone in case we come on him and he thinks I'm "the enemy." I'll need Gus's help to bring him down once we find him, in any case.

My dearest Maud, keep the door barred with a chair, but don't worry yourself too much. I've found every man I've searched for, you know that. Try to sleep, or keep yourself busy, dearest; it is always the best remedy for a troubled mind. Why not make a pan of your wonderful fudge? It will give you something to do while you wait, and distract John once we bring him back home. But save a little for me, will you? Oh, my dearest, I so love your fudge, and your company.

I will be forever your Mr.,
Valentine

April 9, 1965

My dear Valentine,

Thank you for leaving your copy of *The Prophet* on the porch. Beth found it and brought it in. Thank you, also, for volunteering to be the one to tell me the RCMP have called off the search. I know that must have been difficult for you, and I did not make the task easy. You startled me, coming up behind me while I was hanging out the laundry, and then the news rather left me raw. I'm sorry I simply walked off without speaking to you. I cried all afternoon, and even as I milked the cows, but now, it seems that I have been wrung dry.

As I walked to the barn to milk the cows in the twilight, I swore I saw John at the four fenceposts that mark the old well, stooping to pick shooting stars for me as he did each spring without fail. Then he was gone. I imagine it was a hallucination induced by my grief, as you and the others tell me he likely died of exposure in those cold mountain rains. Even so, today after you told me the news, I walked up to the bench land to call his name, as I have done almost every day of the search, thinking that, like a wounded cat, he might come home for me, when he wouldn't for anyone else. He hasn't answered my calls, of course, though he has entered my dreams nightly, taking my hand and offering me fistfuls of shooting stars.

Did Beth tell you the kitchen window broke
when the meteor hit, just before John disappeared?
I was standing at the window—looking over at your
cabin, I'm ashamed to say—when I saw that bright
light travel across the sky, and then there was a
flash like a bomb exploding as it hit the mountain.
The meteor lit up the whole of Turtle Valley as if it
were day; I could clearly see you walking across
your yard with the pitchfork to feed the cows. The
initial streak of light surprised me so much that
I put my hand to the glass, and I was standing like
that when the sound reached us. In the instant
before the meteor hit, I saw John's face reflected in
the window behind me; it startled me as I felt he
had caught me looking across the field at you, and
I feared what he might do. But then there was that
bright flash and the boom shook the house, and his
scream rang out just as the glass shattered.

John fell to the floor, shrieking, holding his
head, just as you described him that day the army
came to blow up the Japanese balloon. I knelt on
the floor and held his head because I couldn't
think what else to do. But he pulled away from me.
His eyes were open, bulging, as they were so many
nights when he sat up in bed with the night terrors, but he didn't see me. I wasn't there for him;
this house, this farm, and everything that was
familiar weren't there for him.

I wish now I had found a way to awaken him
from that horrible dream, to bring him back here to

this kitchen. But I thought at the time it was better to let him be, to let the terror flood over him and pass on as it had during all those nights of our marriage. If I tried to touch him, he only became more frightened. So I withdrew, to sit in my rocking chair. I didn't accompany him down that slide into his nightmare. That was where I first failed him.

He jumped up and grabbed the gun off the rack and put on his glasses, as he did when he was about to go out hunting. I took his arm in some effort to stop him but he pushed me to the floor and lifted the gun over his head. His intent was to hit me with the butt of the gun, but then his eyes focused on me for a moment and he pulled back and headed out the door. "I'm going up there to get the sonofabitches," he said. I called after him but that was the last I saw of him: marching through the rain in that circle of yard light, wearing his puttees from the war, his jack shirt, and the big black hat, before he disappeared into the night.

As for that kiss the next night, there is nothing to forgive. I was finishing up the dishes when I saw the light in the cabin and saw you feeding the cows, and so I ran right over in the rain, hoping for some news of John. As you told me you had found no sign of John, I felt the panic of a mother whose child has wandered out of her sight. I didn't know what to do. But then you wrapped your warm coat around me, and pulled me out of the rain, and held me, and let me cry into your chest. I have always

loved the smell of you: pipe tobacco and coffee, hay
and the balsam boughs you stuff your mattress
with. The kiss was not stolen; it was freely given. It
made everything seem all right, as your kisses
always have.

But everything isn't all right, is it? With Beth's
help I replaced the shattered kitchen window
with a warped pane of glass we had left over from
building the greenhouse all those years ago (so
it's through this memory of you that I now look
over at your cabin and the unfinished house). But
I fear I can't fix what else ails this family.

After that kiss, as you and Gus went out to
hunt for John, Beth kept watch with me in the
kitchen. As you had suggested, I made a pan of
fudge and did housework to keep myself occupied.
And when that was done, I sat in my rocker with
Katrine asleep in her basket at my feet. I must
have fallen asleep because Beth told me that when
she saw the light in your cabin, she slipped out to
take over that pan of fudge, to see what the news
was. It was then, she said, that she saw a cougar
skulking about the barns.

I woke to gunshots, four shots altogether,
and stepped out onto the porch, but I could see
very little past the yard light. Your voices were
murmurings in the black. Then you walked into
the yard light supporting Gus, and his arm was
hanging, bloodied, at his side, and I feared the
worst at that moment, as I still do. You told me

that you had just shot a cougar that had followed
you down off the mountain. You said John had
shot Gus on the mountain, and had then fled.
But it was a fresh wound to Gus's arm, not one
from even an hour or two before, I'm sure of it.
I have seen so many wounds. I was an ambulance
driver in the Great War, you remember.

And it is so odd how you have all withdrawn from
me this week, how it seems there is an invisible,
uninvited guest sitting in on my dealings with Beth,
or Gus, or you. Some ghost listening in, who keeps
each of you from being candid with me.

Oh, Valentine, I want to cry, because right now,
as I'm finishing this letter to you, the radio is
playing our song, "If You Were the Only Girl in the
World." It is such a strange coincidence, not only
because it is our song, but because the lyrics seem
to sum up exactly what I am thinking: if it were
only you and I, if there were no other considerations, then we could go back to loving in the same
old way. But it's not just you and I, is it? There is
this ghost haunting us.

Tonight after I milked the cows, I walked over to
your cabin, to say thank you for all your efforts and
to offer my apology for my behaviour earlier today,
and perhaps to work up the confidence to talk with
you about much that I've written here. But you
weren't there, and so, thinking you were feeding the
cows, I walked over to the pasture by the unfinished
house. It was there that I saw something glinting in

the grass by the old house. Valentine, it was John's glasses. I tucked them away in their case and in an envelope out of view, and I haven't spoken to Beth or Gus about them. But all this has left me with a question, a terrible question that I barely dare to ask. But I will, my love, because nothing can come of us until it is answered.

What happened that night, the night we kissed? Did you kill John?

22.

LIGHTS BLAZED FROM THE KILN SHED and the CD player blasted out J.J. Cale's old tune "Crazy Mama." Jude moved back and forth at a hectic, choreographed pace. Within the seconds that it took him to move the pots from the kiln to the garbage cans, they faded in colour from that glorious yellow to the orange-red of a stove burner, and then to the browns, yellows, and whites of the glazes.

"Hasn't some fire marshal come to give you hell yet?" I said.

"A cop came by late this afternoon, told me to shut it down. I said I would as soon as I had finished firing that load."

"And yet here you are."

"It's my last firing before my show next week. In any case, I'm just about done."

I turned down the volume on the CD player. "You knew I would come. You played our song."

"It was meant as an invitation. I've been playing it on repeat ever since that bizarre little calf-killing episode this afternoon."

"I'm sorry," I said. "I wish you hadn't been there for any of it."

He used the tongs to carry another vase to a garbage can. "I didn't understand what you were up against until I saw it in action today. You and Ezra are in a rut, stuck in this thing that's happened to you. You're both so angry at each other. Just like Lillian and I were before she left."

I shook my head. "He can't help his anger. It's a handicap, a symptom of the stroke."

Jude put the vase in the can and flames flared up as the newspaper ignited. "But it still pisses you off."

"I didn't come here to talk about Ezra," I said. "I wanted to show you something."

"I can't stop to look right now."

"These are letters Uncle Valentine wrote to my grandmother. They were in the partition wall between the kitchen and Val's room. And there's a letter here from my grandmother; she died the night she wrote it so she never had a chance to give it to him. She asks him, 'What happened that night, the night we kissed? Did you kill John?'"

Jude stopped beside me a moment, tongs in hand, to glance at the letter before heading back to the kiln. "Jesus."

I followed him. "Here she talks about hearing 'If You Were

the Only Girl in the World' on the radio just after Valentine told her they had called off the search, the night she died. The weird thing is, this past week I heard the piano in Mom's parlour playing that song, but there was no one in the room and the piano was closed. My grandmother says here that it was their song, Maud and Valentine's song." I sorted through the other letters in my hand. "My grandmother and Valentine *were* lovers that year my grandfather was in Essondale, after the military blew up the Japanese balloon. Valentine wrote to her, trying to make Maud reconsider after she ended the affair." I held up the letter. "Here he begs her to leave her husband. But she stayed."

"And what would you do if I begged you to leave your husband?"

I crossed my arms and looked out the open door. I could make out the lights of my parents' house, but the smoke was too thick to see who was in the kitchen. The wind swirled the smoke and ash into eddies, creating the effect of a snowstorm on this hot August evening. "I don't know," I said.

"Shit!"

I turned back to Jude. He was standing at the kiln, attempting to lift a pot from it. "What is it?"

"I fucked up. I wasn't focussing on what I was doing and now I can't get either of these vases out without lifting one or the other out of the way. This is so stupid."

"Can I do anything?"

"Yes. Get those gloves on." He nodded at a pair of Kevlar gloves sitting on a stack of bricks behind the kiln. "And that shirt."

I quickly slid on the Nomex shirt. When I put on the gloves they extended up to my shoulder; they weren't only dirty brown, but burned.

"I'll hold this vase to the side while you reach into the kiln and grab this other one by the neck."

"With my hands?"

"Yes! There's no time to dick around. Reach in and pull it out in one motion, then set it in one of those cans."

"Are you crazy?"

"I do it all the time."

"No."

"Katrine! Now!"

I reached into the kiln and grabbed the vase by the neck. It glowed yellow, a vessel fashioned from fire, and the molten glazes slipped across its surface like spirits. The heat on my face and chest was incredible, much more intense than the blast from an open oven when I reached in to take out a roast. I felt it through the gloves and tried my best not to touch the stiff material from within; the gloves began to smoke. The smell of burning leather.

"Quick!" said Jude. "Into a garbage can."

I settled the vase into a nest of newspaper within a can and the paper immediately caught fire, sending flames and smoke up around me. I put on the lid and flicked the burning gloves from my hands. Then I watched as he pulled the remaining vase from the kiln and placed it in a garbage can. He removed his gloves to shut the kiln off.

"You all right?" he said.

"I think so." It was then I smelled burning hair; I ran a finger over my eyebrows to make sure I still had them.

Jude smiled. "They're still there," he said. "Your hair is a little singed, though," and he tucked my windblown hair back behind my ear, arranging it as he had for my portrait all those years ago. "That wasn't so hard, was it? If you can handle reaching into fire like that, don't you think you can handle striking out on your own?" He grinned. "Don't you think you can handle me?" But he didn't let me answer. He kissed me.

"We're exposed here," I said, looking over at the road. The wind had shifted, sweeping some of the smoke away. "Someone passing by could see us." But when he kissed me again, I kissed him back. He pulled me closer and ran a hand up to my breast. I felt him grow against my thigh.

His cellphone rang but he ignored it and kissed my cheek, my neck. "You should answer it," I said.

"Let it ring." But the phone didn't stop. "Damn it," he said. He picked up the cell from his worktable. "Hello?" he said, then "Sure," and he held out the phone. "It's for you."

"Me?" I took the phone. "Hello?"

"Kat, you better come home."

"Val?"

"It's Dad. I think it's time."

"Oh, God."

"And Kat, go to the door and look back at the house."

Val stood outside on the steps under the porch light. She waved. Inside the kitchen the dark outline of a figure stood at the window, backlit from the lights within. Ezra.

"We can see you, Kat," said Val. "We can all see you."

23.

THE FIRE WAS NOW SO LOW on the hillside that it filled the room with a reddish glow, lighting up the objects on the bed-side table: my grandmother's carpetbag, the fresh towel I had placed there when we arrived, the baby oil, the little teddy bear tucked into the Kleenex box. I had stared at these objects for more than two hours, unable to sleep. Except for my hospital stay when I gave birth to Jeremy, and those two weeks following the stroke when Ezra was in hospital, he and I had never before spent a night in separate beds. And even then, on that first evening, the nurses had placed a cot right next to his bed for me. I didn't think I would sleep, but I did, and though Ezra's mind was so terribly confused, his body turned to hold mine.

Ezra had once told me that the women of his childhood church would comfort a new widow by sleeping with her, on the night of her loss and for a fortnight after, to make the transition into widowhood less lonely. I had thought it an odd practice at the time, but understood it those first few nights I slept by myself while he was in the hospital. I knew even then that I was losing him. Val came to be with me, and once she arrived in Chilliwack I took comfort from her body in bed next to mine. Her heaviness and warmth were a soothing presence.

I got up and shuffled to Val's old room and pushed the door open slowly so its creak wouldn't wake Jeremy. Ezra slept on a makeshift bed on the floor next to Jeremy's; his sheets were kicked down to his feet. I had come with the intention of running a hand along his cheek to wake him, to invite him back to our bed to talk, as we had not been able to the night before, to end this tension that hung in the house along with the smell of smoke. But now that I was here, I found that I could not. I watched the rise and fall of his chest as it became shallower, and when it stopped altogether I bent over him, waiting, listening, willing his breath to begin again. When his breath did surface, a bubble that opened his mouth, I turned and ran a hand down my son's cheek until Jeremy grunted, turned his face to the wall, and brushed my hand away.

In the kitchen, my mother was asleep in her rocker with Harrison in her lap and the kitten at her feet, the clutch of Grandma and Uncle Valentine's letters in her hand. I pushed open the door to Dad's room quietly, so as not to wake her. The room was dark. Only a small table lamp lit up the corner where Val snored lightly in the easy chair beside Dad's bed. I touched her arm and she startled and looked up at me, confused in her exit from sleep, her eyes dull and cobwebbed with exhaustion. "My shift," I said.

She stood and I took Dad's hand and leaned gently against his chest so I could speak into his ear. "Dad, I'm here."

"He knows you're here," said Val. "He can hear you."

But in the way a sleeper hears the scurry of a mouse, I suspected. The whispers of night sounds were woven into his dreams.

"Has he spoken?"

"At midnight he said, *Mouth,* to get me to take his dentures out. They were in there sideways. He wouldn't let me take them out before. I should have shaved him, but I don't want to bother him with that now."

"His hands are so puffy."

"I wish I'd insisted he let me take that wedding ring off," she said. "But he likely won't swell up much more. The skin on his feet and legs has begun to mottle as the circulation fails. When it reaches his stomach he'll have maybe a couple of hours. The nurse came by after you went to bed. She thinks he'll likely pass this morning."

She drew back the covers to expose the purple web crawling up my father's shins, very like the mottling that Jeremy sometimes woke with on his hands and feet when he was a baby, as his blood learned to navigate his body. Left to our own devices, it appeared, we eased into death in the same way we eased into life. I had never envisioned death in this way before, as a tide washing up my father's body as he stood on a disappearing shore.

"Does Mom understand he'll likely go today?"

Val nodded at my father. "But I think she still half expects him to rally and be out there cutting hay next week."

"He's not breathing!" I said.

"He'll start up again. But the periods of time where he doesn't breathe will get longer and more frequent. Until he stops breathing altogether."

I watched the slight movement in his chest, his heart beating, as I counted to myself, *one thousand and one, one thousand and two*—as I did waiting for a thunderclap—reaching twelve before his breath caught. When it did start again, he sounded like an old glass coffeepot percolating on the stove.

"Fluid buildup in his throat," said Val. "Nothing to worry about. It won't bother him." She patted my arm. "I'm going to try to get a few minutes' sleep. If Dad begins to look at all restless, call me and I'll give him another shot of morphine." She closed the door behind her.

My father's face was turned away but I could see his reflection in the mirror of my mother's bureau; the half-moon whites of his eyes were showing. With his teeth out his cheeks were sunken and his mouth was a small black hole. If it hadn't been for the shallow rise and fall of his chest, I would have thought him already dead.

I stared for a time at the familiar objects on his night table. His old Echo harmonica, the ancient deck of cards in a leather holder that he played solitaire with; his favourite cup; his jackknife and the Gillette razor that he had continued to use, preferring it over the electric one I had bought him one Christmas. Aside from his clothes, these objects were the only ones inside the house that I identified as his alone. He defined himself as a man who needed little, like Uncle Valentine, who had raised him. I picked up his harmonica and played "Good Night Irene" softly for him, just as he had when he serenaded my mother to sleep nearly every night for all those years of their marriage, and I found myself tearing up. Very soon this harmonica and these few objects that he had owned, and the memories they triggered in us, would be all that was left of him. My father's life would disappear into ash and smoke.

I put down the harmonica and leaned against his chest to whisper into his ear. I could feel his heart beating against my breast. "I have something to ask you," I said. "I know this isn't the time, but I don't think I'll get the chance again."

He gave a slight grunt.

"I found the letters Grandma and Uncle Valentine wrote to each other. They were love letters, at least most of them were. Grandma seemed to think Valentine might have killed Grandpa."

My father's mouth puckered just slightly, as an infant's does in sleep.

"Did he?" I asked.

His heart speeded up; as it thudded against my own chest, it felt like a baby kicking me from within. "Squeeze my hand once for no, twice for yes," I said. "Did Valentine kill Grandpa?"

He squeezed my hand once.

"So he didn't kill him."

He squeezed once again.

"Do you know who did? Did someone kill Grandpa?"

His hand went loose within mine.

"Did you?"

My father squeezed my hand and hung on. His chest laboured in breath, caving inward like the wings of a bird coming in to land.

"I shouldn't have asked. It was stupid of me. I know you couldn't have done that." He struggled to open his eyes and his face tensed as if he was in pain. Then he made a sound like the harsh caw of a crow, like a child with croup.

"Val?" I called. "Val!"

My sister hurried in and slid a shot of morphine into the butterfly needle inserted in his chest. His face tightened further from the sting of the morphine entering his veins and then, moments later, relaxed. His hand went limp in mine.

Mom hurried into the room hugging the letters; her face was pale in panic. "What's happened? What's wrong?"

"He just needed another shot," said Val. "He's sleeping now."

Mom sank into the easy chair. "Thank God."

Val took her hand. "You do understand that Dad will likely die this morning?"

"I know. You don't have to keep explaining it to me. I just hate to see him like this. Your father didn't want to go the way Valentine went, all doped up."

"It's better that he doesn't feel the pain."

"I feel so helpless. Isn't there anything I can do? His mouth looks dry. Can I give him water?"

"He can't take water," said Val. "It enlarges the cells, makes the pain worse. You can clean his mouth with a swab, if you like; it will refresh him." She reached for a couple of plastic-wrapped sticks with small sponges attached. "There's a choice of cinnamon and lemon flavors."

"Lemon," said my mother. "He loves his lemon meringue pie."

Val unwrapped the plastic, dipped the swab in a cup of water, and held it out to my mother. "Just touch it against the side of his mouth," she said. "He'll open for you."

"Like a baby," Mom said. And like an infant my father suckled the swab as my mother cleaned his mouth. It surprised me that this relic of infancy, his rooting reflex, remained deep within him, to arise as his consciousness descended.

Val rubbed her brow. "I'm going to try again to get a few minutes' sleep."

My mother watched her leave, and waited to hear the door to my old room close before she spoke. "She thinks I'm a child."

I sat on the edge of the bed at my father's feet. "No, she doesn't, Mom."

She picked up Harrison and put the cat in her lap. "Every time I come in here she's hanging all over him, hugging him, touching his face. She won't give me a moment alone with him. She acts like *she's* the wife."

"Do you want to be alone with him now? I can leave."

"No, not until it's light." She petted the cat. "It's too lonely."

"I'm sorry I woke you. I shouldn't have called out like that."

"He needed an injection."

"It was my fault, I think."

"How could it be your fault?"

"I asked him if he killed your father."

"What?"

"I asked if Valentine had killed him, like Grandma thought. Then I asked if *he* had."

"What did he say?"

"He squeezed my hand, to say no."

"What were you thinking?"

"I don't know." I cupped Dad's hand in both of my own and touched his wedding ring; it was sunken into the yellowed, translucent skin of his finger. "The more I found out about your father's disappearance and Grandma's life with him, the more I felt like I was repeating her life, her choice, to stay with a sick man. I needed to know what happened. I guess I needed to know what will happen, for me."

Mom put a hand on mine. "Ezra is not my father. Jude is not your Uncle Valentine." She patted my hand. "And you, my dear, are not my mother."

We sat without saying anything for a time, staring out the window. Light had begun to spread across the sky.

"The sun should be coming up soon," she said. "Maybe Gus is hanging on to see one last sunrise."

When I stood to look outside, something slammed into the window and we both startled. Harrison leapt from Mom's lap and scrambled, slid into the kitchen. A junco beat its wings at the bedroom window. I turned out the lamp, thinking the bird was attracted to the light, and it flew off. Then there was a face in the window, an old woman's face. I swung around but Mom was still seated in her chair; it could not have been her reflection. I looked back at the window and the bird again bashed into the warped pane. I jumped back. "Jesus!"

"The birds are panicked," said Mom. "The fire is forcing them off the mountain."

"I saw a woman's face reflected there. A woman in the room with us."

"I imagine it's as your father says, a reflection of your own face, distorted by the glass." Even so, my mother stood to join me, favouring her knee. Outside, the day of firefighting had already begun. Firetrucks and army trucks rumbled down the road. Several helicopters flew overhead dragging buckets, rattling the windowpane. Residents drove out with loads, or drove back in with empty trucks. All this business so early in the morning—others ignorant of my father's impending death, focused instead on the crisis at hand—seemed at that moment inconceivably rude.

"Who's that?" said my mother.

"Hmm?"

"There's someone in the field. My eyes are getting so bad."

I searched until I found the dark figure emerging from the smoke and early-morning shadows. "That creepy old man," I said. "I wonder what he wants, hanging around here. I think it might be time to phone the cops. It must have been him snooping around the unfinished house. I wonder if it wasn't him who ran after me in the night."

"It's likely just someone getting a good view of the fire."

"He's been watching the house. I don't want him near Jeremy. He's not one of your neighbours, is he?"

"Have you gotten a look at his face?"

"No."

Jeremy cried out in his sleep and I started for the door, but my mother took my hand. "Why don't you let Ezra take care of him today?"

"He often won't wake," I said. But when I left the bedroom, he was there, wearing only his underwear, carrying Jeremy into the kitchen.

"He had a nightmare," said Ezra. "He wants a mommy hug."

"A mommy hug! You got it!" I lifted him from Ezra's arms and held him close. "Thanks," I said, but Ezra had already turned away. He closed the bedroom door behind him.

I carried Jeremy back into my parents' room, where my mother stood at the window. "The old guy still out there?" I asked her.

"I don't know where he got to."

Jeremy craned his neck back toward the bed. "Can I give Grandpa a hug?"

"You can't hug Grandpa, but you can touch his hand."

I put him down and he stroked Dad's hand as he would a cat. "Grandpa's really sick, isn't he?"

"Grandpa's dying. Just like that bird that died."

"I want to give Grandpa a piece of birthday cake!"

"I'm afraid he can't eat anymore."

"When he's dead can I give him birthday cake?"

"He won't be able to eat then either," I said. "Just like that dead bird won't eat anymore, or drink water."

"Or read books."

"That's right. Grandpa won't read books."

"Or go pee."

I smiled at my mother. "That's right. When Grandpa dies he won't go pee. Or watch TV. Or drive the tractor. Or walk around."

"Dead Grandpa walks around."

"No," I said. "When Grandpa is dead, he won't be able to walk around. Remember the bird couldn't fly after he died."

"No! Dead Grandpa walks around."

"What do you mean?"

He pointed out the window. "Dead Grandpa." I could just make out the dark outline of the old man in the alfalfa field before he was obscured again by smoke. "He walks outside. Dead Grandma walks inside."

My mother put her hand to her mouth.

"Dead Grandpa's scared." He opened his arms wide. "I want to give dead Grandpa a big hug and a piece of birthday cake."

I touched Mom's arm. "Is this the grandma who walks inside the house?"

"No! This is live Grandma. *Dead* Grandma walks inside the house. Dead Grandma wants to burn the house. Ladybug, lady-bug, fly 'way home!" He pointed at the ceiling and both my mother and I looked up: the ceiling was covered in thousands of ladybugs. They formed streams down the walls like caravans of tiny Volkswagen Beetles rumbling down a highway.

"My God," I said.

"Ladybug, ladybug, fly 'way home." Jeremy lifted his arms and danced around the room. Hundreds of the beetles took flight, flying clumsily around our heads, lighting on my arms, on my son's head, in my mother's hair, and on my father's face. Dad's mouth clamped shut as his neck arched backward and his feet thrashed a moment under the covers.

"Val!" I called "Val!"

She stumbled into the room and Ezra followed moments later. "What the hell?" he said, looking around the room at the ladybugs. My father's kicking eased as Val leaned over him. "A seizure," she said, putting a hand on my mother's arm to calm her. "It's common as the body shuts down."

My father's body relaxed for a moment and then his eyes flew open. He stared at the ceiling, the ladybugs there. His breath stopped. I counted the seconds, watching the tick of his heart against his chest, hoping his breath would catch again. But it didn't.

My mother cried, "Oh, no. God, no." I wrapped my arm around her as she sobbed. Val hugged Dad's body, and pressed her face against his. Ezra pulled Jeremy back, away from the bed.

"I want a few minutes alone with him," Mom said, and we all left the room. As I closed the door behind me, my mother leaned over her husband's body, put a hand to his cheek, and whispered, "I love you so very much." The ladybugs descended from the ceiling, whirling in a cloud around her head, lighting on her shoulders and in her hair as if with affection.

24.

I CLOSED THE DOOR to Val's old room, where Jeremy napped, and sought out my mother. She stood in front of the closet in her room, tossing dress shirts onto the hospital bed. A few stray lady-bugs still crawled across the headboard of the bed and over the photos on the bureau, but the bulk of the insects had retreated into the many cracks of the walls. The radio blared in the kitchen as it had all morning, keeping us informed of the latest developments in the fire. Just as my father had predicted, strong winds had urged the fire downhill. It had begun to break through the fire guards and was heading toward the most populated areas of the valley. "You'll tell your grandkids about this, folks," the announcer said.

"The smell of that smoke," said my mother. "It makes me think of all those campfires on the mountains with Gus. I shouldn't be taking any pleasure in it, should I?"

"What are you up to?"

"They didn't take any of his clothes when they came to pick up his body. I'm going to find him a suit to wear."

"Dad doesn't need to be dressed for the cremation."

"I want him to look nice."

"He rarely wore suits."

"This is a special occasion."

I pulled out a coffee-coloured wool suit, something my father would have worn in the early 1960s.

"Not that one," said my mother. "It's horrid."

"It's cool."

"The last time he wore that was to your grandfather's memorial service. I made him buy a new one for my mother's funeral."

"You think Dad would mind if Ezra tried it on?"

She hesitated. "I don't think he'd mind."

Then I realized the absurdity of what I'd just asked; my father was dead, and I was seeking out clothing for my husband even as I contemplated the love of another man. Ezra would never wear this suit in any case. That life was gone. It hit me then, the first blow of my father's death. The prickly tears, the rush of cold running up my arms, then down into my stomach, pulling me onto the hospital bed. I watched my mother as she laid the suit she had chosen on the bed. She glanced at me, but turned away to search for a shirt and tie to match, allowing me a moment's privacy. But then the suit slid from the bed beside me and landed with a thud on the floor. There was something in the pocket. "Mom, there's a wallet in here," I said.

"I once found a fifty-dollar bill in the pocket of Gus's winter jacket. When I told him about it he said he'd put it there for emergencies. He'd hide money away so I wouldn't spend it. It hurt, you know, that he would do that. I looked through the pockets of his town clothes pretty carefully before I washed them after that, but I never found any more bills. I imagine he found new hiding places."

I opened the wallet. "This was your father's."

"*My* father's?"

Mom sat on the bed beside me as I went through the contents of the wallet.

"Why would Dad have your father's wallet?" I asked. "Wouldn't the wallet be on Grandpa's body?"

"This must be an older wallet, something he found when we went through my father's things."

"Here's his driver's licence. And look, a 1965 nickel. But there's no cash." I handed her the wallet. "*Did* Dad kill your father?"

"Gus would do anything, if he thought it was what I wanted. But not that."

"But it wasn't a cougar Valentine shot that night, was it?"

My mother looked past me, and her eyes widened. An RCMP car careered down our driveway, pulling up a plume of dust that was hardly distinguishable from the smoke that swirled all around us. The bantam hen we hadn't been able to catch flew over the fence in panic as the car passed.

My mother followed me into the kitchen. "What do they want?" she asked.

"I imagine it's about the fire."

She stayed inside as I stepped out to watch the police car park in our yard. A woman officer in a yellow jacket opened the door of the car to yell over the wind. "Mrs. Svensson?"

"I'm her daughter."

"An evacuation order has been issued. You have ten minutes to leave the area."

"My father just passed away this morning. They came to take his body only a couple of hours ago. It'll take us a little bit to gather ourselves."

"I'm sorry to hear that." She looked back at the house. "Just you and your mother here?"

"My sister left about an hour ago. My son is napping. My husband must be in the barn."

"That fire is on the move. You need to get out of here. Now."

"I understand."

My mother's face disappeared from the screen door as the police car drove off. When I entered the kitchen I found her sitting in the rocker in the kitchen, pen and paper in her lap, scribbling.

"Mom, we don't have time for that now," I said, but she went on writing. I started for Val's room, to wake Jeremy. Thinking better of it, I turned to the door, intending to alert Ezra first, but there was an old man there, standing on the porch. "Shit!" I said, then, "Can I help you?"

He wore a huge black hat and his face was in shadow. His glasses reflected the light so that I couldn't see his eyes. He just stood there, wavering back and forth a little as if he was unsteady on his feet.

My mother stood up, setting her chair rocking. "Someone's here?" Then she took a step back. "Oh, my God."

"It's okay," I said. "It's just that old guy who's been hanging around." When I turned back to the door, he was gone. I stepped through the screen door and onto the porch. "Hello," I said. "Can I help you?" But there was no one in the yard. My mother came

266

up behind me. "At least we don't have to be afraid of him any-more," I said. "He seemed out of it, like he didn't know where he was. Some kind of dementia, I imagine. You acted like you knew him. Is he a neighbour?"

"No."

"But you do know him."

"My father always said he would stay on this farm after his death, and never leave it. My mother often said the same thing, that she imagined she would be with my father after her death, roaming around this farm."

"She had something to that effect underlined in the copy of *The Prophet* I found in her carpetbag: *You shall be together when the white wings of death scatter your days.* You think she really wanted that?"

"It wasn't so much what she wanted as how she imagined things must be. I don't think she could conceive of a time when she wouldn't care for my father. I remember her worrying over that, what would happen to my father should anything happen to her. She knew I couldn't handle him, and it was obvious that Dan was never going to be around to help."

"So, what? You're saying that old guy was your father? A ghost?"

She glanced up at me, then away, to the bush around the old well site.

"Well, on the off chance the old guy isn't a ghost, I'll get Ezra to take a look for him while I get you and Jeremy loaded into the truck."

I strode toward the barn, leaning into the wind, to meet Ezra as he headed out of the building carrying boxes. When I got close enough that I could hear over the wind, he said, "What did the cop want?"

"The fire is coming our way. We have to leave."

We headed back to the house. "I'll set the stream up on the roof. There's a chance we can recover the house if the roof is wet."

"The sprinkler, you mean?"

"Yes."

"There was an old guy here just a moment ago. He seemed confused. Can you take a look for him first? I'd hate to see him wandering around in this." I waved at the soup of smoke that surrounded us, blotting out Jude's home from view.

I went inside to help Mom gather her things, then carried Jeremy outside to the truck, where I tossed the carpetbag in the front seat. My mother fastened Harrison's harness to the inside so the cat wouldn't get away when we opened the door, but allowed the kitten to hop from the seat to the floor, where it chased bits of dried mud.

"Ezra!" I called out. "Ezra?" But my voice was carried off by the wind. The smoke darkened the day into twilight and obscured even our own barns.

"There he is," said my mother. She pointed at the old well, the figure that appeared and disappeared, revealed and then hidden again by the swirling clouds of smoke. I could hear the crackle of the trees burning on the hills above.

"Ezra?" I said, squinting.

"No."

"The old guy. I guess I better go get him."

"It's no use," said Mom. "You won't find him."

"I'm sure I can catch up to him."

"He's not what you think."

"You don't really think he's a ghost?" I took her hand as well as Jeremy's. "Come with me. He's just an ancient soul, confused by the fire. You can help me lead him back." But when we reached the well, the old man was gone. I searched the poplars, wild rose, and snowberry bushes that waved in the wind around the well, the rotting boards that covered it. "Where'd he go?" I said.

"There." Jeremy pointed toward Jude's place, a dark figure in the smoke.

"You see," Mom said. "We'll never reach him."

"Hey!" I called out. "Wait!"

I walked faster now, taking deep, rapid breaths to get enough air in the smoke. When I reached Jude's yard I waited for Jeremy and my mother to catch up. "Now where the hell did he go?"

"The unfinished house," said my mother.

He stood at the door, his wide-brimmed hat silhouetted by the light coming through the window behind him. "We've got him now," I said. But when we reached the house it was empty. The graffiti on the wall: *This is where I live.*

"You see," said my mother.

"He must be here."

"No," she said. "It was my father."

"Mom, your father has been dead for nearly thirty-five years."

I held Jeremy's hand and followed Mom into what would have become the living room, certain that the old man would be there, but he wasn't. The mouldy mattress on the floor. The graffiti on the walls. *Too bad you found your keys.*

"It was strange how my father's mind worked," she said. "After that meteor hit, he thought that the war was still raging and he was a soldier again, hunting down the enemy on that mountain." She turned to me. "And yet some part of him brought him back here, to this house, where the real threat to his world lay."

"You mean Valentine."

She nodded. "Valentine and Gus had been up in the hills looking for him, even after dark when the police and other searchers had given up. About eleven o'clock we saw lights in Valentine's cabin, so we knew he and Gus were back. I was breastfeeding you at the time, so Mom went over alone to see what the news was. But as soon as you were asleep, I put on a coat and left you with Val. On my way over, I could see Gus moving around in the cabin, but my mother wasn't there. She was in this old house with Valentine. I saw them kiss."

"Did you confront your mother?"

"No. I went to Valentine's cabin to talk to Gus. A little later Valentine and Mom came in, and we ate together before the men headed back up into the hills to continue the search."

She stepped up to the doorway to look at a huge flock of starlings that had swooped out of the smoke and swelled low overhead, black confetti against a dishwater sky. "It's a strange thing to see someone you thought you knew so well, suddenly in a very different light. It was as if my world had cracked and nothing made sense." She turned back to me. "If it was like that for me, for a daughter, think what it was for my father, to see his wife in another man's arms."

"How do you know he saw them?"

"Because I saw him later that night. My mother and I waited in the kitchen, doing what we could to keep ourselves occupied. Eventually, my mother dozed in her rocker but I couldn't sleep, so I saw the light come on in Valentine's cabin. I let my mother sleep and carried the pan of fudge that she had made earlier, along with a carving knife to cut it with, across the field. As I was nearing the cabin, I heard my old cat Midnight following behind me, the jingle of his collar. I leaned down to scratch him and then there was another jingle, of keys within a pocket, and I knew my father was there, in the shadow of this house. He said, 'Come here.' When I didn't, he stepped out of the black and grabbed me by the arm, making me drop the fudge and the knife, and dragged me into this house.

"'You bring that sonofabitch in here,' he said.

"'Valentine?'

"He looked over at the cabin a moment, then said, 'No, you bring your mother here first, and tell her Valentine wants her to wait. Then you bring him over. I would have had them both before if you hadn't turned up.'

"So you see what he had in mind, what he had seen. He planned to kill them both, together, in that house. I bolted for the door and he ran after me. Oh, God! The sound of his keys jingling in his pocket behind me! When he couldn't catch me he yanked Midnight back by the tail, so the cat yowled. I stopped when I heard that.

"'This is Katrine,' he told me, 'if you don't bring your mother and Valentine here.' Then he stretched Midnight out like he would to break a rabbit's neck, and dropped it. I knelt down to hold Midnight in my arms. Its head fell backward loose in my hands, but its heart still beat under my fingers. I couldn't think what else to do, to stop its suffering. So I picked up that knife I brought for cutting the fudge, and I cut its throat, like my father would a calf's, to bleed it. I killed that cat!"

"You put it out of its misery."

"I heard the horses then, and looked up to find Valentine and Gus on their horses with their guns trained on my father, just as he had his aimed at them. Valentine said, 'Put the gun down.' When my father didn't, he fired, not to hit him, but over his head, to scare him. Took out that window."

I looked over at the window. Whatever glass had remained had long since been pulled out.

"My father fired back and hit Gus in the arm, knocking him from his horse. When I crawled over to him, I saw his gun glinting there on the ground beside him."

We both listened as a Bombardier droned low overhead, issuing a piercing warning like an air-raid siren, warning us to get the hell out. Jeremy held his ears and cried. I held him and tucked his head into my chest. "We've got to get out of here, Mom."

"I must have picked up that gun, though I don't remember firing it, any more than I remember throwing that axe at the turkey, or shooting that calf yesterday." She looked down at her lightning arm and stretched her hand as she did when she was in pain. "But Gus and Valentine told me I fired and hit my father twice, once in the chest and once in the head, and I remember walking toward my father with that gun trained on him. The barrel was hot in my hands."

She turned to wander through the house and after a moment I followed her, carrying Jeremy. She stopped in the little room that would have become the bathroom: the painted "mirror" and the face. *How much time have you spent here waiting?*

"After I fired those shots, my mother came out of the house and stood on the porch, squinting into the dark. Val came out a few moments later. Neither of them could see us from the house because the yard light was too bright. My mother said, 'What's going on?'

"'I just shot a cougar,' Valentine called out. 'I expect it was attracted to the scent of blood, from Gus's wound, and followed us down. John shot Gus in the arm, while we were up in the hills. We've got to get him to the hospital.' He helped Gus walk toward the house. I stayed where I was, looking down at my father's body.

"Mom said, 'But where's John?'

"'He's still in the hills,' Valentine said. 'You and Beth get Gus to the hospital and get him fixed up. I'll phone the cops to let them know what happened, then I'll head back up into the hills to look for John.'

"'I don't want you going up alone,' Mom said.

"'I'll wait until the cops and the others arrive.'

"Mom took Gus into the house, to tend to his arm, and Valentine came back to the field for me. 'Beth,' he said, and he made me look at him. 'You're going to go with your mother now to take Gus to the hospital. He's going to be all right.' Then he nodded at my father's body. 'You don't say anything to anybody about this, ever. You understand? It was a cougar we shot here tonight.'"

"He lied to your mother," I said. "To protect you."

"He lied to protect my mother. He buried my father's body in that well so she wouldn't have to know what I'd done, or why I'd done it. He knew it would have all come out. All those things my father did to me, and to Val."

"But your mother must have suspected something of it."

"She didn't want to know. I didn't want to know or I would have seen it much sooner in Val. Valentine forced me to see it. You don't know what it's like, knowing what I allowed Val to go through. How would my mother ever have forgiven herself? How could she ever have forgiven me?"

"Oh, Mom, you weren't responsible for what your father did."

Jeremy pointed at the corner, at a shadow there. "Grandpa's crying."

I squinted to make out what the corner held, and the darkness took on the shape of a man. The shadow moved; it was as if someone had pencilled the outline of a man in the air, and then animated the sketch. It did indeed appear to be a man crying.

Mom stood beside me. "You see him too, don't you? You saw him here when you were a child. It's not just in my head like Val thinks."

"But you say your father's body is in the old well. Why would he lead us here, to this house?"

"This is where he saw them kiss. This is where he died." She pointed at the graffiti on the wall. "This is where *he* lives."

Another shadow slid across the wall. I turned to find Jude at the doorway.

"What are you doing here?" he said. "Didn't the cop come to your place?"

"There was an old man, at least we thought there was an old man—"

"You can explain to me as we get in the car. We've got to get out of here."

"Where's your pickup?"

"Nelson Dalton dropped me off so I could pick up the Impala."

"There's Ezra."

"We'll drive over and get him."

Jude pulled the mannequin and paintings of me out of the car and helped Jeremy into the back seat as I buckled my mother in place. "We can come back with the pickup and get the paintings," I said.

Jude pointed at the hills above. "No time." The boiling cloud of smoke that arched over the valley was flame-orange. He turned on the wipers as pieces of ash fell onto the windshield and

accumulated on the road like snow. The wind howled, whipping
the timothy grass in the field and forcing the bank of Lombardy
poplars into postures of submission. He swerved as one cracked
and fell over the road. As we drove into the yard, the umbrella on
the patio table on the lawn lifted and twirled, hovering over the
table for a few moments before being ripped away.

Ezra was on the roof of the house, nailing sprinklers in
place. A blast of wind came up as I ran over to the ladder, forcing him to hunker down and cling to the cedar shingles. "We've
got to get out of here!" I called up to him.

"What were you attempting at Jude's?"

"The old man led us there."

"Where is he?"

"I don't know."

"We've got to salvage him!"

I glanced at Mom as she made her way over to us. "No, there's
nothing we can do."

"We can tell the cops."

"I suppose we can do that. Someday."

"I don't grasp it."

"He wasn't what I thought. For Christ's sake, Ezra, come
down!"

"You and Mom and Jeremy go away with Jude."

"No!"

A panicked sparrow shrieked as it swooped past Ezra's head,
nearly hitting him. Then there was another, and another, a flock
of terrified birds—sparrows, finches, swallows, and jays, and all
screaming as they flew low overhead. Some, confused by the
smoke, slammed into the roof and the side of the house, rolling
as they were pulled away on the wind.

"My God, the birds," my mother said.

"They're fleeing the fire," said Jude. "We've got to leave, Katrine. Now."

"I can't leave Ezra here!"

"What are you going to do? Drag him down?"

"If I have to."

"We've got to get Jeremy and your mother out of here!"

I looked up at Ezra. "Go," he said.

Jude took my arm. "He's got the truck. For God's sake, Katrine, he's not a child."

Burning pine needles fell from the sky like lit matchsticks that flared up with each gusting wind. They hit my bare arms, curling the hairs, biting briefly like mosquitoes, leaving welts the size of dimes that I wouldn't notice until later in the day.

"Ezra!" I cried. "Please come down!"

He did climb down, and turned on the tap on the outside of the house, releasing a rain of water from the sprinklers above. Then he led me a short distance away from Jude, so that, in the wind, his voice would be lost to him. "Let me do this for you, Kat," he said. "Let me do this for us. I can show you. I can do *something*."

"You want to be the hero."

"No, I just want you to see that I'm capable. An adult. What Jude said just now, you see me as a child, not your husband. We can't survive like that."

His language was uncluttered by stumbling, the voice of my old Ezra and his eyes were free of the confusion and anger that so often yellowed them. I stood a moment, holding his hand, enjoying the relieving rain from the sprinkler. Then the shower stopped.

"The power's cut to the pumphouse," he said.

"The fire's got the lines," Jude shouted. "It's close."

A blast of heat hit us first as a huge cloud of smoke and fire roared down the valley toward us; its vibrations in my chest felt like those of a jet engine powering up. A propane tank exploded at the Petersons' place, sounding like a bomb. "Look!" Jeremy said, pointing at the fireball. "Stars falling on us."

Chunks of burning wood, some the size of a man's fist, fell from the sky. Several landed in the alfalfa field that enclosed the old well, and within seconds the field was alight, as if it had spontaneously combusted. Driven by winds that came at us from all directions, the fire zigzagged first one way and then another. On Blood Road a truck pulled a trailer that was on fire. The driver stopped and got out to unhook the trailer, then drove several feet away before jumping out again to swat at the flames with his jacket. When that had no effect, he stepped back and watched his things go up in smoke. A firetruck with lights and siren blazing screamed past him.

"I've got to get water on the barns!" Ezra said, and he started toward the outbuildings, but my mother took his hand in both her own.

"Ezra," she said. "There's no power." When he looked back at the barn, she put a hand to his cheek to get him to focus on her. "Sometimes," she said, "the only thing you can do is accept things, as they are." She patted his hand. "It's time to go."

I expected him to pull away, to dig in his heels and refuse to leave, as Jeremy would when he refused to go to bed, as Ezra himself had when he fought my counsel so many times before. But he walked hand in hand with my mother to the truck, steadying her when she stumbled, and then sat in the passenger seat staring straight ahead as Jude put Jeremy in his car seat and I helped my mother fasten her seatbelt in the back of the pickup.

"Let's stay together!" shouted Jude as he got in his car. "In case of problems."

"Yes," I said. He held my gaze a moment longer, as he had held it all those years ago at my wedding, and then he ducked into the car and was off. I turned on the air conditioning in the pickup and followed the Impala up the driveway, feeling the winds push at the vehicle as I drove. Someone up the valley had let loose his horses. They galloped ahead of us as we turned onto Blood Road. Jude and then I slowed our vehicles so we didn't panic the horses further, and they ran along either side of us, their manes flowing. When I turned briefly to watch them as we passed, I caught sight of smoke billowing from the back of our pickup. "Oh, shit, Ezra. Our stuff is on fire."

I pulled off to the side of the road near Jude's driveway and we both jumped out. Stepping into that blast of hot wind was like sticking my face into Jude's kiln. I struggled to find breath, and held onto the door of the truck to avoid being blown over. "We're not going to get this fire out before we lose everything," I yelled.

"No."

"Mom, get out," I said. As Ezra unfastened Jeremy from his car seat, I leaned into the cab and honked the horn to get Jude's attention, and he slowed the Impala and turned around. Then I pulled what little I could from the burning truck: my grandmother's carpetbag; the shoebox containing my father's jackknife, cup, razor, wallet, and harmonica; the set of kitchen scales on which my grandmother had weighed her bread dough, an object we had almost forgotten on the top of the kitchen cupboard.

I held those scales close, as if they were a beloved pet I had saved, and we all stepped away from the truck, clinging to each other to keep our footing in the buffeting wind as burning

debris pelted down around us. The lawn around my parents'
home exploded into flame and bits of burning letters and photos
from the boxes belonging to Ezra and me were carried up from
the truck by the wild winds. Some swirled back down again,
landing on the ground at my feet, and I scrambled to save whatever I could. An early love letter from Ezra, Jeremy's drawing of
a snowman, a photograph of Ezra just shortly before the stroke.
As Jude pulled the car up beside us, I picked up a photo of our
little family taken when Jeremy was three, and brushed the cin-
ders off the edges before tucking it into my jeans pocket.

Jude pushed open the passenger-side door. "Get in!" he said.

I unloaded the few items I had salvaged onto the front seat,
then buckled Jeremy and my mother, who held Harrison and the
kitten, into the back. "I'll sit in the back," I said.

"No," said Ezra. "Sit in the front."

"Katrine, in the front, now!" said Jude.

I reached instinctively for the seatbelt, but there was
none. As Jude sped off, overtaking the galloping horses once
again, I felt I was floating, untethered, unsafe, thrilled. I felt
cold, despite the intense heat, and as I clutched my grandmother's scales to my chest, I shook as hard as I had in child-
birth. Harrison yowled and clawed my mother as she tried to
hold it. Trees on either side of us burned. Embers and pieces of
flaming wood and pine cones pummelled us, bouncing off the
hood of the car. Jude clicked on the headlights as the smoke of
the firestorm blackened out the sun, and I turned in my seat to
watch, with my mother and Ezra, as the farmhouse was engulfed
by fire, as the truck burst into flames, as our past burned away.

25·

JEREMY AND I PICKED UP my mother at her apartment at Rotary Gardens and drove her out to Turtle Valley to say goodbye to the farm one last time. The remains of trees on the Ptarmigan Hills were charred sticks exposing the lay of the land underneath, but the rock of those mountains was still there, substantial, faithful; the mountains themselves hadn't collapsed under the weight of the catastrophe, as I had somehow imagined they would. But they were smaller, less imposing, less secretive, without their trees. I wondered now why finding a lost soul within those hills had seemed so difficult.

Jude was in his kiln shed as we passed by, prepping his

garbage cans for a raku firing, presumably for the summer pottery show coming up next week in Sorrento. I waved but he didn't see me, or more likely he pretended he didn't see me. On the other side of the road his neighbours, Tammy and Nelson Dalton, were putting up siding on their new home. They'd been living in the house since spring. The fire was capricious in its hunger: it consumed the Daltons' home, leaving nothing but the chimney, and yet their flag still flew. It took Valentine's cabin and the unfinished house, but not Jude's or his studio or kiln shed. It consumed my parents' home, but not my grandmother's greenhouse or the orchard only a few yards away.

The day after the firestorm, when Ezra, Val, Jeremy, and I drove Mom out to the farm, we found my parents' house distilled to three inches of ash in the basement. I salvaged a frying pan that was half melted; the metal base from one of my mother's lamps; the burned-out frame of my childhood bicycle, left leaning against Valentine's granary all those years before Jude bought the place. In the fallout of the fire, these objects became, for me, beloved treasures, links to a lost past, and even when I left Ezra and moved to my rented house in Salmon Arm, when I threw so much away, I kept them.

As I salvaged the bike frame that day, Jude parked his Impala in the driveway and walked through the blackened field to meet me. "What you got there?" he asked.

I laughed, expecting him to make fun of me. "The bike was mine when I was a kid. I was wondering if I could have it."

"Of course," he said.

I nodded toward my parents' farm, the burned fields, the foundation of their still smoking house. "This the first you've seen of it?"

"No, I came out this morning." He ran his hand through his hair. "I can't believe my house and studio are still standing." Then he turned back to me. "I'm so sorry about your dad, Katrine, and about your folks' house."

"I'm sorry for everyone," I said, as I looked at the smoke-filled valley around us. The firestorm had roared down into the valley bottom and up the opposite mountain range at speeds of ninety miles an hour or more, burning down a half-dozen homes and countless outbuildings.

"At least no one was killed," said Jude.

"But a lot of livestock was lost. Alex Hamilton was talking on the radio about how he shot his emus so they wouldn't suffer a terrible death. The fire moved on his house so fast he couldn't get them out in time."

"No one expected the fire to go up his side of the valley." He put his hands in his jeans pockets and looked down at the charred earth. "So, what now? Are you heading back to Alberta?"

"No, for the meantime at least, I need to help Val look after Mom."

"Does that mean you'll move back here?"

"I don't know what I'm going to do."

He took my hand. "Why not stay with me for a while as you figure things out?"

I shook my head.

"Why?"

I glanced across the field at my mother, Val, Jeremy, and Ezra wandering around the yard. The smoke was dense, but they could see us. "You excite me," I said. "You make me do things I wouldn't have the courage to do otherwise. You always have."

"And you want to give that up?"

"I don't want to rush into anything," I said. "Not this time." I shook my head. "I just don't know what I want, yet."

He stared at me a moment, then he looked at the ground. "Well," he said. "When you make up your mind, you know where to find me." And he turned on his heel and walked to his house. I called out, "Jude, wait!" but when he kept walking I didn't go after him. He hasn't tried to contact me since, as I half hoped he would. So we are back to where we were before the fire: we lift a hand to each other if our vehicles meet along Blood Road or in the parking lot of Askew's Foods, but neither of us stops to say hello.

As I carried the burned bike frame back from Jude's that day, the bantam hen we had not been able to catch appeared, leading a dozen sooty chicks down the driveway and pausing now and again to shake her blackened feathers. Later I found her nest as I walked the yard: a chicken-sized patch of grass in the midst of black near the ashen rubble where the barn had been. I marvel at her survival, at the powerful maternal instinct that kept her tethered to her nest as the fire raged around her. Did she feel the terror I felt at the prospect of either staying or leaving her clutch? Did she shake as I did when the fire raged around her? Every time I tell the story of our exodus, my own fear fades a little further from memory. But even so, when I catch the whiff of a wood fire I'm drawn here again to this place, to the horror I felt as I fled almost all that I had known.

THE REALTOR HAD put up a *Sold* sticker over the *For Sale* sign at the end of the driveway. The new owners would take possession the next day, though I think all of us gave up possession of that farm with the loss of my parents' home. The place was naked and strange without it. Nothing but the foundation was left, and it was crumbling and falling away to expose the stones John Weeks had unwisely mixed in the concrete, presumably to save money. I wondered how the foundation had ever supported the weight of the structure. It was surrounded not by my father's neatly mown lawn but by a field overgrown with blue-flowering chicory and golden tansy. Several panes in my grandmother's greenhouse had been cracked or knocked out by the hailstorm earlier that month.

I parked the truck in the yard and my mother and I sat a moment, looking over the orchard. "Well," I said. "Shall we go for a walk?"

"I'll wait here," Mom said. "You go on."

"This is your last chance to say goodbye to the farm. I don't imagine the new owners will want us stomping through their property."

"I'm done here, I think," she said. "But take a look in the greenhouse, will you? I'm not sure Val ever thought to check if there was anything worth keeping in there."

Jeremy followed me to the greenhouse, dawdling behind to yank the blue chicory flowers from their hardy stems. For a moment I was unaccountably afraid to go inside, and when I did, I found myself stepping into an awareness of déjà vu, though I'd been inside the greenhouse countless times before and knew it well. There was nothing left to salvage.

Jeremy came inside to hand me his fistful of flowers. "Thank you, honey," I said.

He pointed at the corner. "There's a dead bird." A junco had found its way in but had not found its way out again. A bird flying in the house was an omen, a death in the family, wasn't it? But what did a dead bird in a greenhouse mean? In any case, this was no longer our place, our greenhouse. I used a scrap of mouldering newspaper to pick up the bird and carried it outside to place it beneath a lilac bush.

If this last visit to my childhood home had been a dream, how would I have interpreted it? A familiar landscape that was now strange to me. A door I was afraid to open. A dead bird in the corner. But no sign of ghosts.

I'd like to believe that Maud and John Weeks's souls are finally at rest. At least their footsteps no longer followed me as I walked the fields of the farm that afternoon. I saw no figure by the well, as I half expected I might; in fact, there was no longer any sign of the well itself. At Val's request, Jude cut down the bush around the well and filled it in. Val then plowed over the area using Dad's old tractor, planting it in alfalfa so there was no evidence, any longer, of what was hidden underground.

Even so, I did see my grandmother that day, reflected in the greenhouse glass as I strode toward it. Maud couldn't have been forty, but I recognized her: the long nose, the full mouth, the look of anticipation. For an instant I wanted to call out to her across the decades. In that last photo taken of her, when she carried her carpetbag down the street, she bore her past on her shoulders like an overloaded gunnysack. The bones of her thighs ground in the hollow cups of her hips like painful drums: *I ache, I ache.* But that wasn't the music of her body on this day. She created whistling breezes with her stride and wore the day like a tiara. She was beautiful.

"ARE YOU GOING TO WRITE about this place?" Mom asked as we drove back up the driveway. "About what happened here?"

"I've already begun."

"Good. I think my mother wanted that. She led you to that carpetbag the first night you arrived, didn't she? She wanted you to find out, to tell the story."

I nodded. My mother, at least, needed to tell it.

She took my hand. "But you won't show it to anyone quite yet, will you?"

"No, not for a long time yet, I hope."

As we turned onto Blood Road, she looked out the window at the fields she had farmed first with her father and then with her husband. "It's strange how it doesn't feel like home anymore," she said, "as if it belonged to someone else. I don't feel *attached* to the memories I have of this place, if you know what I mean. I wonder, now, why I chose to live here all those years."

"I understand," I said. In a similar way I struggled to remember Ezra's smell, the details of his skin, the way he moved, what moved me to love him. But our lives had diverged. He worked the land that we bought without me, and another woman lived with him, a petite farm girl who seemed more comfortable within that tiny rented house. I had moved back home with my son to help my sister care for my mother in her final years. Although I remembered the events of my life with Ezra, or a good many of them, in any case, I didn't feel the emotions I felt at the time. As my mother said that afternoon, I wasn't *attached* to my memories of him. Even so, when memories of Ezra surfaced I searched them, hoping to capture something of my feelings for him, to gain some sense of who I was when I was with him. There was a summer sometime after Ezra's stroke, when Ezra and I drove Mom and Dad down this same road during a visit. Jeremy was just two. "Butterfly!" he said. Sulphur butterflies danced over the yellow alfalfa blossoms along the roadside, and one dinged our windshield.

"Look at all the butterflies hugging the shoulder," Ezra said, and he pointed out the butterflies that had been hit by cars and gathered by breezes into drifts along the roadway.

"Can I see them?" asked Jeremy.

"Why don't we stop?" said Ezra, and he parked the truck on the side of the road and helped Jeremy out to look at the butter-flies that littered the ground like yellow confetti. Most were dead, but some were injured and still alive, their wings fluttering. Jeremy plucked butterflies from the gravel, and the luminous scales from their wings dusted his fingertips like eyeshadow.

"Can I take some home?" Jeremy asked me.

"Have we got anything to put them in?"

"My hat, I guess," said Ezra.

As I collected butterflies with Jeremy, Ezra came up to us with his hands cupped as if holding something precious within. Then he opened his hands to show me, palms out as if offering me a gift. It was something I never would have taken the time to notice: a tiny, strange green insect with fragile, tear-shaped, iridescent wings. He brushed the insect into my cupped hand and all at once I was *here,* a witness to the moment I inhabited, aware of the hot sun on my back, the sweet smell of my father's cattle across the fence, the pop of broom pods bursting. For that instant there was no past or future; I knew only the pleasures my senses offered me, that I was alive.

We placed the hat full of butterflies on the seat between Ezra and me, and as we drove Mom and Dad home the wind coursing through the open window lifted a few of the dead butterflies so that they flitted around our heads. Jeremy tripped as he carried the hat to the house and the hat tumbled from his hands, shower-ing the gravel on the driveway with a drift of yellow butterflies.

A great many of them were blown away on the afternoon wind, and Jeremy and Ezra and I chased after them, struggling to recover them before they were lost in the thick grasses along the field.

I remember that day now as yellow: the sunlight on yellow alfalfa blossoms in the fields and the brilliant golden tansy in the ditches; the field of huge, flowering sunflowers that hid Tammy Dalton's house from view; the yellow butterflies dancing over the flower heads; the dead ones rolling on the wind like drifts of wisteria petals; the saffron T-shirt Ezra wore, my son's blond hair. A day a long time ago. I remember that I loved Ezra for stopping to show Jeremy the butterflies, and for giving me that moment cupped within his hands, but I don't remember what that felt like, and that saddens me, frightens me. My memories are so like that hat full of butterflies, some already deteriorating the moment they are collected, some breathed back to life now and again, for a brief moment, by the scent on a passing wind—the smell of an orange, perhaps, or a whiff of brown-sugar fudge—before drifting away, just out of my reach. How much of myself flits away with each of these tattered memories? How much of myself have I already lost?

AS WE LEFT TURTLE VALLEY behind that afternoon, we said goodbye to the farm. Jeremy said, "The moon's following us."

I glanced back in the mirror to find my son looking out the window at the sky.

"Why *does* the moon follow us?" Mom said.

"What do you mean?"

"Before we turned that corner it was over there," she said. "Now it's here. Why does it move with us?"

"Move with us?"

"Why does it follow us?"

I swerved to miss a turtle crossing Blood Road and, glancing into the side mirror, witnessed its death under the tire of the Chevy behind us. The brief spray of wet. I was struck at that moment by a sweet grief, a longing to stay inside that day with my mother, because I knew I was losing her. That afternoon was like one of her parting kisses, the press of her lips to say goodbye fading the instant it was planted on my cheek. I knew that at the end of that day the memory of our time together would already have begun to disappear. I'd be left with a crumbling rose and a pot of faded rouge. So as soon as I returned home with Jeremy, I pulled my notebook and pen from my purse to record the day's events, to seize the memory within ink before it faded away.

Acknowledgments

I'D LIKE TO THANK Mitch Krupp for the time and care he took to create the photographs used in this novel, and for helping me to integrate them into the text. So many other individuals contributed to this novel in so many ways that I couldn't possibly thank them all here, but I will list a few: Irene Anderson, Cindy Malinowski, Rick Tanaka, Floyd Dargatz, Jake Jacobson, and the many residents who offered their stories about the Salmon Arm fire of 1998. Thanks also to the Canada Council and the British Columbia Arts Council for grants that assisted me in the writing of *Turtle Valley*.

Jude's love note to Kat was written, in good measure, by Mitch Krupp. The recipe for waxing flowers was paraphrased from a recipe I found in my grandmother's scrapbook. The story "Turtle Valley Is Jarred by Slight Tremor" was taken from the July 5, 1945, *Salmon Arm Observer*. The story "Brilliant Flash Lights Heavens" was taken from the *Kamloops Sentinel*, April 1, 1965. The newspaper depiction of the shivaree is verbatim from an account written by my mother, Irene Anderson. Again, names, dates, and locations of these newspaper stories have been changed. The clippings describing the search for John Weeks are complete fictions.

GAIL ANDERSON-DARGATZ is an award-winning Canadian author whose bestselling novels have been published world-wide. She currently teaches fiction at the University of British Columbia's Creative Writing Program and lives in the Shuswap Valley, the landscape found in so much of her writing.